The Anteater
of Death

Books by Betty Webb

The Lena Jones Mysteries
Desert Noir
Desert Wives
Desert Shadows
Desert Run
Desert Cut
Desert Lost

The Gunn Zoo Mysteries
The Anteater of Death
The Koala of Death

The Anteater of Death

A Gunn Zoo Mystery

Betty Webb

Poisoned Pen Press

Copyright © 2008 by Betty Webb

First Trade Paperback Edition 2010

10 9 8 7 6 5 4 3 2 1

Library of Congress Catalog Card Number: 2008925508

ISBN: 978-1-59058-774-4 Trade Paperback

Poisoned Pen Press
6962 E. First Ave., Ste. 103
Scottsdale, AZ 85251
www.poisonedpenpress.com
info@poisonedpenpress.com

Printed in the United States of America

*To all my friends—both human and animal—
at the Phoenix Zoo. But especially to a certain Giant Anteater
who adores bananas. This one's for you, Jezebel!*

Acknowledgments

Thanks to all the helpful zookeepers and other animal experts at the wonderful Phoenix Zoo, who so generously shared their knowledge about wild animals and their habits. Believe me, any errors to be found in this book are strictly my own. Many of the animals mentioned in this book do live at the Phoenix Zoo, including sweet Lucy, whose real name is Jezebel. To learn more about Phoenix Zoo, click the link on my web site at www.bettywebb-zoomystery.com or www.phoenixzoo.org.

For readers who desire to visit Gunn Landing and Gunn Zoo, I'm sorry to tell you this, but both places are totally fictitious. The tiny fishing village of Moss Landing (population less than 1,000) on the Central California coast, did inspire some of the fictional town's gentler aspects—and none of the negative ones! Thanks here go to Moss Landing's extraordinarily helpful harbormaster, and to the terrific liveaboarders who graciously conducted me on tours around their floating homes. Thanks are also due to the innkeepers at Captain's Inn, as well as to the area's many harbor seals and otters; they all made my visit the Moss Landing an unparalleled delight. To learn more about Moss Landing, check the village web site at www.mosslandingchamber.com.

Chapter One

Intrigued by the commotion underneath the banana palm, Lucy curled her four-inch claws under her leathery pads and moved forward on her knuckles to investigate. It wasn't time for the human-thing with the soft voice to arrive with the morning meal, so what could the noise be?

Ah, there was the cause of the trouble. A strange human-thing had fallen into Lucy's enclosure and now thrashed among the weeds as if it belonged. What nerve! All the ants and big juicy termites in this place were Lucy's, and Lucy didn't share. One swipe with her claws and the human-thing would limp off squealing.

She grunted a warning. *Get out. If you don't get out, I'll uncurl my claws and give you a rake down your belly. Out, out!*

The human-thing ignored her, just kept flailing in the weeds.

Lucy extended her long nose and poked at it. *Better listen to me.*

The human-thing made a rattling sound, slowed its thrashing to a twitch, then lay still. Did it think it could fool Lucy by pretending to be asleep? A sly move, but Lucy was slyer. She knew if she allowed the human-thing to stay it would gobble up all the lovely grubbies as soon as she went back to her nest and fell asleep. Furious now, she flicked out her tongue and slapped the human-thing in its open eye. *I said to get out, out, out. Now, now, now. If you don't, I'll show you what hurt feels like.*

No reaction from the human-thing. Refusing to be taken for a fool, Lucy glared at it for a moment more, then slowly and with great show uncurled her dagger claws. *Here comes trouble.* When it remained motionless, she darted forward and gave it a swipe, little more than a scratch, really, but enough to let the stupid creature know she meant business.

It stayed where it was.

Her tongue flicked out again. Blue and almost two feet in length, it slapped the human-thing here, there, around its head, and in the folds of its dark clothing until it found a sticky spot, a different kind of wet.

The scent rising from the human-thing was different, too. Usually the creatures smelled like fruit, sometimes like flowers—especially the females. But this one reeked musky and sharp, almost like the metal around her enclosure.

And the sticky-wet on its front? Lucy vaguely remembered an encounter with a big spotted cat shortly before the human-things caught her and brought her to this place. The cat had flashed claws even sharper than Lucy's, and when they raked along her shoulder, this kind of smell leaked out. When in self-defense Lucy opened the cat's belly with her claws, curly dark ribbons tumbled onto the ground. After a while, the cat stopped twitching. Like this human-thing.

Oh, she understood now. That sharp scent was the smell of death.

Too bad, human-thing. I told you to leave and you didn't. Point made and the human-thing no longer a threat, Lucy started to walk away, but as she began to turn, she noticed movement out of the corner of her eye. *Now what?* Yes, there was another intrusion into her enclosure, this time a happy one. Ants—juicy, sweet-flavored ants, were now crawling across the human-thing, splashing through its wetness.

Lucy wheeled around, flipped out her blue tongue again, and gave a lick.

Mmm, yummy.

Chapter Two

Zoos are little pieces of Eden. In the morning, before the gates open and the crowds stream in, the groundskeepers trim and sweep so that the scent of greenery blends with the odor of fresh urine as the animals indulge in their first pee of the day. It's the fifth day of Creation all over again, when only animals populated the Earth and God was pleased with his handiwork.

Of course, this was before the Sixth day, when God created Man and Man began tossing his Diet Coke cans around.

For the past year, I've been a zookeeper at the Gunn Zoo, a large private zoo five miles inland from Gunn Landing Harbor, a tiny village located halfway between Santa Cruz and Monterey. I arrive a half-hour before my shift begins, just to spend a few quiet moments meandering through the paths.

Mondays find me in California Habitat with condors and otters; Tuesdays, Tropics Trail with the giant anteater and the spectacled bears; Wednesdays, Africa Trail with rhinos and lions; Thursdays, Down Under with wallabies and emus; and Fridays, at Friendly Farm with llamas and chickens. Saturdays—yes, I work six days a week and would work seven if they let me—I visit the giraffes on Verdant Veldt.

Then I hike down to the commissary and shovel worms onto the food cart.

Today being Tuesday, I finished my early-morning stroll around Tropics Trail by looking over the moat for Lucy, our giant anteater from Belize. She was nowhere in sight. I figured she was sulking somewhere toward the back of the exhibit, maybe near her holding pen.

Lucy had good reason to be in a bad mood. Not only was she pregnant, with a tendency to suffer upset stomachs, but yesterday a visitor had ignored the DANGER: DO NOT FEED THE ANTEATER sign and threw a bag of popcorn over the moat. Before I could grab my safety board to enter the exhibit and retrieve the bag, Lucy snaked out her blue tongue and tried a kernel.

Have you ever heard an anteater gag?

Anteaters have no teeth, so Lucy spit out the hard-bodied kernel immediately, but there was nothing she could do to rid her mouth of salt. Enraged, she reared up on her hind legs, propped herself kangaroo-like on her thick tail, and slashed at the offender. Good thing for him he stood ten feet away behind the enclosure's fence. With their extended noses and oversized tails, giant anteaters may appear cuddly-funny on the ground, but when they stand up they're almost the size of bears. Five feet tall, weighing in at one hundred-and-fifty pounds, with massive shoulders and four-inch claws designed for tearing open logs, they can eviscerate a jaguar in one swipe. In fact, giant anteaters are so lethal zoos everywhere have designated them Code Red animals.

In zoo parlance, that means if one gets loose, run for your life.

The popcorn-thrower, a wobbly-bellied man of around fifty, had jumped back with a frightened squeak but by then the damage was done. In full-bore anteater rage, Lucy swatted the bag back and forth across her enclosure with her muscular forearms, scattering popcorn from one end to the other.

"Get a grip," I'd told her, as I angled around with my safety board, careful to keep it between us. "Be a good girl or you're going off-exhibit until you calm down." Such an extreme decision would be left to Zorah Vega, the zoo's head keeper, but Lucy didn't know that.

I'd eventually corralled her in the chain link holding pen where she continued her tantrum, slashing out at the world in general. Lucy wanted a piece of me. She wanted a piece of everybody. She especially wanted a piece of Popcorn Man. After I'd spent the rest of Monday afternoon picking up popcorn kernels saturated with anteater dung, I wanted a piece of him, too.

But today, on this sun-drenched California May morning, Lucy should have returned to her more-or-less cheerful self. Across the way, the orangutans *huhu-huhu*ed cheerfully as they threw feces at each other. Macaws squawked for joy. Everyone was happy, so why not Lucy? Why didn't she trot out to welcome me as usual?

Then I remembered the Gunn Zoo Guild black tie fundraiser, which had started at sunset the previous night and continued on until the wee hours. The noise had probably disturbed her, and sleepy anteaters were cranky anteaters. Especially when pregnant.

Scanning the area more carefully, I spotted Lucy in the far corner of the public enclosure, her nose sticking out of the large, rattan-covered dog house she used for a nest, her diagonal black-and-white shoulder stripes hidden in its shade. "Lucy not say good morning to Teddy?" I crooned in the baby-talk many zookeepers use with their animals. She grunted once and turned over, but refused to emerge.

"Be like that."

I left her to her sulks and drove my electric zoo cart down to the commissary to fetch breakfast. Mashed Purina Monkey Chow mixed with wiggling termites always cheered her up.

After I'd fed the squirrel monkeys, the capybaras, and the Chacoan peccaries, I waited by Lucy's fence for the head keeper to turn up. Zorah had mentioned that she wanted to check on the anteater herself this morning, but when she hadn't appeared after ten minutes or answered my radio calls, I finished the routine on my own. With the same caution other keepers used with the big cats, I entered Lucy's holding pen at the rear of the enclosure.

Hearing me, Lucy stuck her long nose out of the dog house, lifted it high for a good sniff, then trotted over to the chain link fence that separated her public enclosure from the much-smaller holding pen. While she watched through the links, I poured her breakfast into the Wellington boot we used for her food bowl and turned it on its side so it would look more like a log. Then I picked up the safety board and held it in front of me. Thus assured she couldn't take her bad mood out on me with her lethal claws, I opened the gate to the pen and stepped aside. With a happy chortle she rushed past me, stopping once to give the safety board a perfunctory swipe, then stuck her snout in the boot and began to lick up termites.

Once again I wondered about Zorah's absence, but guessed she had been held up in a meeting with Barry Fields, our new zoo director. Or perhaps she was helping another keeper with a difficult animal, a common occurrence.

I'd saved some of the Monkey Chow mixture for Lucy's public area, and after exiting the holding pen and locking its gate securely behind me, I stuffed the rest of her breakfast into various hollow plastic "logs" placed in several locations around the enclosure. That accomplished, I picked up my bucket and broom and set about the least fun part of a zookeeper's job: picking up poop.

For a giant anteater, Lucy is relatively tidy. She always relieves herself in the deep brush near the banana tree, so I started my cleanup there. But when I leaned over to pick up the first pile, I saw a man in a soiled tuxedo lying half-hidden in the weeds. A drunk left over from last night's fund-raiser?

When the man didn't move at my approach, I gave him a poke with the broom. "Party's over, sir. Rise and shine. And just between the two of us, you shouldn't be in here. Lucy's...well, Lucy's not much of a hostess."

Nothing. Not even a groan. I poked harder. "Sir, didn't you hear me? Lucy's a Code Red animal. If she decides to, she'll rip the skin right off your bones! Let me escort you to safety."

The man still didn't move. "Sir, you need to..." I stepped closer and pushed the weeds out of the way. "*Oh!*"

Lucy had already ripped the skin off his bones.

I made it all the way to the moat before I vomited. It wouldn't do to soil Lucy's enclosure.

The first argument that morning was over how much of the zoo should be shut down while the San Sebastian County crime scene techs did their jobs. Sheriff Joe Rejas wanted the entire zoo closed for the day but the zoo director and Zorah, who'd finally turned up, held fast for Tropics Trail only. Attempting to forget the mess the anteater had made of the dead man, I listened to them argue while I sat on a rock under a eucalyptus tree at the trail's entrance.

"I'm sure you understand, Sheriff, that the Gunn Zoo is a private establishment and as such, receives no government funding," Barry Fields snapped. The zoo director's high voice made him sound like the dingos in Down Under. With his sleek build, pointy nose, and California tan, he resembled a dingo, too, albeit one dressed in Armani. "Besides relying upon the good graces of our benefactors, we must also keep an eye on gate receipts. Two thousand-plus visitors a day adds up, you know, and I can't allow you to cut those numbers. There's staffing, upkeep…"

"Sir, there's been a death." Sheriff Rejas towered over the director, his own bronze skin owing more to genetics than Fields' obviously obsessive tanning rituals. He moved a lot more like a stealthy mountain cat than some scruffy Australian canine, too. If Fields was wise, he'd watch his step.

But Fields had all the self-confidence of the truly ignorant. Dismissing the sheriff's frown, he stroked his sports jacket's expensive lapel. "Oh, something's always dying at a zoo."

The zoo's park rangers, who had come running when I radioed them, gave him a disbelieving stare.

The sheriff looked disgusted. "I'm sure your animals are all very healthy, but this is a special situation. A man is dead."

Aware of his gaffe, the director looked around for a scapegoat. Seeing me, he fired off a series of accusatory questions. "Why wasn't that thing locked in its holding pen for the night? Did you forget? Idiot! Don't you realize the lawsuit your incompetence has let us in for? What's your name? I'm reporting you to Human Resources."

I stood up and brushed away the eucalyptus leaves clinging to my butt. "I'm Teddy Bentley, and I didn't forget to lock the gate. Since being impregnated, the anteater prefers to spend the night in her enclosure, not the holding pen. The man must have climbed over the fence and waded across the moat. It's not as deep as the one the bears have."

"Climb over the fence? Don't be ridiculous! No one would do such a stupid thing. Especially not with that nasty aardvark."

"Giant anteater, sir. *Myrmecophaga treidactyla*."

"Whatever you call it, I want it shot before it causes us any more trouble." Suddenly his face changed. "Wait a minute. Did you say your name is *Bentley*?"

Angered by his outrageous order, I gave my full name. "Yes, sir. Theodora Iona Esmeralda Bentley."

Fields blinked. "Any relation to Mrs. Caroline *Bentley* Petersen, of the Gunn Landing Bentleys, by any chance?"

"She's my mother."

His abrupt manner segued to servile. He did everything but lick my mud-caked work boots. "Then I'm certain you were very careful, Ms. Bentley. And that you always are."

What a jerk. "I was careful."

At this point, Zorah, her big frame sunken in shock, spoke up. "Shoot the anteater? Oh, c'mon! Giant anteaters are on the Vulnerable Species list. We can't go around killing them just because some idiot let himself get clawed. Besides, Lucy's one of our most popular attractions, and if you send her to another zoo, our visitors will raise hell. The publicity for the Name-the-Baby-Anteater contest is all set to go as soon as she gives birth, and that'll give us tons of media coverage."

While the director mulled this over, Sheriff Rejas spoke again. "Here's what we're willing to do. We'll keep the zoo closed until noon, then cordon off Tropics Trail for the rest of the day.

That way, the man's death won't cut into your gate receipts too deeply."

Fields missed the barb. "It'll cut them by half!"

Ignoring him, sheriff turned to me, his frosty eyes warming. "Teddy...ah, Ms. Bentley, perhaps you'll show me what you were doing when you discovered the body? Without entering the exhibit again, of course."

Relieved that my long-ago boyfriend had decided to keep our interaction on a professional level, I led him and his deputies back to Lucy's enclosure and ran through my movements. "I didn't notice the man until I..." I motioned to the bucket and broom I'd dropped on the way out of the exhibit. "...until I started cleaning."

"Did you touch the body?"

I averted my eyes from the ongoing action under the banana tree. "When he didn't wake up I poked him with my broom. He still didn't move so I pushed the brush aside. That's when I saw that he didn't have much skin left. Especially on his face." I swallowed hard.

"What did you do then?"

"Got sick."

"Teddy, that's not what I meant."

Back to first names. Not wanting to let our personal history sidetrack me, I said, "Sheriff Rejas, I'm not sure what I did then. It's horrible, finding someone clawed to pieces." I breathed deeply. "After I finished upchucking, I radioed the park rangers. And the head keeper."

Zorah, who had followed us, looked up expectantly.

Joe ignored her. "When you called in the emergency, did the park rangers respond immediately?"

"As soon as they finished their Earl Grey and crumpets."

He shot me a look. "No point in getting smart, Ms. Bentley. I'm just doing my job."

"Yes, they showed up within seconds. With first aid kits and rifles."

He glanced into the enclosure, where the crime scene photographer was packing up his camera equipment. "Has the anteater attacked anyone before?"

"Her former keeper, whom she didn't like. But Lucy didn't kill him, merely scratched him on the leg." As far as zookeepers were concerned, anything less than twenty stitches was a scratch, and he'd only required nineteen.

The photographer backed out of the enclosure, looking as sick as I felt.

Oblivious, Joe resumed his questioning. "What do you think brought on the attack?"

"It could have been anything. Merely intruding into her territory might have set her off. She doesn't even like it when I enter, and she's used to me. A stranger would be taking his life in his hands." Oops. The dead man certainly had. "Do you know who he is, ah, *was?* I couldn't tell from his face." What was left of it.

Joe leaned toward me, lowering his voice. "I don't want this to get around yet, but his driver's license indicates that he's Grayson Harrill. The deputy I sent up the hill to notify his wife radioed me a few minutes ago that she collapsed. Her doctor's with her now."

My nausea returned, but at least not to the retching point. "Oh, Joe, you can't let Jeanette see him like this!"

"We'll make the official ID from dental records. The condition he's in, it's the only thing possible for now. We can confirm with DNA later."

Grayson's wife was the great-great-granddaughter of Edwin Gunn, the zoo's founder. Jeanette—who'd been my roommate at Miss Pridewell's Academy—was a voting member of the Gunn Trust, the organization which ran the zoo.

Now I was more alarmed than ever on Lucy's behalf. She was just an anteater being an anteater, and as such, blameless in the attack. But I doubted that the billion-dollar Gunn Trust or its insurance carriers would interpret her actions in such a benign manner. Regardless of her popularity with our zoo visitors, the

Trust could order her traded to another zoo. Even worse, they might follow Barry Fields' advice.

Grasping at straws, I said, "When you get through questioning everyone, it might be worth your while to find out what Grayson was doing up here. He wasn't all that cuddly with animals."

Joe frowned. "Isn't he one of the Zoo Guild members? Like his wife?"

"Sure. So's my mother and she doesn't even own a cat. A lot of the Guild members see community service as their civic duty, others perform it for political reasons. Sure, the majority of them like animals. Grayson did, too, at least in the abstract, but he didn't care for close encounters with them. You should have seen his face a couple of weeks ago when someone stuck an adolescent saki in his arms for a publicity picture. He looked at the poor little thing as if it were a bomb ready to explode."

"Adolescent saki?"

"Small white-faced monkey. Weighs about a pound."

"If he was uncomfortable with animals, why did he spend so much time at the zoo? People have told me he was here almost every day."

"That's because he'd taken over for his wife. As one of the Gunns, she did a lot of office-type stuff around here besides her Guild work, but her migraines, which she's suffered from for years, started getting worse, so he jumped in to fill the breach. He's always been good about helping her. And it kept him busy."

"Didn't he have a job?"

"He dabbled in real estate. Some, anyway. Other than that, I guess his job was being Jeanette's husband."

"Sounds like a kept man."

A harsh epitaph, and unfair. Grayson worked harder for Jeanette than most men did at their nine-to-fives. In my mind, I could see his round, eager face turned toward her, anxiously awaiting her next request. Not my idea of the perfect husband, perhaps, but as they say, it takes all kinds.

"You're being unfair. He didn't just sit around counting Jeanette's money. If the zoo needed anything, from a gross of paper clips to new plantings for the cheetah exhibit, he was our point man."

"I'll take your word that the victim earned his keep."

We were both silent until I asked, "What's going to happen to Lucy?"

"Since the San Sebastian County Animal Shelter doesn't have suitable quarters for a giant anteater, we'll have to leave her here until…Well, until the zoo makes up its mind."

Which meant that the anteater's ultimate fate lay in Barry Fields' insensitive hands.

Unless I could prove Grayson was responsible for his own demise, Lucy was doomed.

Chapter Three

About an hour later, the sheriff finished interviewing everyone and released us. The earthly remains of Grayson Harrill were taken away to wherever earthly remains go, and soon afterward the crime scene techs departed.

Lucy remained distraught. Despite my efforts to soothe her, she paced back and forth along the holding pen fence, hissing like a snake. She wanted back into her big enclosure, but on the zoo director's orders she stayed off-exhibit. Perhaps permanently.

Having done all I could for her, I hopped into my electric zoo cart and continued my rounds. Next stop was Monkey Mania, the quarter-acre open-air exhibit where fifteen squirrel monkeys mingled freely with zoo visitors. I'd fed the monkeys first thing in the morning, but because of the unfortunate event in Lucy's enclosure, was late cleaning out their night quarters, a series of room-sized cages hidden amid the brush behind the exhibit itself. As I hosed down the last cage, I heard an all-too-familiar voice.

"Teddy, I need to talk to you!" My mother.

I froze, hoping she wouldn't see me. With everything that had happened, I wasn't ready to deal with her.

"Did you hear me, Theodora? I know you're in there because I can see that red hair of yours through the leaves!"

So much for avoiding her. I turned off the hose and waded through the troop of monkeys that had assembled outside the night quarters door, hoping for an extra handout.

"Sorry, guys, no more Monkey Chow until five."

Marlon, the big Alpha male—if a two-pound monkey can be said to be big—snuck his hand into my pocket hoping to find a tasty worm. When his hand came up empty, he shrieked at me in outrage.

"Told you so, Marlon. Now go entertain the kiddies."

For once Marlon did as he was told and led his troop away from the cages and onto the exhibit's gravel path. A tour group, noisy third-graders bussed up from Monterey, thirty miles south, cheered as the monkeys gamboled among them for several yards before taking to the trees. Having struck out with me, the monkeys began foraging, looking for leaves, beetles, and small birds. An omnivorous species, they weren't fussy.

"Theodora! I'm waiting!"

"Coming," I muttered, as I emerged from the brush.

Today Caroline Piper Bentley Mallory Huffgraf Petersen, looking at least a decade younger than her fifty-two years, was dressed in a fuchsia Lanvin dress offset by a silver Fendi handbag and fuchsia-and-white polka dot Ghesquiere pumps, an outfit hilariously out of place in a zoo. Since she usually dressed appropriately, the outfit confused me until I remembered that one of her favorite charities, the San Sebastian County Library Guild, had been slated to hold its monthly luncheon today. Why was she here, not there?

She wrinkled her nose. "You stink, Teddy."

"Taking care of monkeys will do that to you."

As if to lead me away from my life of grime, she took me by the arm, then immediately let go as if something from the scorpion exhibit had stung her. "What in the world?"

"One of the monkeys crapped on me before I could move out of the way."

With a cry of distaste, she opened her purse, hauled out some tissues and wiped a brown spot off her hand. "You don't have to live like this. Now that one of these nasty creatures has killed someone, you need to resign immediately. In fact, I want you to come home with me now."

Normally she behaved as if we were pals, not mother and daughter, but today she'd slipped back into the over-protective mother who'd driven me crazy throughout my teens. Ignoring her demands, I started up the winding pathway toward the exit, giving her the alternative to stay behind with my furry friends or follow me.

She chose the latter. "Didn't you hear me? If you really want to work, God knows you don't have to, we can find you another job in…"

"Please don't tell me you skipped your luncheon to start that again."

My job at the zoo had been an ongoing source of dissension ever since I'd left my teaching job in San Francisco. No compromise was possible. She didn't like the idea of a Bentley cleaning up after anyone, especially monkeys. I didn't like the idea of being trapped indoors all day with homo sapiens. Not that I have anything against homo sapiens.

Mother gave her hand a final flick with the tissue and handed it back to me instead of tossing it on the path. At least her work on the Zoo Guild, another of her organizations, had taught her that much.

"Since you ask, dear, Jeanette Gunn-Harrill was supposed to be our speaker today, but when we learned what happened to poor Grayson last night, we decided on a quick meeting to discuss what we could do for her. We wound up ordering flowers from La Jolie Jardiniere. Not lilies, too clichéd, but something sleek and comforting."

She waited for me to say, "That's nice." So I did.

"Look, I know you love your job, but I'm afraid you'll get hurt. You're my only child, for heaven's sake!"

One of the squirrel monkeys scampered across the walkway in front of us, carrying her baby on her back. Catching sight of a pink bead on her metal neckband, I identified her as Zsa Zsa, a first-time mom. Because first-borns rarely survive in the wild, their inexperienced mothers frequently being unable to cope, I'd prepared myself to hand-raise the baby. My caution proved unnecessary. Zsa Zsa loved her baby and if she had a flaw as a parent, it was in being over-protective. Gee, who did she remind me of?

"Mother, I'm perfectly safe here."

"I'm sure that's what Grayson thought before the anteater bit him. And don't call me 'Mother.' It's too age-specific. You know I prefer 'Caro.'"

"Anteaters have no teeth, *Caro*. She clawed him."

"Horrible!" Her hair, makeup and manicure were flawless; only the quiver of her collagened lower lip marred the perfection. That, and the slight pinky-orange tint her skin had taken on since she'd begun the La Jolla Strawberry/Carrot Diet a month earlier.

"It's time for you to rejoin the real world, Theodora, maybe go back to teaching."

Real world? This, from a woman who at a size three thought she was too fat?

I looked around at the playful monkeys, listened to their bird-like calls blending with the nearby kookaburra's cackles and the roar of the snow leopard six exhibits over. On the soft westerly breeze I could smell the Pacific, that liquid Eden populated by dolphins, whales and otters. If this wasn't the real world, I didn't know what was.

"I hated teaching. Besides, my teaching certificate has expired."

"You don't have to teach. You can…" Caro had never worked a day in her life, so her career advice tended to lack substance. "You can open a boutique."

"I'm not interested in clothes."

"How about an art gallery? I'll front the money."

"Gunn Landing already has more galleries than the tourist trade can support."

"Go back to school! Study law or something."

"Living with Michael soured me on the law." I wouldn't wish my ex-husband's hours on my worst enemy. Not even him.

"How about medicine? You're smart. You could be a doctor."

The urge to laugh returned. I had never been a good student, frequently nodding off from sheer boredom, ditching classes to ride my horses, guessing my way through tests. I'd achieved my bachelor's in biology and afterwards, my teaching credentials, by the skin of my teeth, so the idea of attempting medical school, even if one would accept me, was beyond ludicrous. All I wanted was to be outside in the sun and the rain and the fog and whatever the Central Coast climate threw at me. I especially wanted to be outside with animals. Like my Lucy.

Which reminded me of something that had been bothering me. "You were at the Zoo Guild fund-raiser last night. Wasn't Jeanette there, too?"

Caro stopped, a strange look on her face. "Of course she was, at least that's what I heard. They say she left early, without Grayson."

"What do you mean, 'they say'? You don't know for sure?"

"I wasn't at the funder. Something came up."

My mother hadn't attended the fund-raiser? Civic-minded to a fault, she never missed any Guild function. For now I let it pass. "You'd think that when Jeanette noticed her husband didn't make it back home, she would have called the police. Or did she? The sheriff didn't say anything like that."

As my mother stood there, one of the monkeys, an adolescent male named DiNiro, ran across her foot in pursuit of a dragonfly. She jerked her foot back as if the monkey were a snake.

"Ugh. Does it have fleas?"

"Probably. Did Jeanette and Grayson have a fight or something?"

"Don't be silly. Those two never fought."

She resumed walking toward the exit, eager to escape the free-range wildlife and return to the domain of human beings. Two more monkeys ran by, giving her a wide berth.

I hurried after her. "Jeanette never went anywhere without Grayson, so why'd she leave early? And later, how could she possibly not notice he wasn't in bed with her? They do sleep in the same bed, don't they?"

"I never asked." As we reached the exhibit gates, where another group of school children waited for their turn to walk among the monkeys, she halted again. "Why are you so interested in Jeanette's comings and goings? You went to school together, but you've never had two minutes to spare for her since then."

"Just curious, that's all."

She put her hand up, keeping me from opening the door and ushering her out of the exhibit. "Teddy, you're not a curious person now, and you weren't a curious child. You never cared for anything other than your horses or going out on some boat. In fact, you were so uncurious that I used to worry about you."

Used to? "Caro…"

"Oh, all right. I heard that halfway through the funder, Jeanette came down with one of those awful migraines of hers, so she left. Once she arrived home, she took enough medication to zonk her out for the duration. When the police showed up this morning she hadn't come around yet, and they had the devil of a time waking her. My maid heard that from her maid, you understand. I wasn't snooping or anything."

"Not you." I tried not to smile. "But if Jeanette was ill, why didn't Grayson leave with her, which is what he'd normally do? And how'd he get home? Walk? It's a half-mile uphill from here to Gunn Castle, and I don't remember him being all that fond of exercise."

"Teddy, I have no idea why he stayed on alone at the party. And as far as walking home goes, he wasn't *that* exercise-averse. Heavens, I could walk the distance in my Ghesquières!" She gave a smug glance at her pretty feet. "If the man was too lazy, well, he and Jeanette had plenty of friends at the funder, people like us who live in Old Town. They'd have to drive right by the castle on their way home, so maybe they dropped him off."

"You live in Old Town. I live on the *Merilee*."

She sniffed. "That ratty old boat's not your home. It's…It's… It's a place you're staying until you figure out what to do with your life. If you moved in with me, you could join the guilds, we could throw parties, take some cruises, and even double date! Wouldn't that be fun? I could take you to my cosmetic surgeon, too. I know Dr. Markgraffe would do a wonderful job on your nose. He's offering a Mother/Daughter Special this month, twenty-five percent off. While we're recovering, we could go hide out in some secluded spa, get seaweed wraps and high colonics."

I shuddered, unable to decide which sounded more unpleasant: cosmetic surgery, high colonics, or double-dating with my mother.

Fortunately, the children lined up at the gate began making enough noise to deflect my mother's latest attempt to lure me away from my job. The noise increased as one of the zoo's many volunteers walked the line, checking the children for any contraband the monkeys might steal. Candy, cell phones, guns. Searches completed, two volunteers escorted them into the enclosure to ensure that they didn't pull the monkeys' tails and to keep the monkeys from doing worse to them.

Stepping aside to let the children flow around her, Caro switched tactics. "I miss your company. Why don't you come up to the house for dinner tonight? When I was shopping in Carmel yesterday I picked up a cute Donna Karan I know you'll love and another one for myself in a different color. We'll look like sisters!"

I didn't want to look like my mother's sister, but I knew she wouldn't rest until she'd seen the Donna Karan on both our backs. I gave it a try, though. "Sorry. I need to sand the *Merilee*'s deck."

"Not at night you don't." She hauled another tissue out of her handbag, and with that clean barrier between her hand and my dirty arm, gave me a pat. "Seven o'clock. Look nice." Before I could come up with a better excuse she hurried out the gate.

Look nice.

It sounded like she'd found yet another eligible male for me.

The rest of the day passed without incident. Satisfied that I'd done everything needed to ensure my charges' welfare, I parked the zoo cart near the employees' entrance, clocked out, and climbed into my battered Nissan pickup. Then I drove home, a five-mile commute west between soft green hills that slowly leveled as they rolled down to the Pacific.

Home for me is a refitted 1979 thirty-four foot CHB trawler moored at Slip No. 34 in Gunn Landing Harbor. Living up the hill with Caro in Old Town was out of the question, but the Landing offered no affordable rentals. No rentals at all, actually, except for a few closet-sized fishermen's cottages and some over-the-garage flats occupied by the same tenants who had lived in them for years.

People don't move around much in the Landing. Once they find a place, they dig in, and for good reason.

Gunn Landing hadn't seen any new construction in decades. Given the restrictions imposed by the California Coastal Initiative, which severely limited development, the village would never sprout apartment buildings and condos. If not for the *Merilee*, I would have had to commute from Castroville or San Sebastian like other zoo employees. Although the boat could be cold and damp, I considered myself lucky.

When I stepped aboard, DJ Bonz, my three-legged Heinz 57 terrier, hopped to meet me. From the galley, Miss Priss, the one-eyed Persian I rescued from the pound's Death Row the same day I rescued Bonz, meowed as if she hadn't eaten for days. Before grabbing the dog's leash, I opened a can of Meow Mix and raked it into her bowl. Priss took one look and turned up her nose. She was just playing hard to get. By the time Bonz and I returned from our nightly walk, the cat food would be gone.

I snapped the leash on Bonz and headed out.

We strolled through Gunn Landing Park with the other dog-walkers. Bonz, amazingly nimble despite his handicap, sniffed along the pathway, stopping to mark every bench and trash can we encountered. He did his major business in the shadow of a red-stemmed filaree plant.

As I disposed of his droppings into a nearby trash can, I heard footsteps behind me. I turned to see Sheriff Joe Rejas, dressed in chinos and a windbreaker that matched the Irish blue eyes he'd inherited from his Dublin-born mother. I tried hard to ignore the easy swing of his broad shoulders, the long stride of his muscular legs, but failed. Just watching him move had always caused my breath to catch.

Fortunately, Joe, who was walking Fluffalooza, his late wife's elderly Bichon Frisé, appeared oblivious to my schoolgirlish yearnings. After the debacle with my ex-husband, I was nowhere ready to risk getting my heart broken again.

Our dogs sniffed each other. Fluffalooza waved her thick tail and Bonz wiggled his hindquarters back and forth in an attempt to wave his nonexistent one. Due to lack of support, he almost fell over once, but righted himself just in time.

"A bit far afield this evening, aren't you?" Joe lived fifteen miles away in San Sebastian, in the small adobe house his Hispanic grandfather had built sixty years earlier using money he had somehow saved from a lifetime spent picking artichokes for Anglo farmers.

Joe smiled. "Fluff wanted to see the sights. Besides, I need to ask you some questions." He moved close to me. Too close. But I couldn't bear to back away. Not while feeling the heat of his body.

"Official questions?"

The smile never left his face, or the warmth his eyes. "What else would they be?"

"I'm busy."

"Really? Doing what?" He moved even closer.

So close I could see the tiny scar near his mouth. I wanted to reach out and smooth it away. "Nothing that can't wait, I guess."

He traced the line of my cheek with his finger. "A new crop of freckles, I see. On you they look good."

Now I could feel his breath on my hair.

"Teddy, I…"

I took two steps backwards. "Let's get the questioning over with."

Pretending a casualness I didn't feel, I suggested we walk over to Chowder 'n' Cappuccino. A few minutes later we were seated at an outdoor table sipping decaf, watching the fishing boats straggle in. The dogs lay happily at our feet.

Making a big show out of looking at my watch, I said, "This'll have to be quick. I'm due at at Caro's for dinner."

When Joe leaned over to pet Fluffalooza, I couldn't see his face, which was probably just as well. "How is your mother these days?"

"Same as always."

"Too bad." Giving Fluffalooza a final pat, he straightened up. "Tell me everything you know about Grayson."

I couldn't hide my surprise. "Why do you want to know?"

He lowered his voice. "Because the medical examiner found a bullet in his abdomen."

My confusion deepened. "A bullet? Like an old war wound or something? Goodness, that is sad. I didn't really know him, you understand, but I never heard that he'd been the military, especially some place where he could have been shot, although considering how things are going in the world these days…"

"Someone killed him, and it wasn't the anteater. Turns out, the wounds that thing inflicted were all post-mortem."

"That *thing's* name is Lucy!"

"Don't you understand?" Joe said, sounding frustrated. "Someone murdered Grayson Harrill. But every time I try to question the folks who knew him, they clam up. There are two strikes against me. I'm the law, which they only respect at a distance, and worse, they're afraid I may be related to their maids. Since you're more familiar with these society types than I am, you could help me. Ask a few questions real casual-like, and find out who was where the night of the murder."

"Be a police snitch? Have you lost your mind?"

"This is serious, Teddy. Or doesn't murder mean anything to you?"

Remembering what was left of Grayson's body, I flushed. "Anything else you want me to do?"

"Tell me what you know about Grayson and his wife. And the rest of the family."

What I knew about the Gunns could fill several sets of encyclopedias, but I stalled for time. "What do they have to do with this?"

He sighed. "You used to be really smart before your mother shipped you off to that snooty girls' school."

Thus breaking up our teenage love affair. "Miss Pridewell's Academy wasn't snooty." But it was located in Virginia, and too far away for a fifteen-year-old girl to sneak back and see her half-Hispanic boyfriend. Which had been the whole point.

"Do I have to arrest you to make you to cooperate?" He tried to make a joke out of it.

Following his lead, I stretched my hands forward. "Cuff me now, Sheriff. Lawsuit to follow."

He laughed. "Now I remember why I fell in love…" He cut the sentence short and pretended to watch a big research vessel leaving the Gunn Landing Marine Institute dock. "About Grayson. He worked in real estate, right? How successful was he?"

"Only minimally. And just because I'm answering your questions doesn't mean I've agreed to do your dirty work."

"Understood. What else can you tell me about him?"

"He loved his wife. A lot. More than was healthy for either of them."

I described the time my mother had invited the couple to one of her parties. Grayson had spent the entire evening following Jeanette around like a puppy, even waiting for her outside the door every time she visited the powder room. Once I'd tried to lure him back into the living room with the promise of a drink, but he refused to leave his post.

"Jeanette wants me here when she comes out," he'd said.

The same behavior occurred at an Animal Welfare League dinner I'd once attended. Every time his wife left his side to chat with someone else, he began to fidget. Not that she was any more independent. When I'd steered him over to an exhibit table to see a model of the League's proposed no-kill animal shelter, she'd hurried along behind, as if fearing I was about to run off with him.

"He was at least twenty years older than her," I said. "Maybe she needed a father figure, and he needed a dependent daughter figure. Whatever their problems, it worked for them."

"They didn't have kids?"

"Nope."

"Her father is dead, right? Everett Gunn?"

I nodded. "Both her parents were killed on a nature expedition in South America, drowned when their boat overturned. She was around twenty when it happened. Since then she's been borderline agoraphobic and for the last year she's been getting worse. Could be that's what those migraines are all about." A seagull flew down and began to peck at the remnants of a biscotti. Bonz and Fluffalooza barked in unison, but the seagull ignored them. When two more seagulls joined him, the dogs hid under the table. "Grayson wasn't much of a traveler, either. He liked to stick close to home. I imagine that's why she married him."

"Or she was in love. Some people do marry for love, you know."

That stung. "I loved Michael!" But not like I'd loved Joe.

"Nothing personal."

I lowered my head so he wouldn't see the misery on my face. Why had I allowed my mother to break us up? And why had Joe given up so easily? Before I'd entered my senior year at Miss Pridewell's, he married his next-door neighbor, and by the time I graduated, they were expecting their first child.

When I left for college, I vowed never to let another man hurt me again. Then Michael came along.

"Teddy, I'm sorry."

I made myself look him straight in the face. "So am I."

He reached for me again, but I jerked away. I wasn't ready. At the sudden motion, DJ Bonz stood up on his three legs and growled. Startled, the seagulls flew off.

Joe moved his leg away from the perceived danger. "That dog better not bite me."

"His name is DJ Bonz. And he doesn't bite."

"Then why is he baring his teeth?"

"He's letting you know what he thinks of you." This is why I like animals so much. They never lie. Well, except for monkeys.

"You'd better tell him that as old as Fluffalooza is, she's at least two pounds heavier. She's protective, too."

"You look like you need protection, with that big gun under your windbreaker."

"The gun goes with the job description, like interrogating suspects. Which brings me to the question of the day. Why weren't you at the fund-raiser?"

I sucked in my breath. "What?"

"You know I have to ask."

After a few more deep breaths, I calmed down. He was right. Given the circumstances, he couldn't give me a free pass. Ex-lovers had to be questioned like everyone else.

"I couldn't attend as Caro's guest because I'm employed at the zoo, but I could hardly work the funder, either. Think how awkward that would be, serving drinks to people I know socially. Not attending was the best way to avoid a potentially embarrassing situation."

"Isn't your mother a member of the Zoo Guild?"

My blood pressure spiked. "Yes, and about every other guild in San Sebastian County. It's what she does." When she's not nagging me.

"I have a list of everyone in attendance, and she's not on it."

"She said something came up. Listen, keep me on your list of suspects if you want, but erase her. She liked Grayson, though she didn't appreciate him always pestering her to sell the Old Town house. He wanted to tear it down and put up condos, like Greenway Development did with the old Santana place. He nagged her for months, until she finally told him to leave her alone."

Joe chuckled. "That must have been a lively conversation. By the way, exactly how long has Grayson lived at Gunn Castle? Several years, right?"

"Since he and Jeanette got married. She insisted, and I don't think he put up much of a fight. The castle's a great place, if you like that sort of thing."

The research vessel had cleared the breakwater and was now headed into open sea, trailed by shrieking battalions of seagulls. They looked beautiful, but they lived on garbage.

Then something occurred to me, and I scrambled to my feet. "Gotta go. Talk to you later."

"I'm not finished with my questions."

"But I'm through answering."

I'd just realized that if the anteater hadn't killed Grayson, there was no longer any reason for her to be confined to the holding pen. On the off-chance the zoo director hadn't gone home yet, I wanted to call him immediately.

My exit across the park would have been more dignified if I hadn't stepped in a big pile of dog poop. But considering my line of work, what was one more dropping here or there?

Chapter Four

Unfortunately, the zoo's administrative offices were closed, and since I didn't have the director's home number, Lucy would stay in the holding pen for one more night. Having done everything possible, I dressed for my mother's Let's-Find-Teddy-A-New-Husband Party and made the short drive from the *Merilee* to Old Town.

Old Town crests a hill overlooking Gunn Landing Harbor, where Gunns, Bentleys, Pipers—Mother's kin—and a scattering of new people lived in too-large houses built in an era when household help was cheap.

Our own place is a Greek Revival topped off by a cube-like cupola where six generations of Bentleys have enjoyed the ocean view. At eighteen rooms, the house dwarfed its single inhabitant, but if Caro sold it and bought something more manageable, where would she put her Victorian sofas, American Empire tables, or Renaissance Revival poster bed? I could hardly see her living in some small condo. The lack of elbow room would make her nuttier than she already was.

Wearing the chartreuse-and-turquoise Donna Karan, my mother greeted my aged Dior with a frown, then force-marched me up the stairs to her bedroom suite, where the same dress as hers, only in yellow and orange, hung from a padded hanger. Once I slipped into it, I resembled a traffic light.

"You look perfect." Caro said. Obviously, not only men suffered from color-blindness. She grabbed a brush and began to rearrange my hair.

My mother was almost as beautiful as she had been thirty-four years earlier when she'd won the title of Miss San Sebastian County and fell in love with my father, one of the judges. After their marriage ended, facelifts kept her looking young enough to snag several more husbands.

Once she had rearranged my hair into a style more to her liking, I pulled away. "Can we go back downstairs now? I'm starved."

The shifty look in her eyes reminded me of the evening's true agenda: fixing up her daughter with an eligible bachelor. "I want you to look especially nice this evening. Maybe a quick manicure. I have some lovely…"

I hurried out the door.

Downstairs, while gobbling canapés, I saw a dark-haired man I didn't recognize hovering with others around the drinks table. Handsome, of what my mother would call "marriageable age," and from the appearance of his hand-tailored suit, the possessor of a marriageable bank account. I felt like a prize pig on an auction block but consoled myself thinking that he probably felt the same way.

Attempting to put off the encounter as long as possible, I loaded up a plate and headed for the French doors that overlooked the harbor. The sun sank toward the Pacific, casting a pink glow over everything. If I craned my neck to the left, I could almost see the lights of the fourteenth century castle that old Edwin Gunn, the family patriarch and the zoo's founder, had transported block-by-block from Scotland a hundred years ago. When I looked to the right, I could see all the way down to the harbor and Slip No. 34, where the *Merilee* bobbed on the incoming tide. How I longed to be there.

"Teddy, I'd like to introduce you to Sheridan Parker, of the Santa Barbara Parkers. He's living in San Francisco now." With those ominous words, Caro disappeared into a crowd of dinner guests, most of whom were members of the Zoo Guild. From their boisterous laughter, I guessed they'd already recovered from Grayson's untimely demise.

I bared my teeth at Parker. "Nice to meet you."

His smile was no more genuine than mine. "The same."

My gay-dar, a sixth sense Caro didn't share, signaled that he was not the eligible bachelor she assumed. His mother probably had cajoled him into this meeting, too. Gay, straight, it never made any difference. No matter who or what you were, mothers never gave up trying to change their children, probably a genetically linked trait.

My compassion activated toward a fellow sufferer, I offered a real smile and shifted the conversation to a neutral topic. "Did you know someone was killed at the Gunn Zoo last night?"

He perked up. "It's the talk of the Castro. Grayson Harrill, husband of one of the Gunn girls, right?"

Way to go, Caro. The Castro's only the largest gay neighborhood in the U.S. Guess you missed that part of the tour. "Yep, that's the guy. He was shot."

"The story I heard must be wrong, then, that the pregnant anteater attacked him. I hope she's okay. And her baby."

Too bad Sheridan was gay. He was my kind of guy. "They're both fine."

He finished what was left of his drink. At these get-togethers, Caro always served wine from Gunn Vineyard. "Strange place to shoot somebody, at a zoo."

"Not really. After the gates close, the only person around is a park ranger. The big cats roar all night, too, which might cover the sounds of any gunshots."

"Then I'll be sure to plan my next murder there. But if the anteater didn't do it, who did? The wife?"

"Jeanette?" Despite the seriousness of the situation, I laughed. "She's eccentric, but as for shooting someone, I can't see it. She was nuts about her husband and he felt the same way about her."

The maid arrived with two glasses of Chardonnay. I took a sip. Yep. Gunn Vineyard, and judging from the too-strong oak, an '05. Good German Rieslings were more my speed, but on my salary, I took what I could get.

Sheridan didn't seem to mind the over-oak, even gave an approving nod after a sip. "I only met them once, and I have to agree with you. They seemed devoted to each other. But if not the wife, who?"

Good question. "You met them? Where?"

"In the City. I'm with Braunstein, Steele, and Mohan. That's all I can say about it, though."

A business meeting, then. The very fact that Grayson and the almost-housebound Jeanette had made the ninety-mile drive to San Francisco to transact some hush-hush business made me curious. Did they belong to the faction attempting to break the Gunn Trust? I hadn't bothered to keep up on who wanted to retain the status quo and who preferred to take the money and run. The only thing I knew was that until this past year, the Trust had been considered unbreakable.

Before Edwin Gunn died on safari in Africa in 1935, he set up the Gunn Trust to ensure that his twenty-five-hundred acre inland estate would be kept intact for his six children and their descendants. Included in the Trust were the zoo, the vineyard with its attached winery, and the magnificent Gunn Castle, where much of the family still lived.

Over the years the estate had increased dramatically in value, as had the Trust's investments, earning the descendants sizeable dividend checks. Now some of the great-grandchildren wanted to cash out. One of the Gunn maids told my mother's maid that the family dinners had become so acrimonious that most of the aspiring Trust-breakers had decamped to San Francisco or Carmel. To the discomfort of the Trust loyalists and especially Aster Edwina Gunn, Edwin's sole surviving child, a few rebels remained.

I took another sip of my Chardonnay and pretended approval. "Nice. Braunstein, Steele and Mohan, hmm? Are they attorneys or…?"

"Yes, attorneys."

"Criminal? Accident?" When I saw no reaction, I added, "Divorce?"

"Trust attorneys."

"Jeanette and Grayson were part of the group trying to break the Gunn Trust?"

"I didn't say that."

"Of course you didn't. But just as a matter of conversation, do you think the Trust can be broken? I heard that one of the sons tried it back in the Fifties and failed. Then he went away to invent TV dinners or something."

Sheridan nodded. "That was one heir against the others. Now fifteen Gunns want to dissolve the Trust. To make matters even more interesting, several of the remaining twenty-three are reconsidering their positions. I'm giving no private information away, you understand. *The Examiner* published those numbers and suppositions a couple of months ago."

I noticed he didn't say the numbers and suppositions were incorrect. Alarmed, I said, "What happens to the zoo if the rebels are successful?" I wanted to kick myself for not staying better informed.

His eyes were wary. "Any particular reason you're asking?"

"I work there."

"Oh. When your mother said you had something to do with animals. I thought you were a horse trainer, hunter-jumper sort of thing. So you're a vet?"

"A zookeeper."

To his credit he didn't look shocked at my lowly title. "Lucky you, doing what you love. It must be nice being outdoors all day instead of being stuck in some office."

Belatedly realizing he hadn't answered my question, he was that wily, I repeated it. "If the Gunn Trust is broken, could it mean the end of the zoo? At five miles inland, it's not protected by the California Coastal Initiative."

He took a deep breath. He shuffled his feet. He looked down at the carpet. "Maybe not."

Never had the word "maybe" sounded so scary.

"Surely the zoo wouldn't be broken up!" What would happen to my animal friends then? Would they be replaced by developers who couldn't tell a Balearic Shearwater chick from a Hispaniolan galliwasp lizard?

He still couldn't look at me. "Trimmed down in size, maybe."

In other words, another Eden lost.

Chapter Five

My conversation with the zoo director didn't go as planned.

When I entered the administration building the next morning, Helen Gifford, his secretary, informed me he had a visitor. "A woman with money," she whispered, looking at the director's closed door. "Absolutely dripping with diamonds." She motioned me to a chair next to a table heaped high with magazines. "It shouldn't take too long. He's pretty fast when it comes to squeezing money out of women."

I started leafing through a copy of *National Geographic*, but, horrified by photographs of poached mountain gorillas and their severed heads and hands, quickly put it down.

To get my mind off the images, I asked, "You like working for Barry Fields?"

She shrugged. "Since I'm over sixty, I haven't had any trouble with him."

Before I could ask what she meant, the office door opened and the aged Lorena Haskell Anders, widow of P. Stephen Anders, who'd founded a national chain of sports outfitters, emerged. A beaming Barry Fields followed behind, wearing a different Armani sports coat than yesterday's. How many did he have?

A ten-carat rock weighed down one of the widow's wrinkled finger, rings with fractionally smaller stones encircled around the others. On her dewlapped neck, a diamond-and-sapphire necklace rose and fell with each breath. Fields' pitch on behalf of the zoo must have been successful, because she still held her checkbook in her hand.

Upon spotting me, Mrs. Anders gave me an air kiss. "How nice to see you, Theodora! I heard you were working at the zoo, but couldn't quite believe it. Yet here you are. How's your mother?" Without waiting for an answer, she said, "So sad about Grayson. Jeanette must be crushed. Have you tendered your condolences yet? I know you two used to be great friends."

There was no point in correcting her. "I plan to visit as soon as I get off work. She…"

Fields shifted his weight from foot to foot, looking anxious. Perhaps he feared that if the widow didn't leave soon, she'd reconsider her contribution. He cast me a look of annoyance. "Do you want something?"

"Yes, I…"

"Wait in my office." He slipped his arm around Mrs. Anders, gave her a peck on the cheek, and escorted her to the door. "Call me anytime," he purred. "I'm never too busy to talk to beautiful women."

Giggling, she left.

Ten minutes later I emerged from the director's office in defeat. While he'd agreed that the anteater had been proven innocent of murder, he still insisted she'd shown her true nature in her post mortem attack and needed to be confined to the holding pen until the zoo board handed down its decision. My argument that the zoo housed many Code Red animals—and in fact, that was what zoos were for—fell on deaf ears.

Frustrated, I left the administration building and headed for the animals' commissary, where I found the other keepers talking about the murder as they loaded lettuce and worms onto their zoo carts. Zorah wondered aloud what Grayson was doing at the anteater's enclosure.

"Maybe he wanted to see how her pregnancy was progressing." This from Jack Spence, the bear keeper.

The Anteater of Death   35

Zorah sniffed. "Not with his fear of animals. Remember how he acted with that little saki?"

A big woman in both height and girth, she seemed more harassed than ever. Her dark brown hair looked like it hadn't been combed in days and she'd inadvertently splashed zoo goo across the front of her khaki uniform. As she picked up another container of mealy worms for the frilled lizards, she mused, "I was too busy serving drinks in that stupid anteater costume to keep an eye on Grayson. Damn Barry, making us dress in animal drag! Where's the dignity?"

She had a masters degree in animal husbandry but had been edged out of the zoo director position by the business-wise, animal-ignorant Barry Fields. It made her more alert to affronts to her dignity than was normal for a poop-scooping zookeeper. When the directive came down that everyone assigned to work the fund-raiser must wear an anteater costume in honor of Lucy's pregnancy, her complaints had been loud and long. Her argument that the costume's long nose might flop into the drinks went unheeded.

Just like my pleas for Lucy's freedom.

I grabbed a tray of meat for the Mexican gray wolves and set it inside my cart next to a Tupperware container of termites. "I'd forgotten about the costumes. Did you tell the sheriff about them?"

"Of course," she replied. "I also told him Grayson partied pretty hard before...Well, before."

There had been rumors Grayson had a drinking problem, which might explain why he'd been foolish enough to enter the deep foliage of Tropics Trail by himself. Or allowed his killer to lead him there. "If he was drunk, he might have said something to upset anyone."

"I wouldn't know. He sure wasn't the only drunk around. By the end of the evening half the guests were in the bag, including our esteemed director."

We worked in silence for a while, but as I climbed into my zoo cart, Zorah called, "Hey, why wasn't your mom at the fund-raiser? She's never missed one before."

I had put Caro's absence to the back of my mind. I decided to ask her again, hoping she'd break down and tell me the truth. The chances weren't good, though. After being married so many times to so many different kinds of men, she'd learned to fib whenever it suited her purposes.

"Who knows why Caro does or doesn't do anything?"

Zorah's scowl disappeared, replaced by a warm smile. "Yeah. Your mom's an original. It must be fun being her daughter."

"It's an adventure, all right." On that note, I started my electric cart and began my morning rounds.

First Lucy, who didn't understand why she couldn't enter her big enclosure, then the squirrel monkeys, the Chacoan peccary, the capybara, and last but definitely not least, the Mexican gray wolves I'd temporarily inherited while their regular keeper was on vacation. On my way to the wolves, the Collie's magpie jay gave a big squawk and flew to the front of the large aviary to see me. I stopped to say hello.

"Good morning, Carlos. How's my favorite cuckoo bird?"

As beautiful as he was, with his royal blue and ebony plumage, the bird was clearly demented. For some obscure reason known only to his tiny avian mind, he had been trying to coax me into mating with him. Every day he offered me a twig to help him build our honeymoon suite. As I approached the aviary, Carlos stuck today's twig through the grid while mimicking the call of the Asian fairy bluebird on the perch behind him.

"Silly Carlos is a love-addled fool."

Delighted by my response, the magpie tilted his head, raised his crest, and pushed the twig out further. Touched, I took it. It's nice to be loved, even if only by a confused bird.

In an attempt to lure me into the aviary, he began running through his entire repertoire.

"*Whit-wheet!*" Curved bill thrasher.

"*Bzzz-zzzz-zzzz!*" Bluebird of paradise.

"*Eine-eine-eine!*" Black-backed gull.

"*Sweet-sweet-sweet!*" Yellow warbler.

"Flattery will get you everywhere, my man." I put my nose up to the aviary mesh and let him peck tenderly at my freckles. "*Sweet-sweet-sweet*," I mimicked back. "Carlos is a sweet, sweet bird."

He closed his eyes in ecstasy.

I stuck my finger through the mesh and scratched his white chest. "Yes, a sweet, sweet, sweet bird."

"*Boom-boom-boom!*" Double-wattled cassowary.

I gave his breast a final scratch. "You had me at 'Hello,' handsome."

Followed by his anguished shrieks—White-crowned fork-tail—I hopped back in my cart and continued on my rounds.

Four hours later, tummies fed and offal shoveled, I was taking a break in the staff lounge when I saw the sheriff heading up the path. The other keepers grinned at me but I tried to ignore them.

"Thought I'd catch you here," His warm smile made things worse.

Behind him, a keeper pretended to play a tiny violin. My former relationship with Joe Rejas had always been fodder for zoo gossip.

"Yep, this is where I am every day around this time, unless someone murders someone."

The minute the words were out of my mouth, I regretted them. The phrase was an old zookeeper's joke, meant to describe the carnivorous behavior of some of our charges, but in light of Grayson's death, it sounded in terrible taste.

"What is it you want, Sheriff?" I emphasized his title, thus alerting the eavesdroppers that this was no personal visit.

"We need to speak in private."

I surrendered to the inevitable. "Let's walk over to the ocelots. They sleep all day so they don't collect much of a crowd."

When we reached Raoul and Elena, they were sacked out under a greasewood bush in the corner of their habitat. I led Joe to a shady area, and we settled ourselves on a bench.

"My break ends in five minutes. After that, I need to give the orangutans some fresh palm fronds. They use them to make hats."

He blinked. "Orangutans *sew?*"

"They drape the palm fronds over their heads to keep off the afternoon sun."

Regaining his composure, he said, "Here's what new information we have. The medical examiner says the victim probably died somewhere around midnight Monday night. I've tried to find out who else was missing from the funder at that time but no one seems to know. Or they're claiming they don't."

He handed me a piece of paper. On it was a list of names that with only one or two exceptions, were people I knew.

"They'll be more open with you, so I'd appreciate it if you'd find out who was where at what time. That includes zoo staffers who worked the party."

I waved the long list at him. "You want me to talk to all these people?"

He nodded.

Not happy, I stuffed the list in my pocket. "I don't feel right about this. Anyway, it'll be next to impossible to find out who was where because at least half of them were wearing anteater costumes."

When he began to laugh, Elena opened one yellow-green eye and hissed. Satisfied she'd frightened him, she went back to sleep.

Keeping an uneasy eye on the ocelot, he said, "I heard about those crazy costumes. Whose idea was that?"

"Zorah thinks it was Barry Fields' but she's wrong. Decisions like that are made by the Zoo Guild president, which is most often Jeanette. Because of her migraines, she didn't run for election last time so Nancy Selby took over. And boy, did she run riot. When the zoo received three kangaroos last August, Nancy made everyone who worked the party wear kangaroo costumes. The keepers kept tripping over their tails and spilling drinks, so our liquor bill was enormous. When the zoo brought the maned wolves up from Bolivia in February, it looked like the days of costumes were over because there's no such thing as a maned wolf costume. But Jeanette, who was feeling better at the time, was able to find some dog…"

"I'd better talk to her again," he interrupted.

"No!" Jeanette had enough grief in her life right now without him breathing down her neck. "She was long gone from the party by the time Grayson was killed. Tell you what. After I walk Bonz this evening, I'm paying her a visit, so I'll ask a few questions. As you pointed out, she'll feel more relaxed with me. Not that I'm going to make a habit out of this sort of thing. I'd prefer you do your own detective work."

His smug smile showed that I'd played right into his hands. "Report back to me tonight. You remember my home number?"

I hadn't dialed it in fifteen years, but he was right. A woman never forgets her first love. Or his phone number.

The rest of the afternoon passed without incident, unless you count the man in Monkey Mania who was bitten while trying to grab one of the squirrel monkeys by the tail, or the toddler who ducked under the rope at Down Under and was knocked over by a passing wallaby.

Before leaving for the day, I visited the anteater again and hand-fed her a crushed banana through the links of the holding pen fence.

"My poor girl's lonely, isn't she?" This was mere zookeeper blather, because in the wild, giant anteaters were solitary creatures, pairing up only at mating time.

Lucy seemed to appreciate my attentions and rumbled *mmm-mmm-mmm* at me while her blue tongue flicked in and out of her long snout as it carried banana mush to her toothless mouth. Once the banana disappeared she leaned her hairy side against the fence, so I stuck a couple of fingers through the mesh and scratched at her.

In order to keep an animal's behavior as natural as possible, zookeepers are warned against establishing close personal relationships with their charges, but few obey the directive. Considering everything that had happened, I needed to remind Lucy that she did have at least one friend left, so I kept up my crooning while I dug my fingers more deeply into her coat.

She continued to respond. "*Mmm-mmm-mmm.*"

"Yes, Lucy, I know you're worried. But your Teddy is doing what she can to keep you right here in Gunn Landing." I kept on scratching and talking until she grew bored and trundled off, snuffling along the holding pen floor for more grubs.

Or perhaps searching for another ant-covered corpse.

As soon as I arrived back at the *Merilee* and took care of my own animals, I showered and changed into civilian clothes. After grabbing the bouquet of white and pink wildflowers I'd picked from the side of the road on my way home from the zoo, I headed inland to Gunn Castle.

In contrast to William Randolph Hearst's light-filled San Simeon a hundred miles to the south, the castle was gloomy and medieval, with six towers, a crenelated roof, and a row of archers' windows. I'd never enjoyed my childhood visits here, but I had to admit that the dour architecture and the moldy smell of centuries-old stone walls was only partially the reason.

Quarrelsome as children, the Gunns had grown even more argumentative over the years, especially now that the Trust and its possible dissolution had driven yet another wedge among them.

The castle wasn't a happy place but its setting was spectacular. The private lane leading up to the hilltop castle was lined with towering eucalyptus trees, some of them a hundred years old. Stretching for almost a thousand acres behind the castle was the famous vineyard with its undulating rows of Chardonnay, Pinot Noir, Syrah, and Grenache grapes.

As a child, I'd sometimes hitched a ride up there with older friends. While they visited the Gunns, I'd snuck out to the vineyard. Lying flat on my belly, I mooched along the rows, picking off ripe grapes and popping them into my mouth. On what turned out to be my final sortie, Aster Edwina herself caught me and, in the accepted custom of the day, tanned my bottom with a riding crop. When my abashed friends had delivered my sniveling self home to tell my sorry tale to my mother, I expected sympathy. To my disappointment, she merely told me to stay out of the Gunn vineyards. Years later, I discovered that as soon as she'd banished me to my room, she'd driven up to the castle and popped Aster Edwina in the nose with a roundhouse right.

To Aster Edwina's credit, she hadn't called the sheriff—Joe's father—but ever since, relations between the two had been frosty.

Fortunately, the old woman never held her sore nose against me. When I arrived at the castle, the housekeeper led me past the immense drawing room where members of the family were having a suspiciously cheerful-sounding gathering, and into the castle's mahogany-paneled library. Aster Edwina put down the book she had been reading—Machiavelli's *The Prince*—and greeted me with a smile.

"How kind of you to visit, Teddy. My niece will be pleased." She took the wildflowers and told the housekeeper to have one of the maids put them in water.

When we were alone, Aster Edwina touched my cheek with a spindly hand. "My dear, you must learn to wear a sunhat while working outdoors. You look positively scalded."

Judging from the youthful portrait hanging over the mantle, she had never been beautiful, but with her upswept snowy hair and military-straight back, she exuded a dignity that made mere beauty seem irrelevant. Her eyes were the same dark blue as the ocean from which her shipping magnate father had made his fortune, her dark eyelashes lending them fathoms of depth. Even her wrinkles, accrued through eighty-plus years of industrious living, only added to her stately presence. Yet she had never married and I suspected why. An eagle of a woman, she'd probably terrified prospective suitors.

"Thank you for your advice on my complexion. I'll remember it in the future."

Her smile made her look ten years younger. "You were always such a polite child. I'm so glad you came back to us. Both Michael and San Francisco were wrong for you. I told your mother that at the time."

"Oh, I, ah…" I didn't want to go where I feared she would go.

"Caroline didn't listen. Michael's family had all that lovely money, and that sort of thing matters to people like her. I guess she didn't know they were stingy, and wouldn't give either of you a cent."

Like my mother had done so many years ago, I was tempted to punch her one, but now she was too old to hit. Remembering Lucy and Carlos and all the other animals at the zoo, I clenched my teeth and took it.

Oblivious to my ire, she continued. "It's hard for these old families to lose everything like Caroline's did, so you must forgive her when she does things that seem incomprehensible to you. She's trying to protect you from the pain she suffered growing up poor."

"Caro's family was never poor." My visit was already turning into a debacle and I hadn't yet seen Jeanette.

"The Pipers weren't eating-out-of-trash-bins-poor, no, but very much so compared to their friends. Why do you think your mother pursued those silly beauty titles so fervently? To catch a rich husband, of course! Which she did, although that didn't last, did it? After your father absconded with all that money and the government seized everything, she had to move in with her brother. I grieved for you, dear, truly I did. Your uncle's quite the sot."

I wondered why she couldn't see the steam rising from my ears. "Uncle Bob's dried out and we got our house back."

"Only because after divorcing your father, Caroline immediately married that fool of a Mallory boy. I had an eye on him for poor Jeanette, but your mother beat me to it. No flies on Caroline! As soon as they returned from their honeymoon she talked him into buying the house and putting the title in her name. Your mother is something, child. You must be proud of her."

Fearing that if Aster Edwina continued in this vein any longer there would be yet another murder in San Sebastian County, I derailed her trip down Memory Lane. "Ma'am, I'm not here to discuss my mother's matrimonial adventures. I came to convey my condolences to Jeanette."

She picked up the small silver bell on the long library table and rang it. One of the maids, whom I suspected of eavesdropping, promptly entered with my wildflowers in a stoneware vase. I guessed they didn't rate one of the castle's many Mings.

"Show Miss Bentley to Miss Jeanette's room, Rose, then come back immediately. That fire's going out."

I looked over at the fireplace, noting that the blaze was already so high it threatened to set an entire shelf of leather-bound first editions on fire. I decided that Aster Edwina simply didn't want the maid to overhear whatever the grief-ridden Jeanette might blurt out. Like tyrants everywhere, she preferred to do the blurting.

In testimony to old stone's acoustic properties, I could hear sobs before we were halfway up the staircase to Jeanette's suite. The castle had twenty-two bedrooms, but now that the anti-Trust Gunns had found other living arrangements, many went unoccupied. Jeanette and Grayson had used the general exodus as an excuse to move into the Reynolds Suite, so-named for the portrait of the Duchess of Marlborough by Sir Joshua Reynolds hanging on one wall. The Duchess was dressed in white but sported a pink sash, and it was this sash which had inspired Jeanette's clumsy attempt at decorating.

This evening the Duchess looked sickly in the dim light, but not half as sickly as Jeanette, who lay slumped on an upholstered pink chaise by the fireplace. Her pink peignoir, the exact shade of the Duchess' sash, also matched the silk hangings on the canopied bed. Even the ice pack Jeanette pressed to her head had been covered in the same pink silk. But the half-empty bottle of Junipero Dry Gin that stood open on the floor next to the chaise wasn't pink. Since I could see no glass anywhere,

I could only surmise that the new widow was drinking straight from the bottle.

Without opening her eyes, she said, "Rose, I told you. No visitors." Her voice sounded hoarse.

"Miss Aster Edwina told me to bring Miss Bentley up, Ma'am."

Jeanette opened her eyes. They were so red they appeared to be bleeding. "Teddy? Is that really you?"

I leaned over the chaise and took her hand. "Please accept my condolences. I brought you flowers but Aster Edwina kept them downstairs." Behind me, I heard the door close softly as the maid left the room. I could only hope that she followed Aster Edwina's orders and went straight back to the library.

Jeanette grasped my hand tighter. "My darling is gone!"

To relieve the pressure, I sank to my knees. "Yes, I know. And I'm so sorry." With her husband's lack of height and too-gener-ous stomach, he hadn't exactly resembled Prince Charming, but she had loved him and that was the only thing that counted. "Is there anything I can do for you?"

"Sit with me and maybe Aster Edwina won't come back in. She's been...She's been..." She trailed off and began to sob again.

Aster Edwina had probably been paying regular visits to her room, demanding that she buck up, pull herself together, keep a stiff upper lip, and all the rest of that insensitive claptrap. But my old friend had never been made of such stern material.

In many ways, she and Grayson reminded me of deep sea anglerfish. Upon finding a mate, the male gives his lady love a bite, attaching himself to her like a pilot fish to a shark. Unlike the pilot fish, the male anglerfish never lets go. Little by little he dissolves until his skin and internal organs fuse with the female's and the male no longer exists as a separate entity. Technically a parasite, he has truly become one with his mate. After a while he dies, but the female, still connected to him, lives on.

As if Grayson was biologically attached to her, no one ever saw Jeanette without him. He took her shopping, he waited in the car while she visited friends, and at the castle dinners I had attended, he sat so close to her that their elbows touched.

"There's nothing you or anyone can do. My life is over." Her tone was dull.

Fearing Jeanette was at risk for suicide, I put my arms around her and began to list all the beauties remaining in the world: sunrises, sunsets, birds, otters, the Pacific lapping at Gunn Landing Beach. I babbled on until she pushed me away.

"You are every bit as crazy as Aster Edwina says you are. I don't care anything about that stuff—*you* do."

At least she was talking. "Tell me what you care about."

"Grayson."

"Besides him."

She lowered the ice bag to her temple, then grabbed the gin bottle by the neck and took a long drink. Ever the polite hostess, she held it out toward me. "Want some?" When I shook my head, she took another slug and set it back down. "What do I like? I never really thought about it. Well, I like winter. There's not as much ragweed then. Ragweed kicks up my migraines."

"Winter, good. How about skiing? You like to ski." Oops. Before they'd become so insular, she and Grayson used to ski St. Moritz every winter. "What else?"

"Horses?" She picked some lint from her pink peignoir. "Grayson and I rode together every morning until their dander started setting off my migraines."

Noting that she had always been a bit plump, I tried something else. "How about Lobster Newburg? Beef Wellington? Fritos?"

"Lobster Newburg was Grayson's favorite dish. He wasn't a beef person. And he said Fritos had too much salt, that they weren't good for me."

It was hopeless. She referenced her husband at my every suggestion, so I decided to just go ahead and ask my questions. "The night of the fund-raiser, why didn't Grayson come back to the castle with you?"

Her brain was so muddled with grief that she actually answered. "He said he needed to talk to the zoo director about something so I drove home alone. Difficult as that was. You know I always liked to have him with me."

She was as dependent on Grayson as he was on her. More so, lately. "The conversation with Barry Fields couldn't wait until the next morning?"

She screwed up her blotched face, which made her look plainer than ever. "He said it couldn't wait. Something he'd heard about, the…what was it? Oh, that independent vet study. He'd just received a copy of the preliminary report."

I failed to control my gasp. Fortunately, she was too far gone in her misery to notice.

After several high-profile animals, including two red pandas and three Asian elephants, had died at a high-profile zoo, some of the more radical animal rights groups had begun lobbying for all zoos to close down and return their animals to the wild. The fact that most zoo animals are born in captivity and could not fend for themselves did not sway them. The radicals believed that as soon as animals smelled fresh African tundra or pure Amazon River water, instinct would take over and they would revert to type.

More likely, the animals would starve to death.

But I didn't judge the radicals harshly because sometimes they had a point. A necropsy proved that the red pandas died from rat poison which accidentally made its way into their food, and that the elephants, although elderly, probably would have lived longer if they'd been given larger quarters and a better exercise regimen.

In a bid to counteract the ensuing bad publicity, the American Zoo and Aquarium Association had asked several zoos to open themselves to inspection by a committee of independent veterinarians from the National Academy of Sciences. To our horror, the Gunn Zoo had been chosen as one of them.

For several weeks, it seemed no one could go anywhere in the zoo without tripping over a vet collecting feces or staring up some mandrill's snout. Like my fellow keepers, I had breathed a sigh of relief when they finished their study and left, but now we were all waiting for the other shoe to drop: their report.

I tried to keep the concern out of my voice. "That's interest-ing, especially since the visiting vets were so close-mouthed about their findings. God knows I could never get a peep out of any of them, and I certainly tried. Did Grayson tell you how he was able to snag a copy of the report before it was released?"

She shook her head. "For some reason he was very secretive lately, which upset me, because normally he and I told each other everything." This propelled her into another bout of weeping.

Secretive? Old anglerfish Grayson, a man so attached to his wife you couldn't tell where he left off and she began?

"Before he was mur...ah, died, did he ever mention any other meetings he might have had with Barry Fields? Or with Dr. Kate?"

Kate Long was the zoo veterinarian. If the zoo didn't look good on the report, her neck would be on the chopping block, and since she had an invalid husband and three young children, I doubted she would mount that chopping block without a fight.

Jeanette shook her head again. "He wouldn't tell me."

"Another thing. Were you the person who decided to put the staff in anteater costumes?"

"We planned everything so long ago that it's hard to remem-ber. I ordered the costumes, I remember that, because getting so many anteater costumes was a real bitch, but I think Barry was the person who made the original suggestion. Or maybe it was...let's see. We had this big planning session and everyone was talking at once, suggesting this and that. The costume thing had pretty much run its course after the kangaroo debacle, but no one listened to me. What difference does it make?"

I shrugged. "An anteater costume with its long nose and thick hair would make a good disguise for anyone who might be up to something."

She began crying again, more softly this time. I kept kneeling there on the floor, holding her hand. When her tears diminished, she took another swig of gin. "I don't understand. Why would anyone want to hurt him?"

"Weren't you two part of the group that wanted to break up the Gunn Trust?"

She blinked at this seeming change of subject but answered anyway. "Of course. It's the only possible position. Unless the Trust is broken, Grayson and I will remain under my great-aunt's thumb." *Will remain.* She spoke as if her husband were still alive. "As Great-grandpa Edwin's last living child, Aster Edwina holds the controlling interest. I'm only fourth generation, and with those niggardly dividend checks I've been receiving, Grayson and I can't afford to strike out on our own. Not if we want to have a decent standard of living, we can't."

Her face changed. "Oh. That's right. He's dead." Through renewed sobs, she wailed, "What am I going to do without him?"

Thirty years old, married for ten years, and she had only recently decided to cut the Gunn apron strings. I'd always viewed her relationship with her husband as neurotic, but today I felt nothing but pity. Love can put a woman through hell, can't it?

"It's never easy after a loss, but you'll begin a new life. Like I did after Michael left me."

Her mouth dropped. "Oh, Teddy! You call what you have a *life?*"

⟨⟩⟨⟩⟨⟩

When I arrived home at the *Merilee*, I made myself a peanut butter and jelly sandwich, poured myself a glass of Riesling and went out on the back deck to watch seagulls dive into sunset-colored water. Their cries accompanied the splashing of waves against the *Merilee's* hull, and from further along the dock, I could hear a woman's gentle laughter, a man answering in a low tone. Further out in the harbor an otter broke the surface.

Smiling in anticipation, I made a quick trip to my small galley refrigerator and took out a dock-fresh herring I'd picked up earlier at Fred's Fish Market. I returned to the back deck, took a sip of my Riesling, and settled myself into the deck chair I'd liberated from the Gunn Landing town dump. DJ Bonz jumped up, curled next to me with his head on my belly and promptly went to sleep. Miss Priss followed, kneading a place for herself across my thighs. She slapped a quick paw at the herring, so I tapped her nose.

"No, greedy. It's not for you."

My muscles ached from the hard physical labor I'd put in, but it was a comforting ache, a tangible reminder of an honest day's work. While the gulls swooped down to grab fish foolish enough to stay near the water's surface, I breathed in the salty air, marveling at how well it went with Riesling and peanut butter.

I smiled, at ease with myself and the world. "This is the life, isn't it, Priss?"

The cat stared at me through her one good eye. While she couldn't answer, her smug look told me she agreed.

I was mulling over my great good fortune to be living here, when my cell phone rang. Annoyed, I took it out of my pocket and checked the caller ID screen. Joe.

Pittypat, went my heart.

"Is this a professional call or personal?" I asked him.

"Either. Or." Behind him, I could hear the TV tuned to something with a laugh track. One of his children begged to be allowed to stay up for a few more minutes to finish the show. In an exasperated voice, he said, "Hold on," and put the phone down.

For about the three-thousandth time I wondered what my life would have been like if I'd ignored my mother's edict and run off with him, as we'd once planned to do. We would have our own family by now. I would never have met Michael.

Or lost my faith in love.

Once the background noise subsided, Joe returned to the phone. "Kids. They drive you crazy and still you love them. Let's get business out of the way, first, shall we? What did you find out at the castle? When I went up there, they'd lawyered up, especially Aster Edwina. Jesus, what a piece of work she is."

Fluffalooza barked on the other end of the line, and Bonz cocked his head. Seeing no nearby threat, he went back to sleep.

"Teddy?"

"You wouldn't need a spy if you read the newspapers."

"I subscribe to three papers, Ms. Smartypants, and read everything from the front page to the obits. Especially the obits. What's your point? If you have one."

"The Gunn Trust is the point. Grayson's death may shift the Trust vote. I doubt if his wife will continue the fight without him." Which was excellent news for the zoo.

A grunt. "Are you saying the Trust might stay intact now?"

"Draw your own conclusions. I'm going to hang up."

"Not yet!"

The otter, who from the white tuft of fur on her side I identified as Maureen, had made it all the way to the dock and was swimming from boat to boat, nosing around for handouts. She'd reach the *Merilee* in seconds.

"Teddy, why wasn't your mother at the fund-raiser?"

Maureen poked her nose up less than three feet from me. I tossed her a herring. "Sweets for the sweet."

"Stop talking to whatever animal you're talking to and answer."

There's nothing I hate more than having people order me around. "If you want to know why Caro wasn't there, ask her yourself."

"*There's* a scary thought. As long as we're on that subject, how many keepers missed the big do?"

"Ask Zorah Vega. She was supposed to keep track of everyone, but I do know there were supposed to be something like a dozen keepers present."

"I'll do that. In the meantime, how well do you know Kim Markowski?"

"Our education director?" Out of sheer surprise, I opened up. "We're not close. She's always looking for volunteers for some goofy new program she's setting up so I try to stay out of her way. Why?"

"She wasn't at the fund-raiser, either."

I frowned. "She should have been, because that kind of thing is her job. She was scheduled to give a puppet show about the anteater." Then I remembered what I should have remembered earlier. "Scratch that. Zorah told me Kim broke her ankle Sunday, so I'm sure it was too painful for her to get out and about yet. And with a cast, there's no way she could have fit into an anteater suit."

"How'd she break her ankle?"

He sounded so suspicious I laughed. "The way I heard it, she was in Carmel shopping and fell off a curb. You know what that town's like, nothing but boutiques, hills, and fog. I imagine the curb was slippery and she wasn't watching where she was going. Kim's always been clumsy. Last winter she broke her wrist just banging into a door."

A splash caught my attention. The otter wanted another herring. With a grunt, I eased my dog and cat off my lap and headed toward the galley, phone to ear. "Look, I'm pretty busy here. Furthermore, this whole idea of playing Spy-on-My-Friends is making me uncomfortable. So goodbye."

I pressed OFF and selected another herring from the fridge.

The intrusions into my peaceful evening continued. As soon as I settled back into my chaise to watch the sunset, the cell rang again. This time it was my mother, her voice grim with determination.

"Teddy, I can't get the idea of what that anteater did to Grayson out of my mind, and the dangerous turn your life has taken. Someone told me you're actually feeding wolves, for heaven's sake! You need to know that I've made an appointment to see the zoo director tomorrow and I'm going to tell him that if he wants the zoo to continue receiving my annual donation—which runs five figures, by the way—he'll terminate your employment immediately."

For some time now I had been expecting Caro to pull a stunt like this so I was prepared. "How are things going with Cyril Keslar, of the Montecito Keslars?" Her prospective Husband Number Five.

"What's Cyril got to do with anything?"

Too bad she couldn't see my smirk. "If you tell the zoo director to fire me, I'll tell the sheriff where you hid Dad's money. That'll screw you with your boyfriend, who's as upright as he is rich." One good blackmail attempt deserves another.

A gasp. "How…how did you know about the money?"

I didn't answer.

My discovery of the whereabouts of Dad's big haul had come about entirely by accident. Before being shipped off to Miss Pridewell's Academy, I had wandered into Caro's bedroom one day as teens are prone to do, and hunted through her dresser drawers for her silk camisole. I didn't plan on wearing it *under* my clothing. Instead, I had a Madonna-style outfit in mind that was certain to shock my teachers and elicit the envy of my classmates, sort of a teenage two-fer.

Imagine my own shock when, hiding under the camisole, I found a letter from my disgraced father, postmarked five years earlier from Costa Rica, where he'd fled to avoid prosecution. After several paragraphs apologizing for the shame he'd brought upon his family, he told Caro how to access a Swiss account where he'd stashed part of the money he'd embezzled from Bentley, Bentley, Haight, and Busby. Paper-clipped to the letter was a statement from a bank in the Bahamas, where my mother had shifted some of the money for her own purposes.

Appalled by my threat, she shrieked, "I'd go to jail!"

This was working better than I'd hoped, not that I'd ever follow through on my threat. "Don't worry. The Feds will probably put you in one of those country club prisons, the kind Martha Stewart was in. Or should I call the lady by her jailhouse name, 'M-Diddy.' Big Bertha, your cellmate, might dub you C-Diddy. Wouldn't that be cute? I promise to visit every Sunday, that is, if I don't have to move out of state to find a job at another zoo. Maybe Miami's Metrozoo, although that is a long way off, and I'd only be able to visit you a couple times a year."

Dark mutterings from the other end of the line. "All right, all right. I'll cancel my appointment with Barry Fields."

"How considerate." Before I stabbed the OFF button, one final word from Caro leaked through. Because the phone was several inches away from my ear by then, the word was faint, but I think what she said was...

"Brat!"

<><><>

I arrived at the zoo early the next day to take my regular Thursday pleasure walk through Down Under, but halfway there saw several keepers running full tilt toward Africa Trail. One slowed for a moment to yell, "It's Makeba!" then sped up again.

With a whoop, I chased after them.

Half a mile and four twisty turns later, I rounded the thick stand of banana trees at the side of the large pasture we'd dubbed the Veldt to see that the tip of a tiny hoof had emerged from the birth canal of Makeba, our Masai Giraffe. In the manner of giraffes in the wild, she remained standing up. Trying not to breathe too loudly, I joined the hushed crowd of keepers gathered to watch the birth.

"She's two weeks early," Zorah whispered, her blunt-featured face pale with anxiety. "I radioed Dr. Kate the second I noticed what was going on."

The zoo's veterinarian lived in a house at the far eastern end of the zoo with her family, and for all intents and purposes was on call twenty-four hours a day every day. When a possibly difficult birth was imminent she sometimes camped out on the sofa in her office, or in a sleeping bag near the animal's night quarters.

Nature, having its own timetable, ignored the vet's plans. Makeba was giving birth on hard dirt instead of in the hay-cushioned birthing stall where we'd planned to move her. Instead of blissful privacy, she was surrounded by keepers and other giraffes. Nearby stood her mate, all eighteen-feet-eight-inches of him, and next to him, Makeba's closest female friend, who would—if everything went according to plan—serve as nanny to the newborn. In contrast to the giddy keepers, Makeba stood quietly.

As another tiny hoof pushed out of Makeba's birth canal, I heard the sound of a zoo cart. Dr. Kate.

She hadn't combed her wild black hair, and had thrown a lab coat over her pajamas. Like everyone else, she kept her voice low. "Anyone know when this started?"

Zorah shook her head. "One foot was already out when I arrived, and that was about five minutes ago. Now I see shins."

Some of the concern left the vet's face. "Good. She's going fast. The feet are pointing down, which means the baby's coming out head first. I want this exhibit cordoned off until the baby drops and we can herd them into the night house. The fewer gawkers the better." With that, she radioed the head park ranger and told him what was needed.

By the time the rangers arrived with yellow tape and saw-horses, the calf's shins had fully emerged and we could see a pair of knobby knees. Then…

The tip of a tiny snout.

"Head down! Head down!" Although Zorah kept her voice so low that it was little more than a rasp, her big body bounced up and down in excitement. "Good to go!"

So far. Sometimes a baby giraffe was born with its long neck bent backwards along its sides, which presented a problem for the mother. Makeba's calf was doing it the right way, with its head out and down, protected between two long front legs. The critical moment would come when the calf dropped six feet to the ground and landed on its head and vulnerable neck. Unable to withstand the drop, some calves died at this stage, which was nature's way of ensuring that only the strong survived.

While the clock ticked on and the birthing process continued, the noise level in the zoo increased. The baboons screamed their hunger. So did the lions.

Once or twice I saw an expression of guilt sweep across a keeper's face when she heard her own charge complain about an empty belly, but no one moved. Sometimes an emergency with one animal screwed up schedules with the others, but it did them no harm. Meals in the wild weren't served by the clock, either. My own Lucy would be angry, but after she ate her first helping of termite-sprinkled Monkey Chow topped off by a banana for dessert, she'd recover.

"Look at the neck! It's so perfect!" Zorah, for whom the giraffe was a personal favorite, almost clapped her hands, but restrained herself in time.

Yes, the calf's neck was perfect. So were the feet, which hung in the air below Makeba's birth canal, as well as the head dangling between them. The calf's eyes were still closed, which meant nothing. Sometimes the baby had to hit the ground before it awoke to the world. Its horns were nowhere to be seen, either, just two small nubs from which they would emerge in a few days.

"Here come the shoulders." Dr. Kate's whisper was so ragged that I took my eyes off the calf for a second and looked over just as she snapped open her emergency bag. From its shadows, I could see the silver gleam of something sharp.

Getting the calf's two-feet wide shoulders out of its mother's narrow vagina was the most difficult and dangerous part of a giraffe's birth process, and if was going to be serious trouble, it would happen now.

If Makeba needed help, Dr. Kate vet would hop the fence and do whatever was necessary. Fortunately for the vet, giraffes were among the gentlest of animals and not even Makeba's mate would attack without cause. If he ever did charge someone, a blow from his dinner plate-sized rear hoof—or worse, his eight-foot-long neck—could be fatal. The same gentleness wasn't true of the ostriches, who pecked at the ground nearby. Big D, the alpha male of the small flock which lived in the big pasture with the giraffes, was vicious and had once almost killed a keeper with a kick from his clawed foot. It would be up to us keepers to ensure that Big D stayed away if Dr. Kate had to enter the enclosure, even if it put our own lives at risk. Zookeepers were members of a mutual protection society.

"Aaaaahhhh!" A collective sigh of relief from the keepers as the calf's shoulders popped through. Now came the easy part, the narrow sides, the hindquarters, the rear legs…

The calf fell.

Six feet to the ground.

On its head.

No one breathed. Zorah grabbed me so hard on the forearm that I knew it would bloom with bruises tomorrow. I hung onto Dr. Kate in exactly the same way.

The calf raised its head and opened its eyes.

"Maaaaaah," it bleated.

Makeba turned around, blinked her long-lashed brown eyes, and stared at the calf as if trying to figure out what this strange thing was. Then she lowered her elegant head and began to clean her baby with a long, sticky tongue.

I wasn't aware that I was holding my breath, or that everyone else was, until I expelled air with a sound that resembled the calf's bleat.

Sounds of snuffling. I turned to see big Zorah, as muscular as a man, with tears of joy streaming down her face. Although too coarse-featured to be considered pretty, she looked radiant. I touched my own cheek and found it as wet as hers. Glancing around at my fellow keepers, I saw that they were all smiling and crying. So were the park rangers.

Just another day at the office.

I hugged Zorah. She hugged back. We both hugged Dr. Kate, who was trying her professional best not to weep along with the rest of us. Not being a good actress, she failed, and a tiny tear dribbled down her cheek.

Suddenly someone pulled Zorah away from me and a deep male voice interrupted our celebration of life.

"Zorah Vega, I'm arresting you for the murder of Grayson Harrill. You have the right to remain silent..." The rest of the words were lost among the loud protests of the keepers as Sheriff Joe Rejas, flanked by two deputies, snapped a pair of handcuffs around Zorah's wrists and led her away.

Chapter Six

"There's no way she killed Grayson!" Dr. Kate stormed, as we watched the sheriff stuff Zorah into his patrol car. "She's one of the gentlest human beings I know."

"With animals, maybe," said Jack Spence, the zoo's bear keeper, a tall, string bean of a man with light brown hair and gray eyes so pale he looked half blind. Yet his vision was sharp and he missed nothing. "Remember what she did to the guy she caught trying to feed a razor-laced apple to the orangutans? Even after he went down she kept kicking him. His teeth were scattered all over the place."

"Are you saying you think she's a murderer?" asked Miranda DiBartolo, a darkly pretty keeper who cared for the marsupials in Down Under. "Because if you are…" She moved toward Jack, her delicate hands balled into fists.

The vet stepped between them. "Miranda, I want you to bring that new wallaby down to the Animal Care Center for a checkup. And Jack, I'm not sure the spectacled bears' play platform will hold up under their weight, so look at it again. As for me, I'm going to lure Makeba and her baby into their night house for an examination. Now let's calm down and get back to work. We all know the sheriff's made a mistake, but there's nothing any of us can do about it now."

Grumbling, we dispersed to our various areas, but I couldn't stop thinking about Zorah. Instead of my standard long chat with Lucy, I merely left her to her breakfast. I repeated my hurried performance at Monkey Mania, where Marlon, who normally was so self-absorbed that keepers didn't exist for him, noticed something was wrong and bared his teeth at me.

For the next few hours, I rushed from one animal to another, not interacting with my charges in any meaningful way. I even brushed away the approaches of the other keepers when they wanted to discuss the arrest. Time was wasting, and I had places to go, prisoners to see.

◇◇◇

After stopping briefly at the *Merilee*, I drove to the county seat of San Sebastian, a small city founded in the late-eighteen hundreds by my great-great-great grandfather, cattle rancher Ezekiel Bentley. Fortunately for Zorah, loyalty to the Bentleys remained strong in the town. The sheriff was nowhere around, but Emilio Guiterrez, the deputy in charge of the lockup and a descendant of one of Ezekiel's vaqueros, agreed to let me see Zorah even though visiting hours were over.

"I'm pretty sure the sheriff's gone for the day, but just in case, don't let him find out about this," Emilio cautioned.

He unlocked the big metal door separating the jail's business area from the netherworld beyond. After a short walk between cells filled with male drunks and thieves, we entered the smaller women's section where Zorah sat slumped on a cot. At least she wasn't alone. In the cell on her left was a raving white woman, on the right, a morose Hispanic. Clad in a bright orange jumpsuit which did nothing for her complexion, Zorah ignored them both and stared grimly at the painted cement floor.

When she lifted her head and saw the deputy pulling up a chair for me outside her cell, the first words out of her mouth were, "How's the baby giraffe? Is it walking around yet? Nursing?"

Not *Get me out of here,* or *I swear I'm innocent.* She never worried about herself, only her animals.

Happy to give her good news, I assured her the calf walked within thirty minutes of birth, nursed in forty.

"It's perfectly healthy, then? No problems at all?"

The shrieks of the white woman in the next cell grew louder, so I had to shout. "It looks that way, but to make sure, Dr. Kate had moved mom and baby to the night quarters and plans to keep them under observation for awhile." I scooted my chair closer until it almost touched the bars.

Although the jail itself was almost a century old, the blanket on Zorah's cot didn't look it. Neither did her aluminum toilet and sink. In fact, both looked brand new. Apparently the sheriff had kept his campaign promise to modernize.

"How about the Bengals? And the frilled lizards?"

The white woman's voice dropped a few decibels so I was able to assure Zorah in a more normal voice that those animals were fine, too. Because the rest of us had taken over a portion of her schedule, not one had missed a meal or a cleanup. I myself had helped feed Maharaja and Ranee, the young Bengal tigers we'd bought from the St. Louis Zoo. The feeding process had been a complicated one, involving two other keepers and various maneuvers through an intricate series of gates.

I related the details. "Ranee was crawling around the enclosure on her belly with her tail in the air, yowling and howling."

Zorah managed a smile. "She's in heat. Did Maharaja look interested?"

"Just confused."

"Typical young male." Her face fell. "I'm in bad trouble, aren't I?"

I kept my tone light, which considering the circumstances, was difficult. Especially when the white woman started raving again. "Only if you killed Grayson, which I'm certain you didn't."

"I never touched him."

"Then why does the sheriff think you did?"

After a quick look around, she answered in a voice so low I had trouble hearing her over the other woman's curses. "For starters, he must have found out that I disappeared for about an hour during the fund-raiser. Right around the time someone offed the guy."

"Where were you?"

Her ears turned red. "I'd been sneaking drinks and wound up getting sick behind the monkey's night quarters. And before you ask why I didn't use the restroom, I didn't want any of our well-heeled guests to see the head keeper barfing up her insides. Fat lot of good it did me, though. I ripped my stupid anteater costume while I was thrashing around in the underbrush."

Light dawned. "You had a hangover when I discovered the body, didn't you? That's why you weren't there to see about the anteater." Knowing she had strong reasons for being unhappy, I couldn't judge her.

A shame-faced nod. "I never could hold my liquor."

"But there has to be another reason. The sheriff wouldn't arrest you just because you disappeared during the fund-raiser."

Her eyes darted away from mine and her voice dropped to a whisper. "I, um, wrote some letters."

"What kind of letters?"

She hunched her big shoulders forward and stared at the floor again. "To Grayson. I hoped that if I told him how badly he'd screwed up when he'd hired Barry Fields, he'd rethink his decision."

Animal smart, people dumb; that was Zorah all over.

I waited for more, but she just continued staring at the floor. I looked down, expecting from her intense concentration to see a cockroach crawling along its gray-painted surface, and saw nothing other than scuff marks.

When she looked up, the glint in her eyes made me glad I wasn't in the cell with her. "Grayson *told* me I had the job. Next thing I knew, he turned around and gave it to Barry. Where's the sense in that?"

It amazed me that Grayson, a man I'd always thought was honest, had not only made such a bad decision but had lied to her about it. Knowing how timid he could be at times, though, perhaps he couldn't face telling her the truth. After thinking over the job requirements, he might have decided that familiarity with fund-raising was more important than familiarity with animals. The zoo was a private facility, and without considerable grants and generous donations from wealthy widows, it couldn't survive. Even though the Gunns paid most of the bills, at least thirty percent of the zoo's operating costs had to come from other sources.

I tried my best to explain. "Fields is good at getting money out of people. I've seen him in action."

She sneered. "It always comes down to money, doesn't it?"

"It usually does."

Now, instead of shouting vague curses, the white woman started muttering something about her neighbor's cat. I didn't want to hear the details.

"The hiring committee should have voided the appointment as soon as they found out," Zorah said.

"They wouldn't dare. Since Aster Edwina stopped being active at the zoo a few years ago, Jeanette and Grayson represent the family interests, so when he picked someone else over you, the hiring committee felt they had no choice but to rubber-stamp the appointment." I'd have to revise my opinion of Grayson, though. It was beginning to appear that he wasn't the wishy-washy little man I'd always believed him to be.

She looked back down at the floor. "It's not fair."

I thought about Michael and the animated Barbie doll he'd divorced me for. "Life seldom is."

Now we both stared at the floor.

After a few moments, I asked, "Do you have an attorney?"

She shook her head. "You've seen that junker I drive. Does it look like I can afford a lawyer? I'll have to take what the county can scrounge up for me."

Meaning a court-appointed attorney, most of whom were too overworked to give their clients the attention they deserved. "When's your arraignment?"

"Monday. That's when I'll find out how much bail's going to be. Not that it matters. My family couldn't raise fifty cents."

I could if I broke an old promise to myself and dipped into the offshore account my father had set up for me in the

Cayman Islands after fleeing to Costa Rica. Shamed by my father's behavior, I'd never touched it, so technically, I was flat broke. However, I held a different kind of currency—powerful friends, some of them attorneys. I decided to make some calls on Zorah's behalf.

In the meantime, I needed to know something else. "I'll do what I can but first you need to tell me *exactly* what was in those letters you wrote."

"I can't believe how stupid I was!"

"If stupid was against the law, we'd all be in jail. Tell me about the letters."

When she summed them up as best she could, I felt sick. After Michael left me I'd written him a few letters, too. Unlike Zorah, I hadn't come right out and said he deserved to die a painful, lingering death; I'd merely implied it.

Giving her a confident smile, I stood to leave. "If those letters are the only things the sheriff has on you, I don't think you have much to worry about. He's flirting with a false arrest lawsuit."

She shifted around on her cot so I couldn't see her face. "There is one other thing."

I sat back down. "Tell me."

"Last week I, uh, lost something."

Before she could answer, the heavy door closing off the cell block opened. I turned to see the sheriff standing in the entryway. He didn't look pleased.

"Hi, Joe!" I called.

"Hi, yourself. You're not supposed to be in here."

Zorah scuttled away from the bars as if they were on fire.

"I thought you were gone for the day."

"You thought wrong."

Thinking furiously, I said to Zorah's back, "Yeah, Zorah, I promise to keep a special eye on that tiger." To Joe, "We were going over some zoo stuff."

He walked toward us, his shoes echoing across the cement. "Didn't you hear me? You're not supposed to be in here."

I forced a laugh. "What did you think I was going to do? Slip her a file?"

He towered over me. "That's not funny."

Refusing to be intimidated by his six-foot, two-inch height, I stood up and met his eyes even though it gave me a crick in my neck. Oh, he was so heartbreakingly handsome. But that was the operative word, wasn't it? *Heartbreaking*. And I'd had enough of that.

"You know my schedule, Joe. There's no way I could leave the zoo and get here in time for regular visiting hours."

"You could have waited for the weekend."

"The animals couldn't."

His scowl slipped. "Don't you people have a back-up plan?"

Of course we did, but I wasn't about to admit it. "For sickness and vacations, not something like this. Look, I can sympathize with your security concerns, but we zookeepers have problems you'll never understand. Beside the Bengals—*Panthera tigria*—there's the snow leopards—*Panthera uncias*—which I'm sure you know also are endangered. Why, less than five thousand survive in the wild today! They have special needs, just like the…" I took a deep breath, then assaulted him with more Latin. "…the *Neofelis nebulosa* and the…"

He raised his hands and backed away. "All right, all right. I'll give you five more minutes, but you stop by my office before you leave, okay?" With that, he fled.

I sat back down. "Let's go back to what we were really talking about."

No reply. Zorah stood against the cell's far wall with her face in her hands. I heard a sniffle. My brave friend, a woman who'd faced down hungry lions and anacondas, reduced to this. The Hispanic woman in the cell next to hers reached through the bars and patted her on the shoulder, murmuring something in Spanish I couldn't quite catch.

I raised my voice. "If I'm going to help you, you need to tell me everything."

Zorah crept back to her cot. With a heavy thud, she sat down, but wouldn't look at me. "Okay."

Like her neighbor, I reached through the bars and gave her a pat of my own. Forcing a bright smile, I said, "Now, where were we? Oh, you were telling me you lost something. What was it?"

Nothing.

"C'mon, tell me. It can't be that bad."

Perhaps strengthened by all those pats, she turned to face me, her cheeks damp. "I lost a gun."

The plastic chair I sat in was shaped to fit the human body and should have been comfortable but now it felt like a torture device. Nevertheless, I kept my voice steady. "A gun, did you say?"

"Yeah."

"And you had a gun because…"

The Hispanic woman moved politely away. The white woman in the other cell muttered to herself about the cat again, oblivious to the world and its inhabitants.

Zorah whispered, "Lean closer, Teddy."

I leaned forward until my forehead touched the bars.

"It belonged to my nephew, Alejandro," she whispered. "I took it away from him."

She seldom talked about her family, but I knew it was large and that they lived in Castroville, a few miles away. "How did your nephew get a gun?"

"Stole it, probably."

I'd heard rumors about her nephew, none of them good. "Don't tell me he handed the gun over peacefully."

"Hardly. A couple of weeks ago I dropped by my sister's house and she was out, but Alejandro let me in to wait. He'd been in his room, I guess, because the door was open and I could hear music. That rap stuff's rank, you wouldn't believe what they say about women. They actually call them…"

"I know all about the ho's. Get on with it."

"Sorry. Anyway, at some point he excused himself to go to the john and I decided to turn the damned CD player off. When I went into his bedroom, there was the gun on the bed, half-covered by a sheet. Alejandro didn't need any more trouble, especially not gun kind of trouble, so I grabbed the thing and took off. I intended to throw it of the end of the harbor break-water, but when I got there, a busload of tourists were tromp-ing around looking at the elephant seals. So I drove home and stashed it under my mattress. Last week, when I figured the beach would be deserted, I transferred the gun to my truck, intending to dump it on my way home from work. But…" Her voice faded away.

"Are you telling me that you kept that gun in your truck all day? In the employee parking lot?"

She shook her head furiously. "I'm not stupid. You know how hot cars get when the windows are closed and they're sitting in the sun all day. I don't know much about guns, but I know there's gunpowder in them, and I was afraid if the truck got too hot, the gunpowder might explode. For obvious reasons, I couldn't keep the truck's window open. So I took the gun inside with me."

"You brought a gun into the zoo?!" That was a firing offense.

"Not near the animals! For safety's sake, I put it in my desk drawer and covered it with papers so no one could see it."

Open-mouthed, I stared at her. Zorah's desk, which had no locking drawers, was situated in the administration building near the time clock used by hourly employees. Worse, everyone knew she kept her desk filled with office supplies, so zookeepers—even though they weren't supposed to—always were rifling it. She couldn't have found a more public place to "hide" the gun if she'd tried.

"Don't look at me like that, Teddy! It didn't seem dumb at the time."

Nothing ever does. "Okay, I think I can figure out the rest. By the end of the day, the gun was gone."

She gave me a weak smile. "Gee, how'd you guess?"

"And you didn't tell anyone." It was a statement, not a ques-tion.

"How could I? Could you see me telling that stupid new director that the gun I'd brought illegally into the zoo, the gun that I'd stolen from my nephew who'd probably stolen the gun himself, had just been stolen by somebody else? Oh, ha. I went home and worried, that's what I did."

The white woman in the cell next to Zorah's stopped mumbling and sat staring into space. The quiet was so loud I almost wished she would start yelling again.

"I hate to ask you this, but at any point did you think to wipe your fingerprints off the gun?"

She gave me a puzzled look. "Why would I do that?"

Why? In case someone took the gun out of your desk, used it to murder a man, then tossed it in a spot where the police might find it, that's why.

Having learned everything from her I could, I stood up. "Here's what I'm going to do. I'll make those calls as soon as I get home and try to fix you up with a good attorney. In the meantime, is there anyone you want me to call?"

"My family already knows where I am. And thanks to your damn boyfriend, the whole zoo does, too."

"Ex-boyfriend. Emphasis on ex."

"Whatever." She resumed staring at the floor.

With nothing more to be gained, I left. On the other side of the cell block door, Deputy Guiterrez gave me a shame-faced look. "Busted. I don't think the sheriff's mad, but he does want to talk to you."

Forcing myself to act as nonchalant as if I visited my friends in county lockup every day, I headed for Joe's office.

Before I could sit down he said, "I noticed that you've wearing *your* uniform, too."

I looked down at my khakis and boots, realizing for the first time that we were dressed alike. The only difference was that his breast pocket sported a badge, and mine an embroidered zebra.

"I didn't have time to change."

"Doesn't matter. Khaki looks great with that red hair of yours. Listen, don't think I bought all that stuff about the tigers. You always were a lousy liar. What did Ms. Vega have to say?"

"C'mon. You know better than that."

He flashed that marvelous smile. "Can't blame me for trying."

Why did I think he wasn't just talking about Zorah? I looked around his office, a Spartan room furnished in fake wood and fake leather. Along with a slew of family photographs, several certificates and degrees hung on the wall, including one from U.C. Davis.

"I didn't know you received your master's," I said.

"In police science, yes. How about you?"

"Bachelor's. And my teaching certificate."

He frowned. "You always said you'd go for a Ph.D. in animal husbandry. What happened?"

Since he knew quite well that Michael had happened, I didn't bother answering. Instead, I studied the photograph of his wife and children. "Joe, I'm so sorry about Sonia."

When he nodded, a lock of glossy black hair fell over his forehead. I wanted to reach across the desk and brush it back, but we were long past that.

"Thank you. You sent beautiful flowers. And a nice card. I appreciated that."

"I'm sorry I couldn't come down for the funeral, but..." No point in explaining that I'd just caught Michael cheating for the first time, and had been busy trying to save my marriage. "Do you have any leads?"

"No."

Three years earlier, Joe's wife had been found slumped over the steering wheel of her car in the emergency lane of the I-5, a bullet in her head. No one had ever been arrested.

"I wish..." I stopped. There was no point in saying what I wished, so I changed the subject. "What's your case against Zorah?"

He straightened some papers on his desk. "At ten tonight KGNN will report that we found the murder weapon tossed into the bushes behind the zoo's Wings of Flight exhibit, with Ms. Vega's fingerprints all over it."

"Based on that you arrested her?"

"That, plus the threatening letters she sent the victim, and the fact that she was at the fund-raiser. Oh, yeah, and because by all accounts she disappeared for a long stretch, right around the time of the murder. So there you have it: motive, means, opportunity."

It sounded too pat to me. "Most of the zoo staff, including her, were wearing anteater costumes, so how could anyone tell whether she was around or not?"

"Hers had a tear in the shoulder. She's kind of, well, large, and as the night went on, the tear got bigger and bigger, to the point where she tacked it together with a safety pin. She was hard to miss, which everyone did when the bartenders ran out of gin. Are you aware how much your rich friends drink? Money sure doesn't buy happiness, does it, just better booze. Anyway, the caterer wanted her to fetch another bottle of gin from the supply he'd left in the administration building. It was locked up tight, and she had one of the keys. When no one could find her, Barry Fields had to trot all the way back there to open up. Fields—who I heard had been sniffing around some recently-divorced socialite—wasn't pleased."

"But Grayson..."

"He was the one who drank the last drop of gin and wanted more. But by the time Fields fetched a new supply, he'd disappeared, too."

I tried to remember what I'd learned from watching *Law & Order* reruns on my thirteen-inch TV set. "If Zorah shot him, wouldn't there be gunpowder residue on her costume? And on her hands?"

"Normally, yeah, but after the fund-raiser the suits got tossed together into a pile in the staff lounge. The next morning someone dumped them into the big sack provided by the rental place. There's residue on several of the suits, not only your friend's. As for her hands, gunshot residue is easier to scrub off than most people realize. She's smart enough to know that."

Which means her hands had been free of the stuff. "Sounds like a weak case to me."

I didn't like the look in his eyes. "Not to me."

Chapter Seven

Since the autopsy on Grayson turned out to be relatively straight-forward—he was in good health, except for being dead—the county medical examiner released the body in time for a Saturday funeral service. Having ensured that my morning shift would be covered, I followed the long line of cars from the San Sebastian funeral home through the iron gates of the private cemetery where generations of Gunns had been laid to rest.

The cemetery perched on a low hill near the back of the Gunn estate. To the east, the terrain dropped sharply until it flattened into the artichoke fields that stretched all the way across the old Bentley ranch. Due west lay the Pacific Ocean, from here a thin blue line.

The view would have been perfect if not for the housing development to the northwest marching down Bentley Ridge toward Gunn Landing. The tract had been built in the early seventies, before the California Coastal Initiative forbidding new development on the Coast went into effect. Now the original houses were being bulldozed one by one to erect gaudy McMansions for new Silicon Valley money.

To Aster Edwin's displeasure, Grayson himself had brokered some of the deals.

The funeral service wasn't bad, as funeral services go. One time Jeanette seemed to realize where she was and loosed a long howl of grief, but her great-aunt quieted her. After the minister intoned the last prayer, everyone filed by the closed casket for a final nod at the mahogany. Then a chauffeur half-dragged, half-carried Jeanette to a waiting limo.

"Interesting, don't you think?" Joe's voice made me jump.

He watched while the chauffeur poured the limp woman into the limo's back seat, next to Aster Edwina. I shook my head. "God knows what's going to happen to her now. She was never strong."

"I wasn't talking about her."

"Then who...?"

A group purr of expensive car engines signaled the Gunn exodus. The cars crept forward slowly, headed for the castle and the funeral brunch. I repeated my question. "Who were you talking about?"

"Barry Fields. The Gunns. A fascinating assortment of emotions."

True. The anti-Trust Gunns looked bereft at the loss of a vote; the pro-Trusters looked positively thrilled. In contrast, the zoo director acted as if he'd lost his best friend, which could be the case since he'd owed his job to the victim's sponsorship. His future with the zoo was now in doubt.

Joe must have read my mind. "I've heard through the grapevine that Mr. Fields' job isn't all that secure. Is he about to get fired?"

"I hope so. But it won't happen before this Trust thing is settled. If the Gunns let him go now, the board would have to replace him immediately. But with whom? The most qualified applicant is in a jail cell, remember?"

Below us, the limos wound slowly along the gravel road to the castle. Bidding Joe goodbye, I jumped into my Nissan pickup and followed them, intent on finding out whatever I could. Zorah hadn't killed Grayson, I was sure of that.

Which meant someone else had. Someone I probably knew.

If Joe couldn't find out the truth, it was up to me.

The funeral reception took place in the castle's drawing room, where I'd once played Monopoly with Jeanette. Furnished with an assortment of antique settees and chairs worth a king's ransom, the silk-covered walls boasted a Rubens, a Turner, and two Monets. These treasures were almost overpowered by the large display of old Edwin Gunn's hunting rifles and pistols that he'd collected before he'd had a change of heart and began saving animals instead of killing them. So many glittering weapons hung on the walls that the room could have done double-duty as an arsenal. As a child, I'd sometimes suspected that Jeanette had chosen this room to play Monopoly in because of its sheer intimidation value. I almost always won, anyway. Once, when I had bankrupted her within a half-hour, she'd slapped me hard across the face.

Today my old Monopoly adversary slumped on a settee rumored to have once belonged to Czar Nicholas.

"I'm so sorry," I said, hugging her.

She didn't hug back, just gave me the vacant stare of the over-medicated. Having performed my social duty I made a wide circle around Barry, who brown-nosed by the Turner, and joined my mother and Aster Edwina by the fireplace. Instead of flames, the hearth burst forth with bouquets of gardenias and mums.

"A lovely funeral, Aster Edwina," I complimented her. "The minister said nice things about Grayson."

"Possible only because the good reverend never met him. Grayson was a spineless man."

Caro raised her salon-plucked eyebrows. "He had redeeming qualities, Aster. Most men do." I could almost hear her add silently, *When they have money.*

Before Aster Edwina could make another disparaging comment, I threw in, "I can't think of anyone who ever had an unkind word to say about him." *Other than you,* I wanted to add, but didn't. "He took his duties at the zoo seriously."

"And he dressed beautifully," my mother added.

This elicited a true smile from Aster Edwina. "Jeanette had his suits hand-tailored in London. The girl has lovely taste."

Remembering that garish pink boudoir, I agreed anyway, which earned me a pat on the cheek. "You are a polite child." With that, the old lady left us to circulate.

"At least you're dressed appropriately," Caro said, eyeing me up and down. She wore a chic smoke-gray silk shantung—Vera Wang, I guessed—with a matching cloche that had a whisper of a veil. She looked like a cover girl for *Funerals Today*.

Knowing I looked much less chic in my all-purpose black dress, I smiled feebly, then seized my chance. "Ah, Moth...Caro, why weren't you at the Zoo Guild fund-raiser?"

She stared at me for a moment. "Something came up. Say, I hear you called Tommy Prescott."

Word gets around quickly in small towns. Tommy, a child-hood friend from Old Town, was now an up-and-coming San Francisco criminal defense attorney. The fact that he'd agreed to become attorney of record for Zorah Vega, pro bono, of course, had leaked out quickly.

"A zookeeper makes a nice change from his standard roster of pimps and politicians," I explained. That wasn't the real reason he'd had taken the case, though. When I called him, I reaffirmed my promise not to tell anyone that when he and I were kids, I'd seen him steal a silver snuff box from the castle's drawing room. He'd later traded it for a dime bag of pot.

I gave my mother a final wave and headed for the door. Before I made my exit, I spotted one of Jeanette's cousins sipping sherry in front of the Rubens.

Roarke Gunn didn't pretend grief. "Yeah, it's a tragedy, blah blah blah. Condolences accepted, blah blah blah." Like most of the Gunns, he was blond, tall, big-boned, tanned, and fit from years of sailing on the *Tequila Sunrise*, his seventy-five-foot custom schooner. Great lovers of the water, he and his wife actually lived on the *Sunrise*, turning up their noses at the land-locked castle.

"Why did you dislike Grayson so much, Roarke? You were hardly ever around him."

His perfect teeth flashed. "I hate all real estate brokers as a matter of principle. But I'll say this for the guy, at least he didn't leech off Jeanette too much. He worked, more or less."

This sounded promising. "Yes, he did. Furthermore, I don't think Zorah Vega killed him and I want to help her. Do you know anyone else who might have…" I left the question hanging.

He picked it up. "…wanted to kill him? Surely you jest. Eighteen people that I know of, all of the Gunn Trust hold-outs."

"Aren't there twenty-three of you voting to keep the Trust intact?"

"Don't believe everything you read in the newspapers." He gave me a mean smile. "I know you saw Grayson as some easy-going guy who lived only to please his wife, but he was more complicated than that. Don't forget that he was the person who brought the anti-Trust coalition together in the first place. With the little weasel working his wiles, we pro-Trust folks were becoming an increasingly soft number."

His face resumed a more genial expression. "Say, why don't you drop by the *Tequila Sunrise* tomorrow. A diver's coming over to scrape the hull and that's always fun to watch. Frieda will be glad to see you."

Frieda was his gorgeous but jealous wife. Ordinarily, she would be hovering at his side, fending off forays from other women, but as I looked around the big room I didn't see her anywhere. "How is she?"

His face shut down again. "She's not feeling well, so I left her back on the *Sunrise.*"

Promising to stop by the boat around noon, I made my escape. I arrived back at the zoo in the middle of lunch—the keepers', not the animals'. After changing into my uniform and stashing my funeral attire in my locker, I went into the employee lounge where the other keepers gossiped near the snack machine.

A hoofed-animal keeper wanted to know if Barry Fields had been fired yet, and a reptile keeper asked if Zorah would be able to make bail, which was certain to be enormous. When I replied in the negative, I received several frowns. Because my name was Bentley, most people believed I was rolling in money, but unlike many of my friends, I was no trust-fund baby. I hadn't emerged from my divorce with much, either. People tended to forget that when Michael and I married, he and I were both college freshmen. His parents—who believed that their son should made his own way—had never helped us out, so for most of our ten years together, we'd struggled to make ends meet. The Bentley name notwithstanding, if it weren't for the *Merilee*, I'd probably wind up sharing government-subsidy housing with the other zookeepers. Or worse, living with my mother.

"Believe me, I'd loan Zorah the money if I had it. But I don't." I couldn't let them, or the Feds, know about that Grand Cayman account, the one I'd sworn never to touch.

Jack Spence, taking a break from the bears said, "You could borrow against your inheritance."

It was all I could do to keep from slapping my knee and laughing. Thanks to my mother's greatly improved financial status, I might come into money one day—*if* she didn't fall prey to some European gigolo. At present, though, I couldn't see myself asking her for Zorah's bail money on the strength of any possible inheritance and told Jack so in the strongest of terms. I also reminded him that she loathed the idea of me working at the zoo and would turn me down flat.

"You could use your boat as collateral." This from Miranda DiBartolo, who lived in a two-bedroom apartment with three other keepers. They commuted to work in an old Volkswagen van that broke down on a regular basis.

Miranda may have given me a solution to my conundrum. There was no way the creaky *Merilee* could serve as collateral for the kind of money I'd need to front bail but I doubted the other keepers realized that. "Oh, my gosh, you're right! Why didn't I think of that earlier?"

A collective sigh around the room.

I made some quick calculations. "Let's see. Zorah's arraignment is on Monday, and after I find out what the bail's going to be, I'll make a few calls and see if I can scare up a loan. Yes, you're absolutely right. The *Merilee*'s the answer."

Before anyone could see through my lie, I hurried away.

When I arrived at Tropics Trail, I found the anteater sulking in the holding pen. For such a solitary animal, she seemed to miss her admiring crowds.

"Lucy lonely? Or is her tummy upset?"

She swung her long nose toward me, walked slowly over to the chain link fence that separated us and emitted a plaintive rumble, which I took as a yes. Giant anteaters have a six-month gestation period and since we'd inseminated her in late November, sperm courtesy of a studly anteater at the Phoenix Zoo, she was due any day. Given her bad temper, I worried that the smaller living quarters might have a negative impact on her mental health, and quite possibly, her physical health as well.

To comfort her, I peeled a banana, mashed it in my hand, and edged up to the fence. That blue tongue snaked out of her long snout and she began to lap up the mush.

"Yes, banana is *goood*, Lucy *loooves* banana. I wish Lucy could talk because then she'd tell me what happened the other night. She'd tell me why Grayson died in her enclosure. And who shot him."

Animals know how to listen, and they're cheaper than a psychiatrist. I've heard Zorah confide her worries about her nephew to a frilled lizard, and I once heard Miranda tell a koala how worried she was about an upcoming mammogram. Male keepers tended to confine their soliloquies to cars. Jack Spence was always bragging to Samson and Delilah, the black bears, about the restoration work he was doing on his '76 Chevy Malibu. Samson, being male, appeared the most interested.

So I didn't feel at all foolish about discussing Grayson's murder with an anteater. "Was there some kind of fight, Lucy? Did he fall into your enclosure after he was shot, or did he jump in, trying to keep from getting shot? Probably the former, since he was so afraid of animals."

Lucy bobbed her head. In agreement? Or in ecstasy over the banana?

I tried to picture Grayson as he'd looked before I found him in the enclosure. Short, rotund, always smiling. Non-offensive, non-confrontational, almost non-there. Aster Edwina's cruel assessment of him was at least partially accurate. Yet according to Roarke, Grayson's manipulative behavior had almost overturned the great Gunn Trust.

"Oh, Lucy, regardless of what he was up to, he deserved better. Yes, I feel bad about him, but most of all, I'm worried about our friend Zorah. She's still locked up in that jail cell when all she wants is to come back to the zoo and be with her lizards and tigers. And with *you*, my sweet girl."

Her blue tongue snaked out again for the last lump of mashed banana. Giving a final grunt, she backed away from the fence.

"The sheriff thinks she's a murderer, but he doesn't know her like I do. So we need to find out who really did it, don't we?"

Lucy didn't answer, just sneezed, blowing banana mush all over my uniform.

Chapter Eight

Sunday was swab-the-deck day on the *Merilee*. After finishing the top deck, I went below and vacuumed the tiny salon's blue indoor-outdoor carpeting and even tinier fore and aft cabins. I followed with a serious polish of the teak cabinets and other fittings. This tired me more than a morning spent cleaning up after the squirrel monkeys, but I enjoyed caring for the *Merilee*. I'd fallen into her ownership after a minor miracle.

When Dad absconded with Bentley, Bentley, Haight, and Busby's millions, the Feds confiscated everything we owned: the house in Old Town, the paintings, the eighty-four-foot schooner, the Rolls, the Jag, my mother's furs and jewelry. One G-man tried to take away the doll I'd been clinging to as they swept through the house, and only the intervention of a soft-eyed agent prevented the outrage.

I grew up believing we'd lost everything except for my mother's hidden stash, but when I returned to Gunn Landing from San Francisco, Albert Mazer, Dad's old poker buddy, visited to relay some stunning news.

"You own a boat at the harbor," he said as soon as my mother left us alone. "I've kinda held it in escrow for you."

The story he told both shocked and pleased me. To escape Caro's eagle eye, my father had secretly bought the *Merilee* to use as a base camp for poker parties and less wholesome gatherings, transferring the title to Mazer so my mother couldn't trace the boat. Over the years Dad paid the *Merilee*'s repair bills, slip fees, and other expenses that came with owning a diesel-powered party boat. The understanding was that if something happened to him, Mazer would fess up and sign over the boat to me.

"The *Merilee*'s not perfect," Mazer had said, handing me the pink slip and keys. "Her engine needs work, the teak needs revarnishing, the hull needs scraping. You won't like the decor, either, since it's kind of, er, male. But she's all yours, and if you ever get tired of living with your mother..." Here, a peek over his shoulder as if he feared the gorgon lurked nearby. "...the boat has a liveaboard permit. All I need to do is put your name on it." Which he promptly did.

His visit proved providential. The next day Caro and I had a falling out over an eligible bachelor she wanted me to meet, "one of the La Jolla Piersons," a much-divorced lout whose goatish behavior eclipsed his fortune. That very night I moved onto the *Merilee*. By the end of the week I'd cleaned out all the liquor bottles, *Hustler* magazines and the breast-shaped toss pillows, replacing the bawdy appointments with bedspreads and cushions portraying Pacific sea life.

I had never been so happy or so lacking in space. Although theoretically the *Merilee*, at thirty-four-feet long and eleven-point-eight-feet-wide at the beam, offered almost four hundred square feet of living space, most of that was taken up by decks, bulkheads, the galley, and various fittings. I once estimated there was less than twenty feet of actual walking-around space in my home. Boat living isn't for claustrophobes.

By the time I finished cleaning and doing my laundry at the harbor's laundromat, the morning fog had burned off, revealing a sky so bright and pure it stung my eyes. Once more I wished my boat had sails so I could take her out beyond the breakwater and hear nothing other than wind and gulls. But beggars can't be choosers.

I stowed the laundry away and made my bed with fresh-smelling dolphin-print sheets and matching comforter. Chores finished, I glanced at my watch and found it already past noon.

Time to take Roarke Gunn up on his offer to visit the *Tequila Sunrise*.

In contrast to the southern end of the harbor, where big salmon trawlers butted up against humble craft such as the *Merilee*, the *Tequila Sunrise* lay berthed at the northern end in the area reserved for yacht club members. The Northies were wealthier, and never worried about rising slip fees or the cost of decent booze, and this fostered an undercurrent of class warfare. Not today, though. When I stepped aboard the *Tequila Sunrise*, Frieda, Roarke's blond wife, handed me a Sunrise Special: a Mimosa comprised of fresh-squeezed oranges, Mumm's, and a dash of Grenadine.

She gave me an insincere air kiss. "Roarke says you should drop by more often."

Her lack of warmth didn't surprise me because she loved her husband almost as much as Jeanette had loved Grayson, and viewed every woman as competition for her man. Given her considerable beauty, I could never figure out why.

I contented myself with a politic reply. "You folks are so frequently away."

Several times a year Frieda and Roarke sailed to Puerto Vallarta, where they partied with an informal armada of similarly wealthy friends. Ordinarily, they would be there now, but the danger that the Trust might be broken kept them in the harbor. They were making the best of their canceled plans by fixing the common problems that plague sea-going vessels. Today's project was scraping the *Tequila Sunrise*'s wooden hull free of barnacles. Left to themselves, barnacles would reproduce and soon cover the hull in a colony weighing hundreds of pounds, creating a drag on the boat. Worse, the pesky crustaceans might bore right through the hull.

Frieda, more gorgeous than ever in a black thong bikini, looked me over carefully. "Been working out?" The acerbity in her voice increased my discomfort.

"Just shoveling sh.., um, stuff."

"That's right. You're a cage cleaner at the zoo." *Meow.*

"No cages. Each of our animals is housed in a large enclosure that resembles its natural habitat."

"Why not leave them in the wild in the first place?"

Good question, complicated answer. "That would be ideal, but what with forest clearings and civil wars and such, the animals' natural habitats are shrinking. There's also the continued poaching of endangered wildlife, which doesn't help."

She took a sip of her drink, which appeared to be pure orange juice. Hard-partying Frieda on the wagon? How odd. "Pass laws against killing them, then."

"There already are such laws, but we're talking international treaties, and with those, enforcement is always the problem. The U.S. can't *order* an African farmer not to kill the endangered cheetah preying upon his goats. The farmer would rather see every cheetah on earth dead than let his children starve. Furthermore…"

Realizing I was becoming agitated about the seeming hopelessness of it all, I changed the subject. "I take it Roarke's down with the diver?"

My old friend loved to watch divers scrape away barnacles with their putty knives, but having tried it once myself and resurfaced with bloody knuckles, I found the process less than enthralling.

She nodded. "He waited for you but got impatient and dove in about ten minutes ago. If you want to let him know you're here, they're on the port side. Jump on in." Her expression told me she'd prefer I didn't. Why, oh why, was she so insecure?

There was no way I was going to jump into the greasy harbor after taking my shower so I resigned myself to wait. Fortunately, almost as soon as I'd sat down in one of the deck chairs, Roarke, wearing full scuba gear, climbed out of the water. After Frieda helped him out of his wet suit, she began rubbing him down with a towel, almost like a medieval servant for her master. I couldn't help but notice how well-matched the two were, at least physically. Both were tall and pretty enough to be models. Next to them, I felt short, flat-chested, and dumpy.

Now stripped to a red Speedo, Roarke gave me a friendly up-and-down. "Hey, you're looking fit, girl. Frieda, top off Teddy's drink."

She threw me a nervous glance, but he kissed her shoulder, her eyes softened.

Love could be so painful.

I set down my half-finished Mimosa and tried to look as unattractive as possible, which isn't hard to do when you have mud-colored freckles and hair the color and texture of an old copper scouring pad. "No thanks. I can't stay long. Too much to do around the *Merilee*."

Roarke nodded sagely. "People don't own boats. Boats own people. Frieda's always complaining that I spend more with the *Tequila Sunrise* than with her."

He probably did, because her obvious insecurity had to come from somewhere.

"I couldn't agree more. Before I get back to the *Merilee*, maybe you could tell me more about the Trust? It might have something to do with Grayson's murder."

At his astonished look, I added, "I know, I know. I'm not a relative and none of this is any of my business, but as you said after the funeral, the Trust business has been all over the newspapers lately. You wouldn't be telling me anything that's not already been printed somewhere."

Actually, I was kind of related to the Gunns. In the late eighteen hundreds, a Bentley great-great aunt had married a Gunn, but they'd produced no children, and that distant connection wasn't close enough to make me a partner in the Trust. *Damn.*

His astonishment faded. "You're right. Everybody knows pretty much everything now, right down to the dollar amount." Frieda handed him a Mimosa and he gave her an absent-minded peck on the cheek. He eased himself into a deck chair and stretched out his long, golden legs. They seemed to take up half the deck. "Ah. You want to know which of my relatives I can implicate in his death, thus gaining a larger share of the Trust for myself?"

"I didn't mean…"

"Of course you did, but so what? Frankly, I think that big zookeeper friend of yours probably did kill him, but if you believe she's innocent, I might be wrong. You always were a good judge of people, which is why you prefer to be with animals." He chuckled. "Anyway, here's the skinny on the Trust. With Grayson out of the way the anti-Trust faction will probably fall apart, and good riddance to it. The whole thing is nonsense."

He paused to take a sip of his Mimosa, pat Frieda on her perfectly shaped fanny, then continued.

"The amount of money the Trust controls has never been a secret. As the newspapers insist on reminding everyone, about one-point-eight billion is invested in corporations ranging from software manufacturers to fast food chains. There's also the land itself, twenty-five hundred acres of zoo pastures, and vineyards located *outside* of the Coastal Initiative's no-build boundary. Wouldn't the developers have a field day with those! As it stands, the income is divvied up among fifty-five of us, which includes thirty-eight adult voting members, so we manage comfortably on our monthly dividend checks. Hell, when heirs live up at the castle, they don't even pay rent! You know what they say: if it ain't broke, don't fix it."

"Then why would anyone want to break the Trust?"

"Hubris. Pride. Whatever word for silly-ass over-confidence you want to use. Most of the anti-Trust people are in their twenties and they have stars in their eyes about overseas investments. I've heard a couple are flirting with the Saudis. Ha! They'd be better off consulting the I Ching. As for Grayson, he was wily enough to bring the anti-Trust coalition together, but believe me, he was no financial genius. He was in way over his head. Local real estate deals are one thing, foreign investments another."

"You're talking about those awful houses up on Bentley Ridge?"

"That's right. Penny-ante stuff but he saw himself as a minor-league Donald Trump. He believed that all he needed to make his own private fortune was the fat nest egg a cash-out would give him. Jeanette never had any business sense—no sense of any kind, actually—so she would have given him free rein. If he'd been able to get his hands on Jeanette's share of the Trust, he would have set a new speed record for bankruptcy filings."

"If you don't mind telling me, what was her share? I can't remember reading that anywhere."

He looked over to where a pelican had come to roost on the end of the boom. "It's hard to estimate but I do know that shortly before the murder she and Grayson turned down an individual buy-out offer worth fifteen mill. Grayson's attorneys countered with twenty-five but I think he was probably willing to settle for twenty."

Twenty million could buy a lot of migraine medication. "What do you mean, '*individual* buy-out?' They were part of the anti-Trust voting block."

"You mean, 'all for one and one for all,' like the Three Musketeers? Hardly. Like I said, when Grayson was so conveniently murdered, he was in negotiations to abandon the other anti-Trust voters in order to feather his and Jeanette's own nest. As to where the money for the buy-out would come from, Aster Edwina and several of the more well-fixed hold-outs, which includes myself and my Uncle Henry—the one who split to San Francisco with his new wife—we pooled our private resources to make the offer. Sure, we'd suffer a short-term loss, but we'd recoup in a few years. But in the meantime, our lovely monthly dividend check would keep rolling in."

If he was telling the truth, and I had no reason to believe he wasn't, not only the pro-Trust Gunns had a motive for killing Grayson, but also the *anti*-Trust Gunns, because they were about to be betrayed. I was mulling over this intriguing development when the pelican, as pelicans are wont to do, took a big dump on the *Tequila Sunrise*'s deck. Roarke merely shrugged but Frieda screamed a curse at the bird, which flapped away, unconcerned.

The pelican had summed up the situation perfectly.

Chapter Nine

At Zorah's arraignment on Monday, which I attended to give her moral support, her attorney was able to knock her bail down to two hundred and fifty thousand dollars. When I walked across the street to the bail bondsman's office, I discovered that I would need to front slightly more than twenty-five thousand cash, and put the rest in an escrow account for collateral. By the time I finished arranging for a wire transfer from the Grand Caymans bank to San Sebastian, I was four hours late for work and Zorah was still in jail.

As I picked up my duties, I saw Kim Markowski, the zoo's education director, headed for Friendly Farm with several puppets cuddled next to a pair of crutches in the cart bin behind her. I slowed my own cart and waved her down.

"How's the ankle?"

She gave me a perky smile. "It's fine, fine. No problem at all. Honestly."

I knew Kim enough to know that if she'd suffered a double amputation she'd answer in the same way. Although only five years younger than me, she retained the bounding optimism of a puppy. Today, though, the dark circles under her eyes belied her smile and her blond ponytail no longer gleamed. I knew that broken ankles hurt like the devil, having sustained one myself when a horse fell on me.

I gestured toward the puppets in the back of her cart. "Putting on a show?"

The smile broadened. "*Goldilocks and the Spectacled Bears,* for some third-graders from San Sebastian Elementary School."

The puppets looked more like raccoons to me, but I wasn't about to say so since she spent hours making them. "Why not the show about the anteater? You were supposed to debut it at the fund-raiser, I heard."

Her smile faltered and her lower lip began to tremble. "Barry Fields said to shelve it, that it might remind people too much of that night, that night…when Grayson…when Mr. Harrill, died." She gulped, then added, "It's hard to believe anyone would hurt such a nice man."

A nice man with a duplicitous side. A nice man who'd been about to sell out his wife's family. "Has Sheriff Rejas interviewed you yet?"

She sniffed. "Why would he want to interview me? I don't know anything."

In the aviary next to us, a Western meadowlark began to sing. Not a flashy bird, with its dull brown-and-yellow coloring, but oh, that voice. Within seconds a mockingbird across the way began to copy him. Soon the air was filled with the sounds of dueling songbirds. I was so entranced that it took a moment for me to turn my attention back to Kim.

"You were out the day he and his deputies talked to the rest of the staff, so I thought…"

Frowning, she cut me off. "Is it true you used to go out with the sheriff?"

"We're ancient history. Besides, he wasn't the sheriff back at the time, just a high school senior. I was a sophomore. We're different people now."

"People can sure change a lot over the years, can't they?"

Suddenly I felt as depressed as she looked. "It's been nice talking to you but I need to take care of the capybaras. Have fun with the puppet show."

As she waved goodbye, she tried another smile, but on a scale of one to ten, the most I could give it was a three.

The capybaras were glad to see me. Two feet high at the shoulder and looking like a one-hundred-pound cross between a Guinea pig and a hippo, they were the world's largest rodents. Gus, the big male, emerged from his slimy pond to greet me and I had to do a quick shuffle-and-slide to keep him from shaking algae all over my uniform.

"*Ick, ick, ick!*" Gus called, in that distinctive capybara voice.

The females—Agnes, Gladys, and Myrtle—followed him out of the water. I threw them all some hay and a few melons, then tidied up their enclosure as best as I could. Since capybaras prefer to defecate in the water, there weren't a lot of droppings to attend to. Like a maid who doesn't do windows, I don't dredge ponds.

A couple of hours later, while I took a break in the staff lounge with some other keepers, the zoo director dropped by and began dolling out Reese's Peanut Butter Cups. At first I was baffled by this rare show of amiability—Barry Fields seldom socialized with lowly keepers, let alone gave us treats—but then I remembered. With Grayson dead, he needed all the supporters he could bribe.

His too-obvious ploy didn't work. Everyone snatched up the candy before he had a chance to renege on his largesse but rejected his conversational overtures. So determined were they to avoid his company that they cut short their break and left the lounge without so much as a goodbye.

The mass desertion suited me perfectly. I gave the director a smile almost as big as Kim's and patted the vacant chair next to me. "It's sad about Grayson, isn't it, sir?"

With a sigh of relief, he sat down. "Call me Barry."

I batted my eyelashes. "Then remember to call me Teddy, Barry." Welcome to my web, Mr. Fly.

His face brightened. "Teddy, then. Yes, so sad. He was a nice man."

Nice. There was that word again. I waited to see if he'd add anything new.

He didn't disappoint. "Grayson was a great loss, a great, great loss. Between you and me, he was a better businessman than most people realized. Perhaps he wasn't a Gunn himself, just married to one, but he definitely shared that family's financial acumen."

As if to emphasize the point, he nodded so furiously I thought his head would fall off, but his dingo-colored hair remained frozen in place. Hair spray? Or, as rumored, Hair Club for Men? His hair (or toupee) was light brown, his eyes were light brown, and although he was Caucasian, his overly tanned skin was light brown. At least his expensive Joseph Abboud sports jacket was blue.

His claim that Grayson shared the Gunn's "financial acumen" intrigued me since I'd heard the opposite from Roarke. "Tell me more about his business dealings."

When the zoo director smoothed his already-perfect hair, I realized he just missed being handsome. But his oily manner negated his-almost perfect physical features. "Grayson understood the amount of funding it requires to keep a place like this running. Our daily outlay would astound you. All these damned animals eating their heads off."

Instead of slapping him like he deserved, I kept smiling. "Yes, the animals are a problem. That independent vet study, for instance, turned the zoo upside down for weeks. Oh, by the way, his wife told me he'd received an advance copy of their report."

He gave me a blank look. "Oh?"

"So how'd we do?"

"What do you mean?"

Could he really be that dense? "Let me rephrase the question. Did the veterinarians from the National Academy of Sciences find any problems here? Or did we ace it?"

He shrugged.

My irritation increased. "It's been a week since Grayson was murdered—the very night he said he wanted to talk to you about the report. He stayed late at the funder to do just that, remember?"

He studied his professionally-manicured nails. "Hmm. I'm not sure if I do. Where'd you get that information, anyway?"

"Jeanette."

"Oh. Well. It was nothing more than a preliminary draft, not the final, so why get all hot and bothered? Whatever detail Grayson wanted to discuss couldn't have been that important because he didn't say anything before he handed the report over to me earlier in the day. I passed it along to the veterinarian, who knows more about that animal stuff than I do, since that's her job."

Technically, Barry was correct. Dr. Kate would be the person most affected by the report, but passing the prelim along to her without so much as a cursory glance underlined what a poor choice he had been for the position of zoo director. What *had* Grayson been thinking?

More curious than ever, I asked, "What exactly are your duties at the zoo? Besides the fund-raising stuff."

He flicked away a tiny feather from his cuff, possibly from an Asian fairy bluebird. "I establish policies. Provide leadership. You know, the usual."

While I'd seen evidence of his skill at rasing money from rich widows, I'd seen precious little else, his management style being best described as one of benign neglect. Sometimes not so benign, as in the case of the still-imprisoned Lucy.

"Not to change the subject or anything, Barry, but don't you think we should let the anteater out of the holding pen? I'm worried about her."

"I'm more worried about lawsuits if that thing gets loose. Don't you remember what she did to poor Grayson?"

Who could forget? "It wasn't her fault."

He gave me a condescending smile. "You keepers are all the same. All you think about are your animal friends. Here in the real world there are larger issues."

Not as far as I was concerned. Disgusted, I rose to leave.

"Say, Teddy?"

"Hmm?"

"Let's you and me go out some time."

After extricating myself from Barry's romantic overtures as politely as possible, I made a beeline for the zoo's Animal Care

Center, where I found Dr. Kate bandaging a tranquilized squirrel monkey. Marlon. I'd brought him over earlier after noticing a couple of nasty-looking bites on his leg. The females had been whipping him into line again.

"Dr. Kate, when you're done there, can I talk to you?"

Marlon, spreadeagle on the examining table, looked over at me with a tipsy smile. The vet gave him a pat. "I'm done. What do you need? Is the anteater…?"

"The anteater's fine, except she hates that holding pen. Isn't there anything you can do?"

She shook her head. "I've talked to Barry 'til I'm blue in the face but he won't budge. Frankly, I'm concerned about her, too. With her pregnancy so far advanced, we could be in for some serious trouble. Stressed animals, as you know all too well, sometimes kill their young." She closed her eyes for a moment. When she opened them, I was shocked at the rage there. "Unfortunately, my hands are tied. Barry made it clear that if I keep pressing the issue he'll find a more cooperative vet."

Damn him! I swallowed my own anger. "I talked to him a few minutes ago and he told me he'd given you the preliminary copy of the independent vet study. Is that true?"

"He did, but we're not ready to go public with the findings yet. We need to wait for the final report."

"I just thought…"

"I'm not going to discuss it further."

"But…"

Ignoring me, she picked up Marlon, and after cradling him like an infant for a moment, returned him to the holding cage to sleep it off. She looked pointedly at her watch. "Don't you have work to do?"

"The Mexican gray wolves, the…"

"Then I suggest you return to your duties."

Stung, I turned on my heel and left.

⟨⟩⟨⟩⟨⟩

The wolves were happy to see me. Cisco, the alpha male, trotted toward me with a sharp-toothed grin when I arrived at their acre-sized enclosure with a cart full of flank steak. Godiva, his chocolate-colored mate, and their four pups followed close behind. Bringing up the rear were the other five wolves in the exhibit, a smaller male and four females. Among Mexican grays, the only pack members that regularly bred were the alpha male and female, so these five served as "helper" animals, regurgitating partially-digested food for the alpha pair's pups.

Lately, however, I had seen Hazel, one of the helper females, casting come-hither looks in Cisco's direction. He remained true to his mate, but Zip, the small male, appeared eager to take up the slack. Given the rigid dictates of pack breeding practices, it would be interesting to see how this soap opera played out.

For now, love was the furthest thing from the wolves' minds. They wanted their dinner and they wanted it now. Although wolves rarely attacked humans, for safety's sake I stayed inside the holding pen while I portioned out the meat. That accomplished, I tossed the steaks far into the enclosure. The wolves sparred briefly and bloodlessly over the selection, and with pecking order re-established, trotted off individually to eat in private.

I watched as Cisco and Godiva waited patiently while their almost-weaned pups took a few practice bites of meat. After the pups grew bored and wandered off to play, the parents ate their own meal, finishing off their steaks in a manner of seconds. Satiated, they settled down with each other for some serious grooming time.

My work with the wolves finished, I headed for Lucy's enclosure, where I found a group of elementary school children gathered around the fence.

"Why won't the anteater come out to play?" asked a child of around six, his face long with disappointment as he stared into the empty enclosure.

Since I couldn't tell him that our ignorant zoo director had put her in anteater jail, I resorted to a white lie. "She didn't get much sleep last night, and she's tired."

"Did she have a nightmare?"

Now there was a question. Discovering a dead human in her enclosure might have affected Lucy deeply, although personally, I doubted if anteaters dreamed. "When she wakes up I'll ask her."

The teacher smiled, then led the group down the path toward the Andean spectacled bears. Once the children were out of sight I took the hidden trail used by keepers to the back of the anteater's holding pen. I found her standing with her head pressed against the gate, rocking back and forth. A sure sign of stress.

"Oh, Lucy. I'm so sorry."

When she didn't even summon up a grunt to greet me, I felt stressed myself. She definitely needed larger quarters, but a reprieve from Barry Fields seemed unlikely. If only...

Let's you and me go out some time.

Judging from the director's behavior in the staff lounge, he was hot for me—or at least hot for the money he imagined I had. It would be easy to turn his greed to Lucy's benefit. Realizing what I was about to do, I almost slapped myself.

Almost.

As soon as the last of my charges were taken care of, I hurried into the ladies' room near the lounge and washed up. Fortunately, I hadn't yet taken home the outfit I'd worn to Grayson's funeral, so I retrieved my black dress and pumps from my locker and slipped them on. Somber, yes, but when I freed my curly red hair from its pony tail and combed it with my fingers, the effect was less funereal. I cadged a spritz of Essence of Lilac off a zoo volunteer, then headed for Barry's office where I caught him as he was leaving for the day.

He gave me his nasty dingo smile. "Teddy! You look..." His eyes narrowed in a calculating manner. "...lovely!"

I put my hand on his arm. "I'm here to make amends. When you asked me out earlier, I was so taken aback I'm afraid I didn't respond properly." For emphasis, I fluttered my red eyelashes.

He covered my hand with his own. It felt clammy. "You've changed your mind?"

Remembering poor Lucy in her small holding pen, I fought back the urge to gag. "Yes, I have."

He looked me up and down, the dingo eyeing its prey. "How about tonight?"

Needing time to steel myself for what promised to be an unpleasant encounter, I shook my head. "I'm busy until Thursday. Or we can wait for the weekend."

Disappointment clouded his face but he rallied. "Thursday it is. Might I suggest Jacqueline's?"

Jacqueline's was a small French bistro in downtown San Sebastian known for its excellent food, but we'd probably run into too many acquaintances, maybe even Joe, who was addicted to their white chocolate mousse. I countered with a less popular restaurant.

"Why don't we try Zone Nine? I hear their steaks are delicious." Zone Nine, on the outskirts of Carmel, was an obnoxiously minimalist eatery where more attention was paid to the food's presentation than its taste. But its greater distance from the zoo suited my purposes.

He beamed. "Then it's a date! What time should I pick you up? You live at Gunn Landing Harbor, don't you?"

I didn't want him anywhere near my beloved *Merilee*. "Why don't I meet you there at eight?" That way I wouldn't have to sit next to him in his car, where he might be tempted to paw at me.

"Eight it is, Teddy. Zone Nine."

I pulled my hand away and wiped it surreptitiously on my dress. "I can hardly wait."

Oh, I was going to Hell, no doubt about it.

On my way home I stopped off at my mother's house to borrow some jewelry for the big date. I also wanted to find out why she hadn't been at the fund-raiser. She turned out to be no more amenable to my questions than Dr. Kate.

Not only that, but her lipstick was smeared all over her face. She couldn't seem to get me out of the house soon enough, either, claiming that she needed to clean the silver (an obvious lie, since Maid-of-the-Week did that), had to go grocery shopping (another lie; Maid-of-the-Week did that, too), and needed to trim the topiary on the front lawn (yet another lie, since Caro had never trimmed a bush in her life. Mr. Gonzales, her combination gardener/handyman, took care of those honors).

As she nudged me toward the door, I asked, "What's going on?" Not for the first time I grew concerned about the side effects of her La Jolla Strawberry/Carrot Diet. Protein deprivation could do strange things to the human brain, hence the ditzy behavior of so many supermodels. "Caro, what have you eaten today?"

She scowled. "More carrots than I can count. Don't you have a dog to walk?"

"I left work a few minutes early so his bladder should be fine." I made a mental note to keep a close eye on my mother's condition during the next several days. Dieting was one thing, anorexia another. "Where's the maid? I didn't see her when I came in. And I couldn't help but notice that the house isn't up to standard." Newspapers littered the sofas and a cat-sized dust bunny lurked under the Georgian armoire. Under ordinary circumstances, Caro would fire a maid for such obvious dereliction of duty.

"I gave her the week off."

"Didn't you hire her less than a month ago?"

"She needed some rest. It was nice of you to drop by, dear, but I have things to do." She opened the door and hip-bumped me gently onto the porch.

"But Caro…"

She closed the door in my face and locked it.

Remembering the other reason I stopped by, I banged loudly on the door. "*Mother!*"

The door opened, but only by an inch. All I could see were a few manicured fingernails and the tip of her surgery-sculpted nose. "Don't make a scene. And stop calling me 'Mother.'"

"But I need to borrow something!"

The door opened slightly wider. Now I could see a mascara-ed eye. It was smudged, too. "What?"

"That diamond necklace Petersen gave you, the four-carat job." I hadn't cared for her last husband, a heart surgeon who seemingly lacked one himself, but he'd been generous with her.

"Hang on." The door closed and I heard the lock turn again.

After a few minutes the lock slid back, the door opened, and she thrust a crumpled paper bag through the narrow opening. "Bye."

The door slammed shut.

Wondering if, like other lepers, I should ring a bell in front of me as I drove through the village, I hurried home, changed into some sweats, and snapped the leash onto DJ Bonz's collar.

"Guess nobody loves me but you, dog."

As it turned out, Bonz wasn't interested in me, either. He was more obsessed with a filaree bush than in keeping me company, so I let him do his business. By the time his bladder emptied and we returned to the *Merilee*, what little good humor I'd had was long gone.

At loose ends, I sat on deck hoping that Maureen, my favorite harbor otter, might swim by for a handout. But she was a no-show.

Other than the occasional bleating of the foghorn on Gunn Point and the *shush-shush* of waves against the *Merilee*, the evening was silent. Most of my neighbors were members of the Harbor Liveaboard Committee, and had gathered at the restaurant portion of Fred's Fish Market to hash through the new ordinance codes recently issued by the harbor master. I'd meant to attend the meeting but what with one thing and another, had let it slide.

Too depressed to watch the spectacular sunset, I went below deck and clicked on my tiny television set. The reception was poor, but at least I was able to listen to the bottom-of-the-hour local news. The news reader—I think he had gray hair, although I couldn't tell for sure due to all the snow on the screen—gave an update on the virus suspected in so many sea otter deaths.

This made me switch my concerns to the Maureen. Could she be sick? Was that why she hadn't showed?

The news reader segued to the results of a kayak race in Santa Cruz. Almost as an afterthought, he added, "The recent murder of Grayson Harrill, husband of one of the Gunn heirs, has curtailed attempts to break the famous Trust." He launched into an account of the monies involved, parroting the information Roarke had given me. "In connection with the murder, Zorah Vega, the Gunn Zoo's head keeper, was booked the other day into San Sebastian County Jail, then released on bond. None of this has affected the day-to-day running of the zoo, administrators tell us. Although the murder did take place on its grounds, the zoo—for years the delight of adults and children alike—remains open."

The camera shifted away from him to a blurry file video of some large animal—I think it was a orangutan—romping through some spotty green stuff that vaguely resembled our Great Apes enclosure. The camera switched to a shot of a bird-like creature flapping around in what appeared to be an aviary. From the multiplicity of sounds the bird made, I concluded it was Carlos, my magpie jay would-be lover.

"Sweet-sweet!" I called to the TV.

"Boom-boom!" the TV bird called back. At least somebody was still talking to me.

Our dialogue ended when Miss Priss jumped on the counter and began pawing at the television screen. Almost as if responding to her attack, Carlos vanished, to be replaced by another talking head, this one a human female, reading the weather report.

"In the Coastal cities, fog in the morning, burning off by early afternoon. Clear inland, temperatures rising to eighty in the valleys."

I turned off the TV and picked up a copy of the latest Jack Hanna book I'd borrowed from the San Sebastian Public Library, but before I finished the first page, I felt, rather than heard, footsteps on deck. The *Merilee* rolled slightly to port, accommodating the added weight. Bonz pricked up his ears but didn't bark.

"Who's there?" I called.

The person had not requested permission to come aboard, as polite sailors always do, so I felt a faint stab of worry. Especially since my mother's diamond necklace lay unprotected on the galley counter.

When the person didn't answer, I raised my voice. "I said, '*Who's there?*' "

No answer. Just stealthy footsteps approaching the open salon hatch. Alarmed, I grabbed a heavy flashlight from the shelf behind me, wishing it were something more lethal. After all, there was a murderer on the loose.

"Identify yourself!"

The footsteps continued until they stopped outside the hatch, where the light spilling from the salon revealed the tip of a shoe. Big. Broad. Rubber-soled.

A man's.

My mouth went dry. If the intruder was a burglar, or something worse, what kind of defense could a three-legged dog and a half-blind cat mount on my behalf?

I'd have to save myself.

There was no place to run, no place to hide. As Bonz continued staring at the salon door, I snatched up my cell to call 9-1-1, but stopped before punching in the first numeral. What would I tell the dispatcher? That someone was standing on my boat and wouldn't identify himself?

It sounded silly, even to me.

I could call Joe, but he lived fifteen miles away in San Sebastian, and by the time he drove down to the harbor, whatever was going to happen would have already happened. I could simply scream my head off, but such behavior would earn eternal contempt from the liveaboard community if my visitor turned out to be a tipsy neighbor who'd stumbled onto the wrong boat.

All those choices being unsatisfactory, I grabbed the bag containing the necklace in one hand, my flashlight in the other, and tiptoed into the aft cabin. Wishing I hadn't left the nightstand light on, I ducked behind the entryway where a shivering Bonz immediately joined me. Tucking the necklace under a pillow, I raised the flashlight and gave it a few practice swings. Due to the heavy lifting I performed every day at the zoo, my arm muscles were well-developed, so with a little luck I could knock the intruder unconscious, then flee.

The *Merilee* rolled again as the man stepped into the salon. Maybe he would take my cheap TV set and leave. But I knew better. A mere thief would target a glitzy sloop like the *Tequila Sunrise* instead of my shabby, de-commissioned fishing boat, so my intruder had to be after something else. Probably not Caro's necklace, because other than her, no one else knew I'd borrowed it.

There was another possibility; the intruder was after me personally. Since Zorah's arrest I'd asked a lot of questions and maybe Grayson's killer had decided to shut me up.

My entire body began to tremble.

Fear was acceptable, cowardice wasn't, so I forced my hands to stop shaking. If the intruder was Grayson's killer, I would fight back and get as much of his DNA on me as possible between my teeth and under my nails. He might take me out, but I'd take a piece of him with me.

A tall shadow fell across the cabin carpet.

I raised my flashlight to bring down on the intruder's head.

As if suspecting someone waited for him, the intruder paused at the threshold.

I held my breath.

Come on, come on. Let's get this over with.

He entered the cabin.

The nightstand light illuminated the intruder's face, revealing black hair, a neatly-trimmed black beard, bushy black eyebrows—and green eyes fringed by red eyelashes very much out of sync with all that black hair.

I exhaled in relief.

"Hi, Dad."

Chapter Ten

"I hardly recognized you with that beard and terrible dye job." I poured Dad a glass of Riesling, and settled next to him on the salon's settee. "You're lucky I didn't bash your head in."

"So that's why you were holding that flashlight up so high." He took a sip of the wine, made a face. "Jesus, this is cheap stuff."

"It's all I can afford."

"Sorry about that."

I gave him a look. "I'll bet."

"We are what we are, Teddy. Besides, you know that I set up a bank account for you in the Caymans. Still not using it?"

"For charitable purposes only." Like bailing friends out of jail.

"Aren't you the self-righteous one."

Since there was no point in discussing ethics with my ethics-challenged father, I changed the subject. "Let me take a wild guess here. You've been hiding out at Caro's."

He pushed his wine glass away. "Off and on. I arrived in town a week ago but your mother was having one of her awful parties, so I drove up to Santa Cruz and stayed on Al's sloop."

Albert Mazer. The friend who'd kept the *Merilee* for me. It didn't surprise me that he would lend aid and comfort to my fugitive father, nor that Caro had, too. Her other marriages aside, he'd been the only man she'd ever truly loved.

"This isn't the best time for you to pay a visit. There's been a murder here and the authorities are, shall we say, acting hyper-vigilant."

He nodded sagely. "The unfortunate murderee being Jeanette Gunn's husband. When you say 'the authorities,' I take it you mean the sheriff."

Annoyed, I grabbed the Riesling he so disdained and gulped it down. "Yes. Him. Anyway, everyone's nervous around here, so while I'm always glad to see you, you'd be better off in a country that doesn't have a tight extradition agreement with the U.S."

"Such as Iran? North Korea?"

"Why not go back to Costa Rica? That's worked fine so far."

"It's too hot for me there right now, and I'm not talking about Global Warming."

I almost spit up my wine. "Don't tell me you pulled another of your scams down there!"

You'd think that when my father absconded with his firm's millions he'd be set for life, but no. After a few years on the relatively legal lam he missed his larcenous ways and began delving into various schemes to relieve the financially unwary of their superfluous money. The only good thing about all this was that he never ran scams on the less-than-filthy-rich, so the poor widows and orphans of the world were safe.

"Dad, I asked you a question."

He flashed a sheepish grin. "That was a statement, not a question. If you must know, there was this young man at the El Presidente Casino in San Jose…"

It took me a minute to realize he wasn't talking about nearby San Jose, California, but San Jose, Costa Rica, and the casino we sometimes visited with him during one of my infrequent trips to Central America.

"…and he was flashing around such a big roll of cash that I knew it would eventually give him back problems, so I just kind of helped him out. Played proactive chiropractor, you might say. I told him I could get my hands on some perfectly executed counterfeit twenties for about three cents on the dollar, a bargain rate…"

"I don't need the details. What was your haul?"

"Less than two hundred thou. Mere pocket change."

With people like my father, it's not the money but the game, the adrenaline rush. This was why, with off-shore bank accounts totaling in the millions, he continued to rob, cheat, and steal as if he was one crust of bread away from starvation.

"If it were mere pocket change, what are you doing back here in Gunn Landing? You know the feds haven't given up."

"And I admire their persistence. But that's why I grew the beard and gave myself the dye job you are so critical of."

"You could at least have used some black mascara. Those red eyelashes are a dead giveaway."

"Not a problem, since I always wear sunglasses when I'm out and about."

Suspecting that I'd need it, I poured myself more cheap wine. "As much as I love discussing cosmetics with you, I repeat my question. What are you doing back here when there's an open warrant out for your arrest? Yeah, it's been twenty years since you've shown your face in Gunn Landing, but still…" The straits must be dire indeed if they'd chased my fugitive dad north of the border again.

"You sure there's no single malt whiskey around?"

"I'm sure."

His face took on an serious expression. "Some warrants are worse than others, Teddy, and while the feds might want to do unpleasant things to me, at least their unpleasantness won't involve cement galoshes. Whereas the young gentleman's relatives… Well, let's just say they're already mixing up the cement."

It took me a moment to understand. When I did, some of my earlier panic returned. My darling dad was talking about a *death* warrant. "Don't tell me you didn't pull a fast one on the Mafia!"

"Not the Mafia. Even *I* know better than that. But as it turned out, the young gentleman in the casino was the only son of Seamus Fitzgerald."

"Jesus, Mary and Joseph! You scammed Chuckles Fitzgerald's son?!"

Mere months before my husband left me, the San Francisco newspapers had been filled with stories about the Seamus "Chuckles" Fitzgerald murder trial. Fitzgerald, who'd supposedly made his fortune in import/export—but everyone, especially the cops, knew better—was suspected of murdering his cousin, James "Little Jimmy" Hannon. Little Jimmy had ratted Chuckles out to the feds over various money-laundering schemes, and soon afterwards, Little Jimmy was found floating down the Sacramento River. Without his head.

Following the disappearance of several key witnesses and two suspected instances of jury tampering, the murder trial collapsed into chaos, and Chuckles walked out of jail, free to decapitate again.

Dad leaned forward and tipped my mouth shut with an elegant finger. "Such a nice girl, so concerned about her wayward father."

"Dad, this isn't funny. That man's a *killer!*"

He raised a too-black eyebrow. "Unlike the person who eased Grayson Harrill out of this vale of tears?"

"That's different."

"I doubt he would think so."

"Don't change the subject. Why in the world, with Chuckles Fitzgerald only ninety miles away, would you even consider coming back here?"

"Because it's the last place he'd think to look."

I didn't buy it. Only fools returned to the scene of their crimes, and Dad was nobody's fool. I was about to point that out when he interrupted me.

"If you're worried about him taking out his pique on you and your mother, rest easy. Even Chuckles has his standards and would never hurt a woman. Now it's my turn to criticize you. While I was staying at your mother's, she gave me an earful about all the snooping you've been doing and, for once, I agree with her. Stop playing amateur detective and leave crime to the experts."

"Experts like you?"

"Don't be naughty."

"Talk about the pot calling the kettle black."

"I mean it, Teddy. There are dangerous people in this world, I should know. You're not equipped to deal with them."

Dangerous.

Like the animals we keepers cared for at the zoo? They were dangerous, too, but as long as we took the proper safety precautions, we were fine.

Then I thought about Chuckles Fitzgerald and headless corpses and began to feel sick. But when I remembered that one of my best friends was facing trial for murder, I decided that safety was overrated.

With my most sincere smile, I said, "You're right. I'll stop snooping around. Now that we've got all that cleared up do you need me to take you back to Caro's?"

He shook his head. "I'm driving Al's Lexus."

Of course he was. Fugitive or not, Dad always traveled first class.

<><><>

The Cayman Islands transfer arrived at my bank Tuesday morning. After receiving the call from the bank manager, I found another zookeeper to sub for me and drove a cashier's check over to the bail bondsman. By early afternoon, Zorah had been released from jail, courtesy of "an unknown benefactor." Her gang-banger nephew drove her home in his low-rider. Gee, what a nice kid.

When she showed up for work the next day, joy reigned supreme in the staff lounge. Later that morning, her face drawn from her week in lockup, she approached while I was feeding the wolves. Without preamble, she said, "How are we going to get that poor anteater out of the holding pen and back into her enclosure?"

Remembering my upcoming date with the zoo director, I said, "I'm working on it."

She gave me a puzzled look. "Care to share?"

"Not yet."

With a grunt, she started to leave, then paused. "One more thing. Thank you."

"For what?"

"Bailing me out."

"I don't know what you're talking about."

"Really? Oh, yeah, I forgot. I have tons of friends ready and willing to pony up two hundred and fifty thousand dollars bail money."

Before I could think, I blurted, "No, no. That's wrong. When you front someone's bail, you only have to pay ten percent of the stated amount, so it would have been no more than twenty-five thousand. Plus a small fee." Seeing her "gotcha" expression, my face flamed. "I learned about that kind of thing when my father had his own, ah, legal troubles. But as to who paid *your* bail, I haven't the slightest idea."

Her mouth twitched into a smile. "The tooth fairy?"

"Or a secret admirer."

"Whatever." She squeezed my shoulder. "I appreciate everything you've done for me. And you don't have to worry about me skipping bail. You'll get your money back." With a final squeeze, she headed back down the keeper's path toward Africa Trail.

Skipping bail? The thought had never occurred to me, but if she did flee and my money was forfeit, I didn't care. The Caymans account was dirty money. At least my father's thievery had finally accomplished something good.

Humming with satisfaction, I went back to feeding the wolves.

The rest of the day passed without a major crisis. The sun shone, the animals behaved themselves, and the zoo's visitors did, too. A cloud of unpleasantness arrived, though, when Joe dropped by as I was feeding the capybaras. He told me my help was no longer needed in the Grayson case.

"But you *asked* me to find out what I could," I reminded him, trying not to notice how handsome he looked in his uniform, and how unnerved his presence made me. I didn't need more complications in my life.

"That was then, Teddy, and this is now. We've made an arrest. Too bad our suspect's made bail. I wonder how that happened."

Just the sound of his voice made my heart pound, though I didn't like what he was saying. "You arrested the wrong person!"

"No, I didn't. Stay out of it."

I glared at him. "Or what? You'll arrest me, too?"

His face grew grim. "Don't think it can't happen."

"Is that a threat?"

"If you want to take it that way, yes."

How could I have ever loved such an immovable man? Unable to meet his eyes, I turned my attention to the capybaras, where Gladys and Myrtle had begun to fight over Gus. Both hungry for love, they nipped at each others' shoulders while the male stood there and watched with what almost seemed like a smug expression.

Men.

"Stop it!" I yelled to the females.

They did.

"You, too!" I yelled at Joe.

He blinked. "What?"

"Stop threatening me! Now I've got work to do, and I imagine you do, too. Elsewhere."

After he stomped off, I finished the rest of my chores wondering why I felt so unhappy.

I felt even worse when, during my late afternoon break, I placed a call to Tommy Prescott. "Zorah's trial date is set for mid-October, right?"

"Yep. Listen, you know I always like to talk to you, but I'm going over a brief right now and I..."

I cut through his excuses. "Be truthful with me. What are her chances of acquittal?"

"Your friend's got one of the best defense attorneys in the state, remember?"

"The sheriff put together a pretty good case, didn't he?"

Sighing, he answered, "That's what the D.A. informs me. The murder weapon may present a problem since Ms. Vega's prints are all over it. Same for her perceived motive. She was pretty angry with the murder victim, remember, and she does have a history of violence. The prosecution will probably call as witness that man she roughed up at the zoo."

I wondered how many animal-lovers would be on the jury. "Point taken. So, back to my original question. How would you rate her chances of acquittal? Eighty percent? Seventy?"

A long pause. Then, "More like sixty. Maybe less."

"Please tell me you're exaggerating."

"Sixty-five percent at best. She's in real trouble, Teddy."

"Thanks for your honesty," I whispered, ringing off. As I shoved the cell back into my pocket, I remembered Zorah's many kindnesses to me, to other keepers, to her animals. For all her perceived toughness, she was as hypermaternal as my mother, only better at hiding it. When I had first been hired, she'd followed me from enclosure to enclosure, making certain I never came too close to snapping teeth or snatching talons. She had also acted as a buffer between me and the other zookeepers, who at first dismissed me as a spoiled little rich girl having a lark at the zoo and who would cut and run the minute the party got rough. She'd wasted no time in setting them straight, and within weeks, they'd accepted me as an equal.

Leaving her fate to the caprices of the criminal justice system wasn't acceptable.

I needed to find out who'd really murdered Grayson. Especially since that closed-minded sheriff wouldn't do it.

The fateful day for my date with the zoo director dawned without any morning fog. As I fed a crushed banana to an unhappy Lucy, I pondered how far was I willing to go to get her released from the holding pen. First base? Second? Third? A home run? Definitely not a home run. Nor third base, either. Or second. But then what? More eyelash batting?

This quandary remained uppermost in my mind throughout the day, right up until I was back on board the *Merilee*, surveying wardrobe choices for the evening.

I owned a sum total of three dresses: my basic black, the lavender gauze, and the yellow-and-orange Donna Karan. Deciding that a dress might seem too eager, I briefly considered my beige pants suit, then changed my mind. Too "businessy." And what about footwear? My one remaining pair of Jimmy Choo pumps? My Valentino flats? And hair—down or up? If I dressed too conservatively, my wiles might not work, and Lucy would remain in the zoo's version of lockup. If I overdid the vamp thing, I might have trouble fending Barry off.

In the end I chose beige linen slacks (purity), a black cashmere sweater open to the third button (wickedness), the Valentino flats (Barry wasn't tall), fluffed my red hair down around my shoulders (more wickedness), and slicked on a peach-toned lipstick (more purity).

Time for the *pièce de résistance*: Caro's necklace.

The four-carat square-cut diamond sat in the center of a white gold pendant, with four smaller diamonds perched at each corner. While some might consider it vulgar, the thing could excite a dead man.

◇◇◇

Barry, dressed in yet another expensive-looking sports coat and reeking of too much aftershave, was waiting at a secluded corner table when I arrived at Zone Nine. As he pulled out the chair for me, I murmured with as much sincerity as I could muster, "Such a gentleman."

He gave me a carnivorous smile, but riveted his eyes on my necklace. "And you are the loveliest of ladies." Smarm meets smarm.

We chit-chatted while waiting for our server, and I was again reminded why so many of San Sebastian County's wealthy widows turned to putty in his hands. He knew exactly what to say and when to say it.

When our waiter arrived, I opted for a not-too-expensive Riesling and what turned out to be a tasteless ziti in an ersatz Romano sauce. Barry chose a steak so rare it dripped blood. With a few drinks, his thin veil of courtly manners began to slip. He'd started on a relatively harmless Pinot noir to go with the steak, but when we ordered dessert—a tarted-up peach strudel served "tall"—he switched to bourbon straight. As the alcohol built up in his system, his teeth seemed to grow longer and sharper at the same rate of speed that his brain diminished.

Then, as the tipsy are prone to do, he talked about his ex-wives, both—according to him—gold-digging, adulterous bitches.

"Sounds like you need a woman who appreciates you," I said.

With an exhale of bourbon, he leaned across the table and took my hand, all the while staring at Caro's necklace. "You are so right. Let's talk about you. Given your sophistication, why are you working at a dirty old zoo? It's such an odd career choice for a pretty little socialite."

I tried not to grind my teeth too obviously. "I'm not a socialite." Nor pretty. Nor, at five-foot-five, particularly little. Concerned that my tone might sound sharp, I flashed a smile. "I'm like everyone else at the zoo, working for a living and happy to be doing it caring for animals."

"But you don't have to work, right?"

Ordinarily such blatant gigolo-ism infuriated me, but the memory of Lucy's misery funneled my ire into a fib. "My family believes in hard work." I delivered this whopper with a straight face.

He nodded so strenuously that a lock of tan hair fell over his tan forehead. "That's what old families like yours are all about, the sterling qualities that made America great." While I stifled my guffaws, he snapped his fingers at a passing waiter. "*Garçon!* Another Maker's Mark for me and another Riesling Beblenheim for the lady."

I leaned forward and tapped him playfully on the hand. "So decisive! No wonder Grayson hired you!" I almost gagged on the words.

He wriggled with pleasure. "Not everyone recognizes my leadership qualities."

"That's because you're so subtle. Which reminds me. Now that the heat's died down over the mur...er, unfortunate event at the zoo, isn't it time we put the anteater on exhibit again? The visitors have been asking about her, which means we can turn all this bad publicity to our advantage." By calling our recent media coverage "bad publicity," I'd grossly understated the problem, since several newspapers and one local TV station had started calling us, "The Zoo of Death."

Before Barry objected, I added, "Kim could rework that puppet show she was planning to debut at the fund-raiser to take into account our problem. I've even come up with a new plot. When the curtain rises, Lucy has been accused of eating Little Red Riding Hood's grandmother. Hood, who's a private detective, discovers that the anteater is merely hiding Grandma to keep her safe from Mister Wolf. In the end, they chase Mister Wolf out of the forest and everyone lives happily ever after."

I forestalled argument by fiddling with my mother's diamond necklace until it caught the candlelight. Rainbow prisms danced across his face. *See how much money I represent? Don't you wish you could get your hands on it?*

He stared at the necklace, his eyes almost as large as the steak he'd just finished. "That's, wow, pretty."

"This old thing?" I hunched my shoulders forward to make my modest bit of cleavage thrust the necklace closer to him. The ploy worked, and I could almost hear his hormones screaming, "*Boobs! Diamonds!*"

Sweat popped out on his forehead. "You're so...so..."

Confident that he was tipsy enough not to realize he was being played, I took his hand. "Now, about that anteater..."

"Put her back on exhibit!" He actually shook with excitement.

I almost wept with relief. Tomorrow I would drive to the zoo at dawn, spruce up Lucy's exhibit, then free her from the holding pen. The evening's objective secured, I made a great show of looking at my watch.

"My goodness, it's ten o'clock already! If we want to get to work on time tomorrow, we'd better leave."

He looked at my necklace again, flames of avarice burning in his eyes. "Let's go to my place for a nightcap."

Here came the most delicate part of the evening. Not only did I want to free Lucy, but I wanted to keep her free, too. If Barry ever saw through my act, he might lock her back up out of spite. Something told me he was a spiteful man.

"Let's not move too fast, okay? This is only our first date." To remind him what the stakes were, I flashed the necklace again.

Eyes glued to it, he fell silent and stayed that way until we reached the parking lot. There, fueled by diamonds, boobs, and bourbon, he lunged at me as I was about to open the door to my truck. Before I could dodge out of the way, he pinned me against the door and groped at my breasts, such as they were. Since the anteater's fate hung in the balance, I pushed him away more gently than he deserved.

"Good *night*, Barry!"

"There's this spark between us, can't you feel it?" He grabbed at me again but this time I moved away quickly, and he came up with a handful of Nissan instead of a handful of Teddy.

I slid to the side and positioned the front fender between us. "Let's talk about this tomorrow. For now, I have to get home because I want to be at the zoo by five." To spring Lucy from anteater jail.

His next words would have been more convincing if he'd addressed them to my face instead of the necklace. "If that's the only problem, come in late. Hell, take the day off! I'll tell everyone you're working on a special project."

He started toward me again.

This is what happens when amateurs try to act the part of *femme fatale*. Biting back a curse, I scuttled around the Nissan's front bumper toward the passenger's side. Fortunately, I was able to open the door, spring in, and locked up before he reached me.

He pressed his face against the window, an unlovely sight. "Don't go, Teddy! I have so much I want to say…"

I crawled over the gear shift to the driver's seat and turned on the ignition. Rolling the window down a hair, I called out, "See you tomorrow!"

I peeled rubber out of the lot.

<>‹›‹›

The next morning Lucy rushed into her roomy enclosure with a joyful bound. I leaned against the railing and watched her run back and forth to each of her faux logs, then start the circuit all over again. Seeing her caper like this was worth every minute of the ghastly evening I'd endured.

"You go, girl!" I called, my heart lifting to see her happiness.

She spun, reared up on her tail so high that I could see her protruding belly, and pointed her long nose at me.

Grunt, grunt!

Then she gave a hop and buck, and sped around the enclosure again, her tail waving behind her like a furry flag.

‹›‹›‹›

The wages of sin came due when the zoo closed for the day and I rang the squirrel monkeys' dinner bell, signaling it was time for them to return to their night quarters. As I led them toward their spacious, two-story-high cage, Barry emerged from the underbrush, making Marlon shriek in alarm. The zoo director looked as sleek as usual, give or take a bloodshot eye or two.

"Please accept my apologies for my behavior last night," he said nervously. "I don't know what came over me."

A diamond necklace and several bourbons, that's what came over you. For Lucy's sake, I swallowed my irritation. Setting down the monkey's water bucket, I said with as much tolerance as I could muster, "We all have our off nights." I gestured toward the monkeys swarming around our feet. "By the way, never approach animals so quickly. When startled, they might bite."

He threw Marlon a contemptuous look. "They don't scare me. After all, how much damage can a two-pound monkey do? Anyway, I wanted to say how much I enjoyed being with you."

"I had a nice time, too." Pretending that I was merely brushing away a fly, I felt my nose to see if it was growing longer. Nope. Still the same short, bumpy thing.

Hoping to get away from him, I ushered Marlon and the girls into the night quarters and followed close behind to turn on their heat lamps. Barry hurried along, too, but in his haste bumped hard against Lana, one of the younger females. When she gave a frightened scream, the monkeys scattered. All except Marlon, who froze beside an empty water bucket.

The zoo director ignored the monkeys' fright. "Let me prove my contrition by fixing you a great big sirloin at my place tonight."

Like previous zoo directors, he lived in a house in a secluded area at the rear of the zoo, a place where—as the movie line goes—no one could hear you scream. I wasn't about to let him lure me there.

"Tonight?" To give myself more time to think, I poured fresh water into the monkey's bucket.

I was still scrambling for an excuse when Marlon, furious at Barry's rough treatment of Lana, darted forward and nipped him on the ankle. Barry responded by aiming a kick at the monkey, who deftly dodged it.

"Don't!" I warned.

Too late. Several enraged squirrel monkeys leaped on the zoo director, nipping at his hands, his ears, his cheeks—everywhere their teeth could find exposed flesh. For a moment I just stood there shocked. Such orchestrated violence among squirrel monkeys against humans was rare, which is why we allowed them to roam freely with children in the exhibit. Monkey-against-monkey violence was more common, but although the females often ganged up on Marlon, they apparently didn't want anyone else doing it.

Barry flung a few of his attackers away, but for every one he got rid of, two more took its place.

"Get them off me!" he yelled.

Careful not to step on tiny monkey toes, I waded into the melee but had no more luck peeling them off him than he did. Defense was the only possible strategy. "Cover your face and hold still. And for God's sake, stop yelling."

He didn't listen.

Yelling curses that would horrify a gangsta rap star, he swatted at the monkeys, which only enraged them further. Every now and then, his hand or elbow would find its target, but not often enough to make any difference. Worse, Marlon, now recovered from the affront to his dignity, joined the females and gnawed at Barry's ankle with renewed gusto. As the monkeys swarmed over him, the air in the cage grew musky with the scent of urine—the monkeys, I hoped. A humiliated zoo director might be even more dangerous than a bitten zoo director.

Fearing that he might hurt one of my little friends, I stepped away from the brawl, picked up the water bucket and upended it over everyone, drenching the director in the process. With a chorus of screeches, the monkeys—who loathed getting wet— fled into the corner of the cage. I took advantage of their retreat by pushing Barry out the cage door and locking it behind us.

When I patted his arm, water squished through my fingers. Still, I tried for a smile. "That wasn't so bad, was it? We keepers routinely suffer far worse injuries than monkey nips."

Now that it was too late to do him any good, Barry covered his scratched face with his hands. "I want you to put those little rats down. All of them!"

"Euthanize the monkeys?"

"Wring their nasty necks, give them lethal injections, shoot them, feed them to the crocs, I don't care."

He was being hysterical, I decided, and didn't mean it. Then again, maybe he did. While I knew Dr. Kate would rather be fired than carry out such a Draconian order, Barry did have the power to make life hell for everyone until the situation sorted itself out. Meanwhile, it was obvious that he was in pain. When he lowered his hands, I saw a long red mark across his cheek. It resembled a dueling scar, which in a way it was.

"Euthanize them, I said! Or do I have to do it myself?"

Hoping to calm him, I switched to the same soothing voice that usually worked with upset animals. "There, there. Everything will be all right." As he began to settle down, I reverted to human-speak. "Look, these things happen when you work around animals. At least the monkeys have never attacked the kids, but I guess that's because kids have the common sense to pay attention when we tell them…"

Oops. I cleared my throat and blundered on. "From what I can see, the monkeys didn't do any real damage. We'll slap on a few bandages, get you a tetanus booster, and you'll be fine."

He blew his nose on a soiled handkerchief. "Are you nuts? They tried to kill me!"

"When an animal is serious about killing you, it's quick."

"I want those monkeys *dead!*"

"But…"

"As for you, Ms. Bentley, I'm holding you responsible for what happened."

Ms. Bentley? The return to formality wasn't a good sign. But why be mad at me? I hadn't bitten him.

His next words answered my question. "And why the hell did you have to throw water on me? Don't you know how much this sports coat cost? It's a *Cavalli!*"

With that, he stalked off.

The monkeys hurled curses at him as he disappeared.

Chapter Eleven

There are things you can fix and things you can't. Fortunately, the memory of my mother's necklace must have put Barry in a forgiving state of mind, because when I dropped by his office first thing the next morning to plead the monkeys' case, he rescinded their death-by-crocodile sentence.

"I was upset," he admitted, speaking to the spot on my throat where Caro's necklace once dangled. "And for what I said to you, I apologize."

For his words, not his actions? "No problem. You were having a bad time of it."

At that, he rose in his chair, rushed around the desk, and before I could stop him, wrapped his arms around me. Apparently he was one of those men who thought physical contact solved everything. Without letting my disgust show, I stepped out of the embrace.

"How long do I need to wait, Teddy?" he whined. "You know I'm crazy about you. Let me come over to your boat tonight and make it up to you. I'll bring champagne…"

I'd rather have a hungry python slithering around the *Merilee* than Barry, but he did look lonely. Maybe, just maybe, I could teach him to love animals the way the rest of us did. After all, there was a chance he wasn't as bad as I thought. It never hurt to give someone another chance. "Tonight? I'll have to check…"

Sensing capitulation, he attempted to hug me again. This time I was ready and he bounced off my raised hands.

"Gotta go!" With that, I hurried out of his office, climbed into my cart and took off.

I was thinking so hard as I sped toward the anteater's enclosure that I almost had a head-on collision with the vet. After we both braked, Dr. Kate leaned out of her cart and said, "Hey, do you know what happened to Barry? I saw him leaving the zoo last night and he looked like he'd gone ten rounds with an alley full of cats."

The circles below her eyes had deepened, which made me wonder if the combination of job stress, the demands of her three hyperactive children, and the declining health of her husband were overwhelming her. But I didn't dare ask. She was a very private person, so I kept the conversation professional.

"He had some problems in Monkey Mania but it wasn't anything serious. The report's in your mailbox."

Whenever there was an animal-versus-human incident on zoo grounds, the keeper had to file a report in quadruplet: one copy for the head park ranger, one for Zorah, one for the vet, and—ironically, in this case—one for the zoo director, who was supposed to file additional paperwork with the necessary agencies.

Alarm leaped in Dr. Kate's tired eyes. "Perhaps we should close the exhibit for a few days until things settle down. We can't risk having a child injured."

"They gave him a nip or two, that's all. He provoked the incident himself when he hurt one of the females, then kicked Marlon." After the monkey bit him, but no need to mention that.

At this, the vet looked like she wanted to bite him herself. "What was he doing up there in the first place? He hates animals."

"He needed to talk to me."

Her next question proved she didn't miss much. "Then why didn't he summon you to his office?" She motioned to the radio hanging from my belt.

Since the truth was embarrassing, I merely shrugged.

My nonanswer didn't get by her. "Are you having a problem with Barry?"

I tried to force a smile, but those muscles were already exhausted from their performance in the zoo director's office. "What makes you ask?"

"There's been talk."

"About the director and me?"

She shook her head.

I said, "I can assure you that there's nothing to worry about, at least where I'm concerned." After all, I'd brought my problem on myself, hadn't I?

"Positive?"

"Yes. Listen, about that independent vet study…"

Before I could finish my sentence, she started her cart again. Without another word, she headed toward the lemur enclosure, steering carefully around the visitors now trickling into the zoo.

As I watched her go, I wondered where she had been when Grayson was shot.

The squirrel monkeys still appeared agitated when I arrived at Monkey Mania, but after I released them from their night quarters and fed them large helpings of fruit mixed with mealworms, they settled down. At one point Marlon crept over to give me a conciliatory stroke on my ankle.

"Yeah, you're tough," I told him. "Personally, I sympathize with last night's temper tantrum, but you need to steer clear of Barry for a while. He has more clout than you."

Poor Marlon had no clout at all. Granted, he was larger than the other squirrel monkeys, which theoretically made him the alpha male of the exhibit, but in reality he was Big Boss Man only when the females allowed it.

Satisfied that life in Monkey Mania had returned to crazy-normal, I continued my rounds, eventually winding up at the anteater's enclosure. When she spotted me bustling around her holding pen, she gave a happy buck and rushed over.

"How's my Lucy?"

As if in response, her blue tongue snaked out, flapping against the chain link fence that separated us.

"I'm fine, too. Ready for breakfast?"

"Grunt."

"I brought some nice termites. And a couple of bananas."

"Squeak!"

"No, they didn't come all the way from Belize, but I'm sure they're lovely bananas anyway. Teddy wouldn't give her Lucy second-rate fruit."

"Grunt."

After stuffing a small portion of termites into the Wellington boot in her holding pen, I held up the safety board and opened the gate, expecting her to rush in. She didn't. Instead, she backed away, emitting what sounded like a growl. Apparently she'd had enough of the holding pen and wanted nothing else to do with it.

Somehow I had to transfer her to the pen. Regardless of her new loathing for it, I couldn't let anteater droppings pile up in the large enclosure until they became a health hazard. The mess would not only impact Lucy, but her baby, too.

"Lucy, I…"

Before I could react, she reared back and slashed at me, knocking the safety board out of my hand and tumbling it against the gate, which exposed my torso to those four-inch talons. Instinctively, I snatched up the safety board and slammed the gate closed between us.

"That was rude!"

I didn't take the attack personally. After all, she was a Code Red animal, and such behavior was to be expected given what she'd gone through the past week. For a moment I considered radioing another keeper and asking for help, but my pride kept me from it.

As I watched from behind the safety of the sturdy gate, she moved to the edge of her enclosure slashing at everything in her path: flies, a stand of bougainvillea, a clod of dirt. She was in what zookeepers call "attack mode," and there was nothing I could do until the mood wore off.

Moments later, it did. Once she finished her circuit and returned to the holding pen gate, her eyes looked into mine, imploring. With a low groan, she leaned against the links.

My heart ached for her. "Lucy doesn't understand why she tried to hurt Teddy, does she?"

Another groan.

Animal behaviorists say animals can't feel guilt, but I'm not sure I believe that. Talking softly, I fished a banana out of my pocket, mashed it into my palm and pressed it to the gate. Lucy's blue tongue flicked out and made short work of the mush.

"Feel better now?"

With another plaintive groan, she turned sideways and pressed against the fence. I reached out and scratched her coarse fur.

"Still friends?"

"*Grunt.*" And something that sounded oddly like a sob.

"I'm sorry, too. And don't worry. I still love my sweet girl."

To make certain she and her unborn baby were all right, I decided to remain with her for a while. I peeled the other banana and squashed half of it into my hand. While she lapped it up, I began to wonder what Grayson was doing alone by the anteater enclosure, since she was Code Red and he was afraid of even the meekest animal. Had he made an appointment to meet his killer there? The more I thought about it, the more I wondered about something else: why had Grayson appointed Barry Fields as the new zoo director? The ability to raise money was important, yes, but it wasn't everything. Other candidates were much more qualified—Zorah, for instance—yet he chose that idiot over her.

Grayson himself remained an enigma. Was he the nice man I'd always believed him to be, or the manipulative double-dealer Roarke had described?

Still baffled, I discussed my quandary with the anteater.

"What do you think, Lucy? Was Grayson a good person? Or like most of us humans, was he a mixture of good and bad? Whatever he was really like, he never locked you up in this awful holding pen, did he?"

At the words "holding pen," I thought I saw another flash of anger in her eyes, but I may have imagined it.

"If Jeanette ever gets her migraines under control, maybe she could come back and work here. Maybe even become director! She has the contacts, and it would certainly help keep her mind off her troubles. Don't you agree?"

Lucy lapped up more banana.

Jeanette had always enjoyed her days at the zoo. Three times a week she and her husband walked the zoo's trails, assuring themselves of each animal's comfort and condition of its enclosure. He always hung back, as if afraid something might escape and bite him, but she, the recipient of old Edwin Gunn's genes, was fearless. Sometimes she even helped the vet with an animal. She was the one who'd demanded Grayson take over her duties when migraines rendered her helpless. For his part, he could have refused, but didn't.

Something occurred to me. "On one of his walks through here, did he see something he shouldn't have?"

The anteater didn't answer.

A few minutes later, having finished her treat, a calmer Lucy moved away from the fence and ambled over to a faux log, snuffling for termites. Since she hadn't allowed me into her enclosure yet, she found none. Whimpering, she returned to the holding pen gate.

"*Whumph?*"

I felt bad for her, but couldn't enter the enclosure without having her stashed safely in the holding pen. Once again I cursed the ignorant Barry. The anteater needed to be fed, and just tossing a bucket of termites over the fence wouldn't do it. To best accommodate her long nose, the insects should be stuffed into the logs.

I decided to give it another try. After mashing the other half of the banana, I crammed it inside her Wellington boot and threw it in the holding pen. Then, hefting my safety board up, I inched open the gate.

"Teddy's going to try to feed you again, so please cooperate this time."

Smelling the banana inside the boot, she rushed into the holding pen and I slammed the gate shut behind her. After casting me a betrayed glance, she licked the boot.

Problem solved, I got busy in the enclosure. I dumped an extra helping of termites into the various logs, and as quickly as possible, swept the area clean. As I worked, I forgot about Lucy's behavior and began thinking about the murder again.

Since I couldn't seem to find any actual clues, the solution to the mystery might be found in behavior. For all their purported brainpower, people are still animals. Deny them food, exercise, or sex, and they get cranky. Threaten them and they become downright dangerous.

Had anyone been behaving as if he—or she—felt threatened? Or at the very least, more wary than usual?

Zorah, of course. But since I knew she had to be innocent, I moved onto someone else.

How about Dr. Kate? Usually the soul of openness and geniality, the vet had seemed edgy lately. As an example, whenever I had tried to ask her about the independent vet study, she gave me short shrift, and I didn't think it was because the study was confidential.

How much did I really know about her? She and her husband, Lowell, had moved from the Kansas City area several years earlier when he'd been offered a job with a Silicon Valley dot-com. Shortly thereafter, he had been diagnosed with multiple sclerosis, and as his health declined, was forced to leave his job. Dr. Kate, who'd given up her own associate vet position at the Kansas City Zoo to follow him to California, found a job here, where her salary took up some of the financial slack. Selling their large home in San Jose and moving into the smaller, on-site house the zoo furnished had helped, too.

Which brought me right back to the independent vet study.

A few hours before the murder, Barry had given Grayson a copy of the preliminary report without reading it. I was certain

Grayson had read it, though, and if serious flaws had been discovered in the zoo's treatment of its animals, he would have held Dr. Kate accountable.

Her continued evasiveness troubled me. The zoo hadn't escaped its own health dramas. No zoo does. Barely a month earlier, one of our lemurs died while undergoing a routine checkup. Granted, the ensuing necropsy revealed a cancerous lesion on its left lung, but questions had been asked in a staff meeting. Had Dr. Kate been too slow in noticing the animal's declining health? And had Grayson demanded her resignation over it?

Talk about a motive for murder.

A wave of guilt washed over me. What was I doing, suspecting a sick man's wife, the mother of three children, of murder? But Zorah hadn't killed Grayson, and since Joe was so firmly convinced of her guilt, I had to do something about it no matter how much my actions displeased him. Or even myself.

After stuffing termites into the enclosure's last log, I walked back to the holding pen where the anteater, having finished her banana, waited anxiously.

"I need to talk to Dr. Kate again, Lucy."

"Grunt!"

Holding the safety board carefully between us, I released her back into the enclosure. Then I blew her a goodbye kiss, and exited through the pen's back gate.

Late in the afternoon, I stopped my cart in front of the Andean spectacled bear exhibit, where a boisterous crowd had gathered. In the bear pit fifteen feet below, Willy, the smaller of the two bears and who'd been at the zoo for less than a month, had backed himself into a clump of bamboo. Despite keeper Jack Spence's urgings, he refused to emerge. The reason for Willy's timidity soon became apparent. Francine, the large female we hoped he'd eventually mate with, paced back and forth along the bamboo's perimeter, growling threats. She obviously resented having to share her enclosure with a relative stranger.

Despite the cute white-outlined black patches across their eyes that gave the species its name, the bears were more dangerous than they appeared. Topping out at almost four hundred pounds, a female could remove a male's eye with a casual swipe from her paw. Given the chance, a male would return the favor.

I climbed out of the cart and stood next to Jack at the fence. The fence's security was increased by a steep-sided drop into the bear's island-like enclosure that was surrounded by a deep, twenty feet-wide moat. Spectacled bears can swim, but unlike polar bears, prefer not to.

"Has he tried to mate with her yet?" I asked Jack. May was breeding time at the zoo and most of the animals were getting it on with enthusiasm. Except for the bears.

A rangy six-plus feet in height, Jack towered above me, but his expression was that of an anxious mother at an inner city playground. "Are you kidding? At this point he's just trying to survive. Francine's mean as a grizzly."

Spectacled bears are on the Vulnerable Species list and few zoos own a breeding pair. Since Willy's introduction to the exhibit wasn't going as well as we'd wished, I worried that the zoo might have to resort to a sperm bank, a risky proposition since animals needed to be anesthetized during artificial insemination. The anteater had undergone the procedure with great success, but spectacled bears didn't have a good track record with anesthesia. Sometimes they simply forgot to breathe.

Jack knew this, which probably accounted for his strained expression. After I'd commiserated with him a while, he said, "Say, could you stick around for a few minutes? I haven't had my lunch yet, and my stomach's about to gnaw through my spine. But I've been afraid to leave them alone together. As long as Francine's acting this way, someone should keep an eye on her." He lowered his voice. "That noisy crowd's not helping."

Zoos do get people excited, so crowd control is always an issue. Today, parents and their laughing, shrieking children strained against the fence around the bear's enclosure, but I wasn't too worried. The four-foot high fence, built of reinforced

concrete painted to look like thick wood logs, could hold back
an elephant. A clear Plexiglas barrier between the "logs" ensured
that no one could slip through and fall into the moat below.

I looked at my watch. Three o'clock and Jack hadn't eaten
yet. No wonder he was so thin. "Go ahead. I'll watch them until
you get back."

"I'm already gone." He climbed into his cart and took off.

Just as he disappeared around the bend toward the snack bar, a
mother with more enthusiasm than sense lifted her kindergarten-
age son and sat him on the top rail of the fence, right above a
sign that warned *Do Not Sit Or Lean On Fence.*

"Hey! That's a fifteen-foot drop!" I called, hurrying toward her.

The woman looked annoyed. "I have a good grip on him."

Not good enough, apparently. Before I could reach her and
snatch the child back, he twisted forward to get a better look at
the bears. And he twisted right out of his mother's "good grip."

The boy fell.

Fifteen feet.

Straight into the moat.

He landed with a screech and a splash, then disappeared
briefly underneath the scummy water. A couple of seconds
later his head broke surface and he began to dog-paddle.
Unfortunately, he aimed toward the bear's "island," the shore
of which sloped down to the moat.

Both Francine and Willy—who had emerged from the
bamboo—waddled to the edge of the moat and watched him, noses
twitching. The male appeared merely curious, but I didn't like the
look on the female's face, nor the way her ears flattened against her
enormous head. Jack was right; she was one mean bear.

The crowd's screams dwarfed the mother's, who tried to
struggle over the rail after her son. Two Hispanic men hauled
her back.

"Bears in there, miss!" one cried, while the other studied the
moat carefully, as if preparing to dive in after the child.

"No!" I shouted to him, then took one precious second
to grab my radio and scream a *"Child in spectacled bear pit!"*

warning to the park rangers. Before the Hispanic man could act and perhaps get himself killed, I took a deep breath and vaulted over the fence.

Like the boy, I landed in the middle of the moat and sank below the surface. For a moment I continued plunging straight down through the dark green nothingness, but my descent was stopped by the moat's concrete bottom. A shiver of pain shot through my heel as it touched down, but I ignored it and headed back toward the surface. As my head entered the sunlight, I shook the water and offal out of my eyes. Immediately I saw the boy, swimming in the wrong direction for all he was worth. Within seconds, he would reach the bears.

As if eager to embrace him, Francine reared up on her hind legs, arms open wide. Her teeth flashed a murderous smile.

Spitting out moat water, I struggled toward the child. "Stop! Don't go near her! Swim to me!"

He either didn't hear or was so eager to get out of the filthy water that he ignored me. Like so many zoo visitors—including his foolish mother—he probably thought Francine was no more dangerous than an overgrown teddy bear. But I knew better. That two-legged stance of hers meant only thing. If the child reached shore, he was dinner.

The realization lengthened my stroke and I surged forward. Mere inches before the boy reached Francine's welcoming claws, I caught him by the collar and dragged him away. Enraged, Francine lunged. She was so close that I could feel the air move as her horrible claws swept by. Finally aware of his danger, the child screamed. This only enraged Francine further, and for a moment it appeared she would jump into the moat after us.

But then Willy, darling little Willy who had retreated all the way into the bamboo again, began to bawl in distress. Francine turned to see what was wrong.

Suddenly debris rained down on the bears and I took a moment to look up. The two Hispanic men were bombarding the bear pit with rocks and soft drink cans. Their aim was so good that a Diet Coke bounced off the female's nose. The boy momentarily forgotten, Francine snapped at the air.

Breathing a prayer of thanks for the distraction the men were providing, I tucked the boy's head into the crook of my left arm in classic lifeguard fashion and back-stroked toward the steep enclosure wall.

"Let go!" the child screamed, and bit my arm. "Want Mommy!"

My arm, now imprinted with two rows of tiny teeth, began to bleed, but I didn't release my grip although my arm now hurt as badly as my heel.

"Stay calm," I urged. "I'll get you back to her." I'd read stories where lifeguards had to knock flailing swimmers unconscious in order to rescue them, but I didn't have the heart for that.

So he bit me again.

"Stop biting!" I snapped, hoping I sounded parental.

Apparently I didn't, because his teeth clamped down on me once more. "Mom!" he screamed.

As he opened his jaws for another munch, Jack Spence leaned over the fence, dangling a rope. "Grab on!"

I did.

Aided by the two other men, Jack hauled us up, the child first, me a soggy second. As I floundered onto the asphalt like a landed trout, Zorah and three park rangers brandishing rifles came tearing up the path in a zoo cart that was trying its best to speed.

"Is the kid okay?" Zorah called, jumping out of the cart and running toward us.

I was too busy vomiting up dirty moat water to answer, so Jack did. "He's fine. But do me a favor and shoot his idiot mother."

Zorah bent down and brushed a lily pad away from my face in order that I could vomit better. "You all right, Teddy?"

"Just peachy." I heaved again. Throwing up at the zoo was becoming a habit.

Within minutes the boy was whisked away by ambulance, trailed by his lawsuit-threatening mother. The two Hispanic men disappeared into the crowd. The rangers drove me to the First Aid station, where they patched up my bleeding arm and pronounced my heel merely bruised. They gave me a tetanus booster (forget the moat water; human bites are *really* nasty) while Barry, summoned from the administration building, hovered nearby.

"Are you sure you're okay? That moat, God knows what's floating around in there! I've given the order to have it cleaned more often."

I waved his concern away. "How're the bears?"

He scowled. "As if I care. The legal ramifications…"

Jack, who with Zorah had followed me to First Aid, interrupted. "The bears are fine. Willy's hiding in the bamboo again and Francine's enjoying a snack of strawberries and beetles."

He'd said the wrong thing.

I leaned over and vomited up more scummy water.

As I stepped out of the shower in the zookeeper's locker room, my cell phone rang. A glance at the display revealed my mother's number. She seldom called me at work, so I guessed that word of my afternoon's adventures had already gossiped its way to Old Town.

Not yet ready for *that* kind of trouble, I turned the cell off. Then I changed into a clean uniform and returned to my duties.

By the time the zoo closed for the day, I was sore and exhausted. I hungered for the comfort of the *Merilee*, but determined to find out more about that independent vet study, I summoned enough energy to visit Gunn Castle. Aware of my bedraggled state, I drove around the back to the castle's more secluded rear entrance. As it so frequently had been during my teenage years, the heavy oak door leading to the stables and other outbuildings was unlocked. I slipped in, relieved that no servants lurked nearby.

I found Jeanette dressed in the same tatty old peignoir, lying on the bed with one of Grayson's suits laid out next to her. Her face almost as gray as the suit, she stroked and murmured to it as if her husband remained inside. Uncomfortable with the intimacy of the scene, I froze in the doorway.

Seemingly oblivious to my battered condition, she threw me an imploring look through tangled strands of greasy blond hair. "His suit still smells like him, Teddy. Do you know how long that will last?"

"I don't know," I answered softly, not getting too close, so that any residual whiff of moat scum wouldn't reach her.

She pressed her nose against the suit's shoulder. "I had his cologne blended especially for him at one of those San Francisco scent shops. Maybe I'll order a few more bottles, make sure I don't run out."

Although there was no alcohol on her breath, she smelled pretty much like I had after emerging from the bear's moat. When had she last bathed?

"You need to start taking care of yourself. Shower. Get out of the house."

She shook her head. "Why?"

"It might help take your mind off things." My advice was inadequate, but it was the best I could do.

"That's what Aster Edwina keeps telling me."

For once I found myself agreeing with the old harridan. Although Jeanette and I had never been close after that Monopoly slap-down, it hurt to see her like this. For her sake, I summoned up some enthusiasm. "Listen, tomorrow's Sunday and I have the whole day free. Let's do lunch somewhere!"

"There's food here."

I tried again. "We could drive down to Carmel and troll the boutiques! A new pair of shoes might lift your spirits."

"I don't want my spirits lifted. All I want is to stay here with my husband." She began caressing the suit again, this time south of the waistline.

I felt like a voyeur. She needed professional help, not my clumsy words of comfort. Before I left, I'd suggest a round of

therapy, but first I needed to ask a question that had been preying upon my mind.

"Did Grayson discuss the independent vet study with
you?"

"The what?"

"That report written by the vets from the National Academy of
Sciences. Knowing how involved you used to be with the zoo's day-
to-day business, I figure he must have talked to you about it."

She shook her head. "Not in any depth. With the Trust and
everything, there was a lot going on before…" She gulped.

I phrased my next question carefully. "Yes, I understand. But
the study might contain a clue about what really did happen that
night. Is there any chance Grayson made a copy?"

Her proud smile showed I'd hit pay dirt. "He copies everything. When it comes to the zoo or anything else he does, he's
very meticulous."

I didn't like the sound of that present tense. "Yes, he *was*
meticulous, *wasn't* he, Jeanette? Did he leave it around here,
perhaps? In his desk? If you tell me where, I could go look…"

At this, she half-raised herself from the bed, one of the suit's
sleeves clutched to her breast. *"You're not touching his things!"*

Alarmed by the venom in her voice, I drew back. As I knew
full well, she could pack a punch. "Sorry. I just wanted to…"

From the doorway, Aster Edwina's voice interrupted my
apology. "Leave her alone, Teddy."

How long had she been standing there? Almost grateful for
the reprieve, I walked out of the bedroom and followed the old
woman down the staircase.

Instead of having a servant throw me out of the house, she
beckoned for me to follow her into the library. "We need to
talk, dear."

Dear?

After she closed the library door behind us, she surprised me
even further. "What's the name of that therapist your mother
went to after your father embezzled all that money? I think you
saw him a few times, too."

You can't hide anything in a small town, especially not visits to the local shrink. I'd seen him twice: once before Caro shipped me off to Miss Pridewell's Academy, and more recently, when my marriage collapsed.

"Dr. Steven Katzenberg. His office is in San Sebastian."

Aster Edwina's wrinkled face betrayed no emotion. "The man's discreet?"

"Very." And perceptive. Dr. Katzenberg had told me that finding meaningful work would help me recover from my heartbreak. Remembering all my talk about animals when I'd seen him as a teen, he'd suggested the zoo. When I'd acted on his suggestion, my mother threatened him with a malpractice suit. She knew full well what dangers zoo work would entail, "Are you thinking about taking Jeanette to see him?"

"I'm not interested in therapy for myself, I assure you," she answered acidly. "You saw that suit on the bed. My grand-niece won't stop talking to it. Or doing other things."

I didn't ask what other things. "It's so sad."

She snorted. "It's pathetic, that's what it is, caring so much about another person that you're completely directionless without them." This from a never-married childless woman. What could she know about loss? "As much as I dislike the idea of Jeanette airing her dirty linen to a stranger, at least I'll have the security of knowing that a psychiatrist must adhere to some sort of ethical code which keeps him from blabbing. Unlike her so-called friends."

That stung. "I don't blab."

"So you say. Until she pulls herself together, I prefer you stay away from her. The next time you come sneaking in here like that, I'll call the police. Are we understood?"

I nodded.

"Good. It's bad enough that the newspapers had a field day with the murder and the Trust fiasco. There's no point in letting them crow over our sorrows, too."

I noted the way she'd phrased, "*our* sorrows," as if the entire Gunn clan wailed with grief over Grayson's death.

Chapter Twelve

As the sun sank toward the Pacific, I hurried home to the *Merilee* only to find a note from Caro taped to the door: I HEARD ABOUT THE BEARS. CALL ME!

I stuffed the note into my pocket and limped inside, where I saw that DJ Bonz had already piddled on the carpet. After spending the next few minutes sponging up, I took him for his regular walk, albeit slowly. Everything hurt, especially my bruised heel and bitten arm. All I wanted to do for the rest of the evening was to pour myself a glass of wine, slump into a deck chair, and *not* think about bears.

But when I returned to the *Merilee*, I found two members of the Harbor Liveaboard Committee standing on the dock, eyeing my boat. They carried clipboards.

"What's up, guys?" Bonz whined at my feet. I freed him from his leash and let him jump on board, where he immediately vanished into the salon.

"We've got trouble," said Linda Cushing, who lived on the *Tea 4 Two*, a Catalina 30 sailboat. Years of seaside living had been rough on her, and she looked every one of her sixty-odd years.

"Big trouble." This from Walt McAdams, a burly San Sebastian firefighter with a hair-trigger temper, whose *Running Wild*, a decommissioned trawler similar to my own, lay berthed three slips away. "Maxwell Jarvis is on the warpath again, but this time he's got Eleanor doing his dirty work."

Maxwell, a San Francisco-based society orthodontist, owned the biggest yacht in Gunn Landing and held considerable sway over Eleanor Jacobs, the harbor master. Although everyone liked the eminently fair Eleanor, it remained her job to enforce rules and regs. Giving other anal-compulsives a bad name, the orthodontist kept her supplied with a list of harbor rule breakers, updated weekly.

I sighed. "What's Maxwell carrying on about this time?"

Walt thrust his clipboard at me. "See?"

Attached was a copy of the latest harbor ordinance codes, all forty-five pages of them.

Belatedly remembering my manners, I asked the pair, "Come aboard for a glass of wine. I have some Riesling that's not too bad."

Walt shook his head. "No time for that. We have to make several more stops."

Linda, her furrowed face grim, said, "Look at that paragraph defining 'sea-going vessels.' It means that if you want to stay in the harbor, you'll have to do something about the *Merilee*."

Which I would if I had the money. "Someday," I promised.

Walt sounded as unhappy as Linda. "You don't get it, do you? The *Merilee*'s on the list."

"What list?"

He looked at Linda, then back at me. "Didn't you read the new ordinance codes?"

"I haven't even read the old ones yet." All I knew about ordinance codes was that boat owners needed to take out the trash before it started stinking, and were forbidden to flush their bilges into the harbor. Maxwell's efforts notwithstanding, rule enforcement had always been relatively lax, which explained some of the more peculiar boats tied to the slips.

Close by was the *Tipsy Teepee*, a hand-built, shingle-sided contraption that looked more like a backwoods shack than a boat; the *Cruisin' 4 A Bruisin'*, a one-time garbage scow that sported the tail fins of a 1963 Chrysler; and my personal favorite, the *Mickey*, a Boston Whaler painted to look like a mouse.

At my confessed ignorance, Linda flipped through the papers on her clipboard. Once she found the page she wanted, she handed it to me. "This is the list of boats slated for eviction unless they pass the test voyage."

"*Eviction*? Test voyage? What are you talking about?"

Walt jumped in, a dangerous note in his voice. "Maxwell's been bitching about the way the south end of the harbor has started to look. The other day he stormed into the harbor master's office screaming that we Southies are destroying the—I'm quoting from his typed complaint—the 'property values' of the Northies' slips. The bastard."

When Linda elbowed him in the ribs, he took a few deep breaths. I remembered, then, that after he'd once punched a suspected arsonist, the fire captain had forced him to enroll in anger management classes.

He continued in a calmer voice. "Maxwell wants every liveaboarder gone, hopefully to some inland river marina far away, and he's demanding we prove the seaworthiness of our 'vessels.' By the end of the month, every boat on the list has to complete a round trip to Dolphin Island with the harbor master on board to make sure there's no cheating. You're expected to contact her no later than the end of the week to get the *Merilee* on the schedule."

He pointed out into the Pacific where the dark bump of tiny Dolphin Island, no more than a glorified sandbar, shimmered in the fading light. Although only eight miles away, it remained an impossible destination for a diesel-run engine that hadn't been overhauled within living memory. Dad had bought the *Merilee* for poker games, not boating, and his friend Al had continued the tradition. Oh, sure, Al had started the engine on occasion, but never ran it long enough to stave off the inevitable deterioration.

Truth be told, I hadn't done much better. In the time I'd lived on the *Merilee*, I'd taken her out only once, intending to picnic with friends on Dolphin Island. Halfway there, strange noises began emanating from the engine, and I turned tail back to the harbor.

I stared at the island, then at the *Merilee*. "But that's crazy! Half the liveaboards around here couldn't complete that trip!"

"That's the whole idea, to get rid of us," Linda snapped. "It's the same thing marinas up and down the coast have been doing for years."

"But not *our* harbor!"

She gave me a sour smile. "Wake up and smell the bilge water, kid."

"We're all in the same boat, not-so-metaphorically speaking," Walt said. "Linda's *Tea 4 Two* leaks like a sieve, and my *Running Wild* should have slept with the fishes decades ago. The *Silver Shoal* has a broken keel, the *Nancy's* sails are ripped all to hell, the *Tumbling Dice* has…"

I waved away his recital of sea-going sorrows. "Okay, okay, so some of us live in floating slums. The question is, what can we do about it?"

"Fix the problems or find another marina."

"Or move back to dry land," Linda added. From her tone, I knew she'd rather drown.

"But none of us can afford to…"

Seeing the look on their faces, I shut up. As nearby slip-owners, they'd frequently heard my mother pleading with me to move back to Old Town. Like everyone else, they confused her bank account with mine.

I didn't bother to set them straight. "Thanks for the warning."

Bad news officially delivered, the two walked away to ruin another liveaboarder's evening.

Feeling more miserable than ever, I joined Bonz and Priss in the salon, where I debated the ethics of using my father's embezzlement money to help myself instead of someone else.

What were the ramifications?

On the ethics side, helping myself to "dirty" money would be wrong, which is why I'd never done it.

But my legal situation? I was no Pearl Pureheart. As soon as I'd made that withdrawal to cover Zorah's bail, I'd become

Dad's partner in crime, even if only after the fact. Once she was cleared—and I was doing my best to make certain of that—I planned to return every penny to the off-shore account. What judge could fault me for that? I tried to ignore the voice that whispered inside my head: *Any judge who cares about the law.*

Worry haunted me throughout the night, following me into a dream, where I stood on the *Merilee*'s deck as she sank on the way to Dolphin Island. When I dove into the water, followed by Priss and Bonz, we were immediately surrounded by a school of sharks. One of them, a sharp-toothed Great White decked out in a black leather bustier and cheap blond wig, was singing Celine Dion's sappy "My Heart Must Go On," while a chorus of otters—two of them with the faces of Joe and my ex-husband—sang off-key backup.

I woke up, laughing and crying at the same time.

For a while I lay there listening to the waves bump the *Merilee*. Too restless to sleep, I tried to read, but couldn't keep my mind on the book. Priss, curled against my hip, questioned me in a sleepy *meow*, then went back to sleep, but Bonz, lying at my feet, crawled along the comforter until he reached my face and gave me a sloppy kiss.

"Oh, dog," I whispered. "What are we going to do?"

He didn't answer, just gazed at me with his trusting brown eyes.

When the sun rose behind the hills of Old Town, I made my decision.

If worse came to worse, I would give up my *Merilee*.

Chapter Thirteen

After taking Bonz for his morning walk, I was about to cobble breakfast together when I heard footsteps coming along the dock. The dog pricked up his ears, but didn't growl. Priss, who hated any visitor, scampered into her favorite hiding place in the forward cabin. The footsteps stopped and someone gave several raps against the *Merilee*'s hull. More bad news from the Liveaboard Committee? Another nagging visit from my mother? I'd wondered how long it would take for her to find out about the new ordinance codes and renew her efforts to move me back to Old Town.

"Permission to come aboard, Captain!" Joe, attempting wit. Apparently no one ever told him that once you start locking up a woman's friends, your witticisms tend to fall flat.

Intending to shoo him away, I stuck my head out of the salon hatch, but after noting the large sack from Chowder 'n' Cappuccino he held, I invited him aboard. He wasn't wearing his uniform, just civvies and a windbreaker to cover his holster. Good. The visit wasn't official.

"Shouldn't you be in church?" I asked. His Irish mother never missed Sunday Mass, and insisted that the family accompany her.

Without waiting for his reply, I opened the sack, took out two Mucho Grande lattes, and transferred some warm croissants to a plate. The scent of hot yeast and coffee overrode the smells of dog, cat and dirty harbor water.

Sitting down with me at the galley table, he took a sip from one of the steaming containers. "Church? Probably. But I thought we need to clear the air, and since Sunday's your only day off…"

I took a bite of my croissant, which gave me time to think about the ramifications of air-clearing. People who say you can be friends with former lovers don't know what they're talking about. There are too many memories, too many wounds.

Chasing the croissant with a slug of latte, I said, "Sunday's my heavy cleaning day. I have the laundry, the…"

He smiled, almost breaking my heart all over again. "Yes, yes, you're a busy woman. I thought—considering what happened in the bear pit and all—that you might take it easy today." The smile wavered. "When I heard…"

I looked away, refusing to let myself be vulnerable again. Not ever. It hurt too much. Steeling my voice, I said, "Don't you have work to do? Like, *real* criminals to catch?"

Instead of answering, he began to trace my cheek with his finger. Without thinking, I leaned against him and put my head on his shoulder like I used to when I was fifteen and he was sixteen.

Also apparently without thinking, Joe slipped his arm around my waist. Just like he used to do. "Oh, honey."

Realizing what was about to happen, I jerked away and in desperation, grabbed my latte. "Boy, this is great stuff!"

"Teddy…"

"It's Jamaican Blue Mountain, isn't it? Delicate, but with a hint of smoke."

"What are you…?"

"Maybe I should switch to decaf because the doctors say decaf's better for you, but it seems to me you'd lose most of the flavor."

He put his hand on mine. It was warm, dry. "Can't you look at me?"

Until then, I hadn't realized I was staring at the galley faucet. Not a particularly attractive piece of hardware with its calcium buildup, but at least it provided a focal point away from those blue Irish eyes.

"Of course I can look at you." A hefty dose of vinegar water would help with the calcium buildup, not that it mattered, what with the harbor master's death sentence hanging over my poor *Merilee*.

"Teddy."

On the other hand, why let my boat go to rack and ruin because…

Strong brown fingers cupped my chin and turned my face to his. Soft lips brushed mine.

I jerked back. "Don't!"

He let me go. "Sorry." Now *he* developed a fascination with the faucet.

I let a moment pass. Took a deep breath. "Joe, what's wrong with us?"

The faucet lost its attraction for him. "We both feel guilty as hell, that's what's wrong. Which is the reason I drove over here. Teddy, we can't go on like this. You've been back from San Francisco for almost a year, and you haven't returned any of my calls. Don't you think it's time we hashed this thing through so we can at least pass each other on the street without looking the other way?"

He hadn't called that many times. After four or five calls every week for the first month or so, they'd dwindled down to one or two a week, then after a few more months, nothing.

"Your timing wasn't good, Joe. I was still hurting over Michael, and I didn't trust my own judgment anymore." And I was so afraid. Of him, of love, of the whole man/woman thing.

"I understand that now."

"Anyway, I'm not sure…" I stopped, uncertain whether I believed what I was about to say, that I wasn't sure we could pick up where we left off fifteen years ago because we were different people now, grownups with all the complications maturity implied. But with Joe sitting so close to me, and my body crying out for his, my intended words sounded inane.

"I'm not sure either, honey," he said.

"A lot's happened. Too much, probably."

"Yeah."

"After all, we're not in high school anymore."

"Nope."

"People can't go back to where they started. It's not realistic, however attractive it might seem."

"Good point."

"I'm glad you see it my way."

We both stared at the faucet for a while, then as if on cue, closed the distance between us so that my leg pressed against his all the way from the ankle to the top of the thigh. Neither of us moved further, just sat there trembling, waiting for the other person to make a move.

"This is dumb." I said, after a few minutes.

"When you're right, you're right."

"Not that we've been smart so far."

"Ha."

"So what do you think?"

He pulled me into his lap. "I think we both think too much."

Once I got my breath back, I said, "Yeah, when *you're* right, you're right."

Two hours later, Joe left. I breezed through my Sunday chores, humming the tune we'd decided so long ago was "our" song. Dolly Parton had written and recorded "I Will Always Love You" the year he was born, and his father sang it to his mother.

The first time Joe and I made love, parked in his father's truck on the beach at Otter Point, we heard Whitney Houston's version on the local San Sebastian radio station. Two years later, alone in my room at Miss Pridewell's Academy in the heart of rural Virginia, I turned on WHRO, hoping for some cheerful Vivaldi. Instead I heard flutist James Galway performing a classical take on the song. By the time I heard Melissa Etheridge's power-ballad version on San Francisco's KSAN, my marriage was falling apart.

I was feeling cynical at the time, and the anguish in Etheridge's voice suited my mood perfectly. Now *I* was humming the thing, but darned if it didn't sound downright jaunty.

Love can make you see stars in sewers, heaven in songs about heartbreak.

Besides, my own heartbreak was in the past, wasn't it? There remained no need to mourn, no need to anguish over men's inability to remain focused on just one woman.

Some men were different.

◇◇◇

Caro took a long time to open the door, and when she did, her hair was a mess, yet she'd never looked so beautiful. "What are you doing here?" She sounded out of breath, too.

No lecture about yesterday's adventure in the spectacled bear pit?

I held up the paper bag. "Just returning your necklace." I lowered my voice in case any neighbors had their windows open. "Dad's here, isn't he?"

She grabbed me by the sleeve and pulled me inside. "What makes you think that?"

"Your blouse is on backwards."

Her face reddened. "I don't know what you're talking about. I'm not…" At the sound of springy footsteps descending the stairs, she stopped.

"Hello, Teddy." Dad's shirt was buttoned crooked and a trail of lipstick traveled from his jaw to his ear, but at least he'd combed his hair.

Caro led me into the living room and briefly disappeared to plop a teabag into a cup of nuked water. Upon her return, she delivered her hundredth-or-something warning about the dangers of zoo life in general, anteaters and spectacled bears in particular.

Dad just smiled fondly and asked, "What's that song you're humming? It's pretty."

My turn to blush. "Song?"

Caro narrowed her eyes at me. "It's that wretched thing Whitney Houston used to sing. You and that moony Rejos boy called it 'your' song." She sketched the quote marks in the air. "Surely you're not seeing him again!"

"It's Rejas, not Rejos. If I'm dating him, it's none of your business."

Dad leaned forward. "Wait a minute. Rejas. Joe Rejas. Isn't that the sheriff?"

"So?"

Appalled, he yelled, "You're dating the *sheriff* now?! And me sitting here with federal and state warrants out for my arrest? What if during a...a heated moment you slip and say something? Don't you understand what could happen to me?"

"But I..."

Caro jumped in. "How dare you, Teddy! It's bad enough that Joe whatever-his-name-is almost ruined your life once, now he's actually trying more of the same."

"But..."

With great effort, my father pulled himself together. "He's not the problem. It's me and my foolishness in coming here to visit you both in the first place, but I missed you both so much that...." His voice broke, but he recovered quickly. "Perhaps I should clear out and leave you two in peace."

Caro made panicky noises, but he merely shrugged. "Don't worry, I'll find someplace safe. Teddy shouldn't have to redesign her whole life just to keep me safe."

At his miserable expression, I realized the complications my runaway heart had caused. "Leaving won't be necessary. I'll figure out something to keep the sheriff away."

After all, hadn't I been doing exactly that for more than a year?

Chapter Fourteen

I stayed at my mother's long enough to suffer through a tense lunch. As I'd feared, she carried on and on about the bear incident, renewing her pleas for me to quit my job.

Since arguing never worked, I simply ignored her. While I was finishing up my asparagus-mushroom crepes—compliments of my father, not Thumbs-in-the-Kitchen Caro—I remembered Roarke telling me that his uncle, Henry Gunn, was a member of the anti-Trust contingent, too. Henry had always been one of my favorite Gunns. Whenever I'd gone up to the castle to play Monopoly with Jeanette, he'd sneak us forbidden pieces of Aster Edwina's jealously-guarded marzipan. Although I hadn't seen him since he divorced Eleanor, his first wife, I figured he could give me a different slant on the Trust.

After calling ahead to make certain he was at home, I jumped in my truck and started the ninety-mile drive north to San Francisco. Sunday traffic was light so by two p.m. I was searching for a parking spot near his Pacific Heights house. After another fifteen minutes I found one, although my rusty Nissan pickup looked woefully out of place among the luxury sedans and SUVs lining the street.

Henry and Pilar, his second wife, owned a large Victorian two blocks off Divisadero, with a stunning view of the Golden Gate Bridge. When he opened the door, I tried not to reveal my shock at how much he'd aged. Remarried less than a year, he looked ten years older. His face appeared gaunt and most of his hair had vanished. Divorce had been rough on him, too.

"How's that rogue nephew of mine?" he asked, offering me a tray filled with marzipan. He'd remembered.

"He's fine," I told him, selecting a marzipan topped with candied orange garnish.

Oblivious to my gastronomical ecstasy, Pilar snorted. "Roarke will always be fine."

Henry chuckled. "Pay no attention to her. She had a thing for him once, all the girls did, but then I came along, didn't I, babe?"

She forced a smile.

A thing for Roarke? Henry had met Pilar two years earlier at a party aboard the *Tequila Sunrise*. Had she been husband-hunting among the yacht club set? Filing his comment away for further reference, I looked around. Judging from the antiques in the living room alone, they'd spent a fortune furnishing the place. But when I complimented Pilar on her taste, she waved away her surroundings with a dismissive hand.

"They're Henry's old things, left over from the divorce."

Like so many wealthy men are prone to do, Henry had traded in his increasingly-broad-in-the-beam first wife for a sleeker model. Pilar was a tall brunette at least twenty-five years his junior, with sharp features that kept her from being convention-ally beautiful. As if to distract from her razor-blade nose, she wore a pink silk scarf around the neck of her mauve track suit. Perhaps the track suit was a mere wardrobe choice, but I doubted it because she had the nervous energy of a runner. After settling me on a fawn-colored Chippendale sofa, for the rest of my visit she paced back and forth through the light-filled living room, touching a priceless porcelain here, a silver candlestick there. It tired me just to watch her.

When Henry spoke again, the sharpness of his voice hinted that the honeymoon was over. "I told my wife that with Grayson dead and the move to break the Trust now stalled, she'd better make her peace with the Victorian era."

She flushed, whether with anger or embarrassment, I couldn't tell. "Just because he's no longer in the picture doesn't mean the Trust can't be broken." She gave me a quick look. "No point in being secretive about it. The damned *Wall Street Journal* has already printed everything there is to know."

"And the damned *San Francisco Examiner*," Henry grumped. "Next comes *The National Enquirer*, I guess. I can see their headlines now. GUNN FORTUNE FUNNELED TO ALIEN INVADERS."

I laughed, but the humor-challenged Pilar frowned.

After helping myself to another piece of marzipan, I followed up on the opening they'd so kindly given me. "When did Grayson first approach you about breaking the Trust?"

Henry started to answer, but she spoke first. "In February. After you called, I looked it up in my appointment book. Like you, he visited on a Sunday, which is the only day I'm at home because I work for a living." She shot a meaningful look at her scowling husband. "Anyway, he arrived around two o'clock and we spent the rest of the day formulating a plan. I must say that I was impressed by the thought Grayson put into his strategy. He knew who was ready to jump ship, who planned to stick, and who hadn't yet made up their minds."

"With you two firmly on the 'jump ship' side." I glanced at Henry, waiting for him to speak. He was, after all, the one with the money. But he continued letting his wife do the talking.

Vibrating with energy, she stalked around the room, her blue-black hair gleaming in the sun that streamed through the tall window behind her. Beyond, I could see the blue waters of San Francisco Bay, the green hills of Marin beyond—a view most San Franciscans would cheerfully kill for.

"It makes no sense whatsoever allowing that money to sit around earning little more than interest," Pilar continued, her mind fixed on things less pedestrian than hills and water. "If money doesn't work for you, there's no point in having any."

I looked around and spotted among other treasures a Duncan Phyfe sideboard and a George III center table. Originals, not copies. It seemed to me that the "little more than interest" Gunn Trust worked well enough. But Pilar was a stockbroker, a member of a profession allergic to letting money just sit there, which was probably what had attracted her to Henry in the first place. All that unused money lying around for her to "work" with. How had she reacted when she discovered that the family fortune was tied up in the immovable Trust and all she'd ever see was a monthly dividend check?

She must have noticed my expression. "This place may be nice if you go for the embalmed look, but we're tired of it and want something modern, like those new towers over on Van Ness. All steel and glass." Then she remembered her husband. "Don't we, Henry?"

On cue, he nodded. "If you say so." His tone wasn't as amiable as his words.

"Yes. I do."

Henry reminded me of Abayo, the zoo's aging lion. Content to lie in the sun all day, Abayo was healthy enough to sire cubs but not agile enough to evade the occasional slaps from Elsa, his mate.

"Did Grayson say anything else of interest while he was here?" I asked. "Maybe he mentioned someone being angry with him."

Pilar raised her sharp nose in disdain. "Are you kidding? Everyone in the pro-Trust camp was furious with him. The lazybones were afraid they might have to get out there and work for their money."

I snuck a look at lazybones Henry, who'd never held a job, wondering if her barb had gone over his head. Except for a slight narrowing of his eyes, his face didn't change. I wondered if he missed his easy-going first wife. "What about Jeanette? Did she say anything?"

Pilar turned away from the Renaissance Revival clock she'd been fingering and shook her head. "She didn't come with him. Suffering from another of her week-long migraines, I guess."

Henry spoke up again. "I doubt that because I saw them together the next day at that little restaurant down the street. Grayson…"

His wife interrupted. "I've told you time and again that her headaches are psychosomatic! She fakes them to get attention."

Having experienced a few migraines myself during the waning days of my marriage, I was certain Jeanette's suffering was the real thing, but Pilar was obviously one of those women who enjoyed perfect health and had nothing but contempt for others who didn't. Not the most comfortable woman for a man to be married to as he marched up the ramp from middle to old age.

She interrupted my musings. "Teddy, how's your own portfolio?"

"Excuse me?"

Abandoning her pacing, she sat down next to me on the sofa. "Your portfolio. There are some interesting opportunities out there I'd like to talk to you about."

Henry stifled a laugh. He knew all about the vanished Bentley millions, not to mention my father's embezzlements and the Feds' subsequent grab-all. But his wife, her eyes fixed so firmly on the prize that she missed the alarm in mine, proceeded to rattle off a long list of stocks that she guaranteed would double in value within six months. All it took, she said, would be backbone on my part.

"I don't have much backbone," I told her.

This time Henry didn't bother to stifle his laugh. "Ease up on her, Pilar. She's flat broke."

She snapped, "But you said…"

"I said she was one of the San Sebastian Bentleys and you interrupted me before I could tell you that they lost their money during the Crash."

"Crash?"

"The Depression, dear. That little financial mess in the Thirties? What with one thing and another, the Bentleys never recovered."

"Oh." She looked at her watch. "My! I didn't realize it was so late. Henry and I are getting ready for a theater matinee, aren't we?" She rose from the sofa so quickly it groaned.

I stood up, too. "It's been nice visiting with you, Pilar."

She bared her teeth. "We must get together for lunch."

I bared back. "I'll call."

"You do that." After making certain I was right behind her, she headed for the door.

Behind her, Henry's smile looked strained.

When I reached the Nissan, I checked my cell to see if the zoo had left me any messages; it hadn't. But I counted seven other messages—five from Caro, two from Joe. With a sigh, I climbed into the truck. Without consciously planning it, I found myself driving south on Castro Street and into the old Noe Valley neighborhood where I'd once lived with Michael. It wasn't actually out of my way, I argued with my more common-sense self, because once through Noe, I could pick up Mission, take that down to the 280, and then transition onto 101 south. Almost a straight shot.

The minute I turned onto Church Street, where my husband and I had leased our own small Victorian, I saw the folly of my ways. The periwinkle blue-and-cream house was still there but now two sandy-haired children played in front, watched over by a woman dressed as a nanny. I'd wanted children but Michael wasn't enthusiastic. At first his excuse was that he wanted to pay off his school loans, later that he needed time to settle in at Hoffman, Williams, and Williams. After that, he said we should start saving for our own house, and stressed that children were a financial drain we couldn't yet afford. Still later...

There was no later. By the time I emerged from denial, it was too late.

As I passed the house, the door opened, revealing a blond man and woman who resembled the children. The man held a golden retriever on a leash. Both children ran toward him, clamoring for the rights to walk the dog. When the older child won, the woman gave the other the consolation prize of a hug.

Together the small group set off in the direction of Mission Dolores Park.

I wondered if the woman realized how lucky she was.

Back in Gunn Landing the early evening sky was still clear, but a fog bank crept steadily toward the harbor. Checking my cell again, I found two more calls from my mother. The drive past my old house in San Francisco had left me feeling bereft, so as soon as I parked my pickup I headed toward the *Tequila Sunrise*, hoping a chat with Roarke would chase away my loneliness. Halfway there I caught sight of Maxwell Jarvis, that enemy of all liveaboarders, lolling on the deck of his gas-guzzling eighty-four-foot West Bay Sonship. After giving me a smirk, he reached over and slapped the thigh of the sexy-looking redhead lolling with him. They were both half-naked (Jarvis' big stomach spilled over his black Speedo) and totally drunk.

When I reached the *Tequila Sunrise*, I found Roarke and Frieda standing on the dock debating whether to eat dinner at the castle, the yacht club, or slum it at Fred's Fish Market. He wanted roast pork in mango sauce, the yacht club's Sunday Special, but she, looking more rosily beautiful than ever, held out for Fred's famous oyster stew, which was served in a small loaf of hollowed-out sourdough. She got her way but tossed Roarke a bone by inviting me along as their guest. The source of her good humor revealed itself while we strolled to the restaurant.

With a rare display of friendliness, she hooked her arm around mine. "You're the first harbor buddy we're telling, Teddy. I'm pregnant."

For a brief moment I felt a pang, but it was immediately dulled by my happiness for her. "How wonderful! When's the baby due?"

"*He* is due in December," Roarke said, drawing her to him. "We didn't want to tell anyone until we were sure. She's miscarried twice, both times during the first six weeks, but her ob-gyn says she's past her danger stage now."

I hadn't known about their attempts to have a baby, putting their childless state down to their lifestyle. Now her insecurity made sense. Or did it?

A shadow dimmed the joy on his face. "This means we'll have to sell the *Tequila Sunrise*. I know that some people raise their children on boats, but I'd worry every minute once he started walking. Schooling would be a problem, too. At the very least, we'd have to home-school if we sailed any distance at all, and I can't see Frieda playing schoolmarm."

"I'm willing to give it a try," she said, surprising me. "I do have a degree, you know."

As she spoke, the wispy front of the fog bank reached us, making her shiver. Roarke whipped off his sweater and draped it across her shoulders. "I'll run back for your jacket."

She shook her head. "It's only a few steps to the restaurant."

He ignored her protest. "In this case, Mama doesn't know best." With that, he turned and ran back to the boat, disappearing quickly into the hatch. Within seconds he reappeared clutching a jacket in each hand, one for her, one for me. My jacket was warm enough but Frieda's could have warded off an Arctic winter.

Picking up the conversation where he left off, he said, "I'm not having Frieda slave away on the boat all day, teaching the kid to read and write. He's going to attend school like a normal person. And we'll buy a house, although God knows how much we'll have to pay, with prices being what they are these days. I don't think anything in Old Town's going for less than three-point-five mill, which means we'll have to sell the boat to help make the down payment."

She gave him a peck on the cheek. "Or we could keep the *Sunrise* and move back into the castle."

He shuddered. "And have dinner every night with Great-aunt Aster Edwina? No thanks!"

"If you can stand it, I can." She was serious now. "Maybe raising the baby in the same house as your extended family isn't such a bad idea. Europeans have done it for centuries. But, really, the *Sunrise* could…"

A sixty-foot Bayliner, returning to its slip from an ocean charter, gave a blast on its horn, causing the seagulls and cormorants
to rise into the fog bank like a noisy cloud.

By the time the main body of the fog arrived, we'd reached
Fred's. Located inside an old cannery, one half of the building
was a busy fish market, the other half a bare-bones restaurant
that served up everything the ocean had to offer—poached, fried,
baked, broiled or sushi-style. The food's excellence wasn't the
only thing that packed the restaurant. Sunday night was blues
night—free music, free second beer—and a goodly portion of
the harbor liveaboarders were already ensconced at the long
tables. Delta Force, the local blues band, was in the process of
setting up.

Some of the liveaboarders glared at Roarke, who, as one of
the harbor's well-heeled Northies, they viewed as an ally of the
much-loathed Maxwell Jarvis. Oblivious to their ire, he grabbed
a table uncomfortably near them.

"You can be as selfish as you want when you don't have
children," he said, resuming the conversation. "Now it's time
to grow up."

"Don't be too quick to make a Draconian decision," I coun-
seled, over the *ta-wang* of Delta Force's guitarist as he tuned his
Dobro. "I know how you both love the *Sunrise*."

Frieda reached across the paper-covered table and took my
hand in a sisterly gesture. "That's what I've been telling him, but
he's determined to do what's best for me and the baby whether
I like it or not. Maybe you can talk sense into him."

Me, talk sense into anyone? Me, with my problematical love
life, my hardly-more-than- minimum-wage job, my falling-apart
boat? But when I remembered Lucy and the rest of my animal
friends, I decided I hadn't done so badly after all.

Discretion overrode valor. "Sorry, I have no advice to give
other than to get a good real estate agent." Too bad Grayson
was dead. He'd have them fixed up in no time.

Whatever Roarke was about to reply was interrupted by Walt
McAdams, who called out, "Better mind your table manners,

Southies! I spy two high-class Northies among us." His table mates, other liveaboarders whose boats were on the dreaded Dolphin Island voyage list, muttered angrily at his words.

Then Walt turned his attention to me. "Hey, Teddy! Whose side you on, anyway? You're a Southie. Come on over here with your real friends." He'd slopped beer all over his blue San Sebastian Fire Department tee shirt.

Before I could open my mouth, Roarke shouted, "Leave her out of this! For your information, I fought hard against those new ordinance codes, so take your complaints to Maxwell, not me."

The drunk fireman stood up as if he were about to stagger over to our table, but his table mates pushed him back into his seat. He couldn't resist throwing another insult. "You Northies are all birds of a feather, spoiled rich snobs flocking together."

Roarke shook his head. "I've played golf with Maxwell a couple of times, that's all."

Walt didn't buy it. "A golf buddy with the very guy who put the harbor master up to the Dolphin Island thing. Hell, you know most of our boats will never make it."

Trying once more to deflect his beery anger, Roarke said, "You have more sympathizers than you realize. Most of us, myself included, believe that the liveaboard community gives the harbor its flavor. It's good for extra security, too. But yeah, Maxwell and maybe a few others would like to see you gone. As for their names, all you need to know is that he's the only one who filed a complaint."

The angry mutterings grew louder.

Walt stood up again. "More golf buddies, right? Why keep their names secret? You afraid we peasants will march on them with lit torches and pitchforks?" As if to illustrate, he held his fork high.

The others tried to shove him down again, but he resisted, making a few stabbing motions toward Roarke with the fork.

"Settle down!" I snapped. "A brawl's the last thing we need."

He pointed the fork at me. "Judas!" Then, knocking over his beer, he stormed out the door, leaving his friends to clean up his mess.

The waiter, who had been hovering nervously nearby, began to take our orders; but by then I'd lost my appetite. Ignoring Roarke's and Frieda's pleas for me to stay, I tendered my apologies and headed for the door. Behind me, Delta Force launched into their first set.

Outside, the cool fog came as a relief from the hot tempers inside the restaurant. And as much as I enjoyed blues, I welcomed the cushioned silence. Walking along the pier back toward the *Merilee*, I could barely make out the *shush-shush* of the incoming tide lapping against the pylons, the soft peeps of shore birds. Entranced by these gifts of twilight, I opened my mouth and breathed in the fog's salty wetness, glorying in the dampness against my cheeks. How could Roarke and Frieda turn their backs on this?

Footsteps intruded on my reverie. I turned.

"Walt?"

No answer.

The footsteps grew nearer. Had Walt changed his mind and decided to return to the restaurant?

"Come on, Walt, let's make up. We've always been friends."

Still no answer. I decided it probably wasn't him after all, but someone who needed to keep his presence a secret.

My father?

I had just started to smile when a sunburst lit up the night. Then a darkness deeper than fog embraced me.

Chapter Fifteen

Lights again. Noise that hurt my head. Some woman asking stupid questions.

"Can you remember your name?"

What an idiot. "Theodora Iona Esmeralda Bentley, of course. Leave me alone."

"Do you know where you are?"

Two times an idiot. "On the *Merilee*. Now would you please switch off those lights? I want to go back to sleep." I tried to turn to a more restful position but couldn't, so I closed my eyes tightly to block out the glare.

A sharp poke in the left leg. I opened my eyes and saw a woman with hair redder than mine hovering over me with something sharp in her hand.

"Don't do that again," I warned her.

"Good response to pain. How about here?" Another poke, this time in the right leg.

"Stop it!"

She ignored me. "Reflexes fine, but she's still confused. Let's get her over to X-ray."

"Hey, lady, I'm not going anywhere with you."

"Teddy, be nice to Dr. O'Hare."

Where had I heard that voice before? Oh, yes. Caro. What was my mother doing here? She hated the *Merilee*, wouldn't visit on a bet. Except to leave notes.

"Tell her to get away from me."

"You have a big bump on your head, dear, and she wants to make sure there's no fracture."

"Humpty Dumpty."

"Who?"

"Had a great fall."

"You didn't fall. Someone attacked you."

"All the king's men?"

"Probably some nasty homeless person."

As whatever I was lying on bumped along, my eyes found their focus. I wasn't on the *Merilee*, but rolling down a wide, white corridor on a gurney. "Did Lucy bite me?" I asked. But how was that possible, considering that anteaters had no teeth?

Giving up on making sense of the world, I went back to sleep.

<> <> <>

When I woke later to a strong chemical smell, my head throbbed. Had I been careless and mixed bleach with ammonia, thus gassing myself while cleaning the *Merilee*? Then I saw the television set bracketed high on a plain white wall. Ignoring the pain in my head, I surveyed my surroundings. Wilting flowers on the nightstand next to my bed, a carafe of water with a plastic straw protruding from it, no dog or cat anywhere in evidence. Stranger still, across the room, Caro slept in a chair guarded by a man, who, although the temperature was pleasant enough, wore a heavy coat with its collar turned up.

Oh. A hospital room.

The man approached the bed. "Feeling better?" he asked. After a closer look, I recognized him as my father.

"My head hurts," I complained. The light streaming through the half-closed blinds merely made it worse.

He gave me a concerned look. "That's because someone hit you over the head."

I decided to worry about this strange piece of information later. "What time is it?"

He looked at his watch. "Almost seven. And keep your voice down. Your mother's been up with you all night. This is the first time she's slept."

"Up all night, you say? Is this seven in the morning or seven in the evening?"

"Ante meridian."

"Then I need to go to work. Outta my way, I'm getting up."

Dad pushed me back down. "The only place you're going is to your mother's, and that's only if the doctor says you can."

"But I need to walk my dog. And feed the anteater. And the wolves. And…"

"Like hell you do. I called the zoo, got passed around from person to person, and eventually wound up talking to the head zookeeper and told her what happened, so she's feeding your precious animals. Don't worry about your pets, either. Some fireman named Walt is taking care of them. On a less pleasant note, your cop friend just left to get some coffee, but says he'll be back."

The world, and my father's problems with it, began to come back to me. "Did Joe recognize you?"

"Let's hope not or bundling up like this was all in vain. He only poked his head in here for a second, then left, so it's doubtful he saw me at all. Now tell me who did this to you so I can kill him."

"What?!" In my alarm, I raised my voice, and Caro began to stir.

"Teddy? Are you awake?" she called. She stood up, revealing that she was wearing pajama bottoms and an old tee shirt. For the first time I could remember, she looked like hell.

My father called to her. "Yeah, she's awake, and I'm clearing out before the fuzz comes back."

"Dad?"

"What?"

"They're not called 'the fuzz' anymore."

"See what happens when you lose touch?" He leaned over and gave me a peck on the cheek. "I don't want to push my luck, so I'll wait for you both at the house." To Caro, he said, "Make her tell who did this."

He started to say something else, but at the sound of nearing footsteps, hunched into his coat and scuttled out the door in the opposite direction.

Caro trotted over and kissed my forehead. "Oh, baby, you could have died! First the anteater, then the bears, now this. Move back to Old Town where you'll be safe!" As she caressed my cheek, her hand trembled.

Joe entered the room in full uniform, his own reaction more subdued. "Awake, I see."

"I don't understand what's going on."

"Those harbor low-lifes tried to kill you, that's what happened!" Caro hissed. "The only reason you're alive is because of Roarke." She gave Joe a stern look. "She's too ill to see you."

"No, she's not. Mrs. Bentley, um, Mrs. Hufgraff, uh…"

Her voice could have cut glass. "It's Mrs. Petersen."

That's the problem with multiple marriages: the police have trouble staying current.

Joe matched her frown with one of his own. "Please leave us alone for a minute. I need to question her."

She squared her slender shoulders. "No."

He squared his broad ones. "Ever see a jail, Mrs. Petersen? Looking *out* from the inside of a cell?"

As much as I enjoyed their pissing contest, it was time to interrupt. "I'm dying for a glass of orange juice. Caro, would you please bring me one from the cafeteria?"

Her face fell. "But I…"

"The vitamin C will do me good."

"Oh, all right." With a beauty pageant flick of her hips, she strode out of the room.

With her gone, I hoped to make some sense out of the night's events. "Joe, what happened?"

"Somebody clocked you, but Roarke Gunn and that fireman…"

"Walt McAdams."

"Yeah, him. They prevented whoever it was from doing any-thing else to you. After chasing the guy away, McAdams held your hand while Roarke called 9-1-1. When the EMTs brought you in, you were kind of goofy, and you stayed that way for a while. You just don't remember. The doc kept you here overnight. If you feel the back of your head, you'll find a bald spot where they had to shave your hair to stitch you up."

Obviously I was no longer "goofy" because Roarke and Walt acting in concert didn't sound right. "Who reached me first?"

"Roarke, as I understand it. Seconds later the fireman came along."

"But Roarke was back at the restaurant having dinner. And anyway, the *Tequila Sunrise* is in the other direction from the *Merilee*. There's no reason he'd be walking toward the harbor's south end. And Walt, well, he'd been drinking. He and Roarke exchanged words before he left Fred's in a huff."

"The guy was hammered, all right. Both of them admitted there'd been some kind of altercation at the restaurant with you in the middle. Roarke said that as soon as you left, a couple of the liveaboarders headed for the door, too, so he told his wife to stay at the restaurant while he made sure you got home okay."

I tried to envision the scene. Me, lying on the pavement, Roarke running to my rescue, Walt staggering along behind. "He left Frieda with the liveaboarders?" This didn't fit with the new and improved Roarke, the Roarke who ran back to his boat to get a jacket for his wife, the Roarke who was already planning his son's on-land education.

"That's what he said. What do you remember before the lights went out?"

I closed my eyes but the darkness just made me more aware of my headache so I opened them again. "Fog. Maybe footsteps, but they might have been my own."

He sat on the side of the bed. Now that my mother wasn't there to disapprove, he took my hand and kissed it. "That's not a love tap on the back of your head, Teddy. Whoever hit you meant business. Look, I know you've continued to ask around about Grayson's murder and for that I blame myself. We've made our arrest, so drop it, okay?"

"You arrested the wrong person. By the way, where *was* Zorah last night?"

He couldn't meet my eyes. "Attending her niece's *quince*."

A *quinceañera* was the coming-of-age celebration for a Hispanic girl, carried out with all the hoopla of a confirmation, bat mitzvah, and high-school graduation party combined. There would have been at least one hundred witnesses who would swear up and down Zorah never once moved from her niece's side for the entire day and evening.

"So she has an alibi," I gloated.

"Family members always lie for each other, that's nothing new." He didn't sound like he believed his own argument.

"You know darned well Zorah didn't 'clock' me, as you so delicately put it."

"She's strong enough."

"But not sneaky enough. She can't even hide a gun without screwing up."

He spread his hands. "What can I say?"

"You can say goodbye, that's what. I'm going home." During my earlier look around the room, I had seen something that looked like a closet door. My clothes were probably in there. I'd slip them on and leave.

Joe gave me a pained smile. "To your boat? Your mother will never allow it. Obviously you don't remember the hell she raised last night, screaming about you living alone on that thing."

I tried to shrug, but it hurt too much. "That's nothing new."

"Right now she has a point. As sheriff, I'm saying it's not safe to go back there. And as someone else who loves you, I'm in total agreement with her. She may not be the easiest person to live with but she'll make sure you're safe. Knowing her, she'll probably hire an entire battalion of security guards."

"I'm going back to the *Merilee*."

"You do and I'll come up with an excuse to have it impounded!"

What an impasse. If I stayed at my mother's, he'd find an excuse to visit and might catch a glimpse of my father. It may have been twenty years since Joe had laid eyes on him, but he had a policeman's memory. I searched for a compromise.

"Okay. I'll stay at Caro's for a day or two. But then I'm going back to the *Merilee*, where—I'd like to remind you—I have a guard dog."

"That three-legged mutt of yours?"

"He's vicious." I didn't tell him about the night my father snuck aboard and DJ Bonz failed the guard dog test. In an attempt to solve my other problem, I added, "Um, I was going to discuss this before my, uh, accident. I think we need to..." I searched for the proper phrase, something that wouldn't be too harsh. "...put our personal relationship on hold for a while. Give ourselves some breathing room."

He stared at me as if I'd lost my mind. "On hold? Has your mother issued another edict against me?"

"It's just that I...I..." Obviously I couldn't tell him the truth, that I was afraid he'd run into my father at the house and arrest him. But since I hadn't yet come up with a believable excuse, I said, "So much is going on, Joe. We need time to think about us, our future. If we have one, that is."

His face intent, he leaned over the bed. "Teddy, are you dumping me again?"

I turned away so he couldn't look into my eyes. "No, no. I just need a break for a while. Some space."

"Space?" Then his expression changed and he grew terribly quiet. "What's the matter? Don't you trust me?"

I didn't answer. How could I?

With a sigh, he stood up and walked out of the room. I could heard his footsteps echoing all the way down the hall.

It was the loneliest sound in the world.

Later that afternoon the hospital released me, and by dinnertime I found myself ensconced with Bonz and Priss in the bedroom where I'd grown up. Caro had kept it unchanged, apparently believing the posters of Jon Bon Jovi, Gloria Estefan, and the Thompson Twins I'd collected as a teen would lure me home. While the Nineties' Gloria still looked stylish, I now realized how weird all that hair looked on Bon Jovi and the Twins. I didn't much care for the room's turquoise and lime green color scheme, either. The bright colors hurt my eyes.

Although I felt fine except for the raw spot at the back of my head and some residual light sensitivity, Caro, changed into a yellow Betsey Johnson frock that hurt my eyes even more than the room, wouldn't even let me out of bed to eat. She served my dinner on a silver tray piled high with rosemary chicken, roasted potatoes, a steamed artichoke in garlic butter sauce, and for dessert, a strawberry-kiwi torte. Obviously, my father remained in residence.

After watching me gobble down the food, she asked, "Ready for seconds?"

"What I need is to walk this off, so I'll take Bonz out. Where'd you put his leash?"

She set the tray aside and leaned forward to dab at my chin with a snowy linen napkin. "He can use the old doggy door. You're staying in bed."

"I'm not an invalid."

"Yes, you are."

"Oh, please. I'm thirty years old and I've been living on my own for more than ten years."

"And look how that turned out." With that, she picked up the tray and left the room.

She did have a point, I mused, as I lay there staring at the ceiling with Bonz snoring at my feet and Priss curled on my stomach. My life choices had worked out so well that someone was trying to kill me and the man I loved had just walked out of my life.

I didn't know which was worse.

Chapter Sixteen

The next morning I was finishing up a chorizo omelet topped with tangy salsa and a dollop of sour cream, another of Dad's culinary creations, when my bedroom door opened. Stiff with disapproval, my mother let in Walt McAdams. She waited by the door like an irritated pit bull.

Looking hung over, with red eyes but at least a different tee shirt than he'd worn the night of my attack, Walt carried a handful of wildflowers. "How you doing, tiger?" His breath still smelled like the Budweiser brewery.

I beckoned him closer for a kiss. Cheek-peck duly rendered, I said, "I hear you helped save my life."

He shrugged, then winced, as if the movement hurt him. "All in a day's work."

I thanked him for the flowers, and stuffed them into the water glass on my nightstand, since if I didn't, my mother would throw out such a proletarian offering. We chatted for a while about boats and things, but when Caro grew increasingly restless, I asked him the question that had nagged me all night. "Do you know how long Roarke had been with me when you arrived?"

"It could only have been seconds. I'd just gotten back to the *Running Wild* and was taking a leak over the side when I heard what sounded like a scuffle. So I zipped up and went to investigate. That's when I saw Roarke bending over you. Then I saw some guy running off and I went after him, but I...Well, I wasn't moving all that good. I was..."

"Drunk," I finished for him.

"Yeah. He took a deep breath. "Look, I'm sorry about my behavior at Fred's and what I said to you. It's the stress. We're all worried about what'll happen to our boats with the new harbor ordinances. None of us wants to move to another marina."

"I don't either."

"I know. That's why when I called you a…"

Time to stop the guilt-wallowing. "I've been called worse. Hey, what's it like outside? Morning fog burned off yet?"

"An hour ago."

We chatted until Caro, whose eyes had never once left him, said, "You'll have to leave now, Mister McAdams. My daughter needs her rest." With a look of distain, she added, "And shame on you, urinating into the harbor!"

She hustled him out the door, following close behind to make sure he didn't steal the silver.

I lay there, hoping Joe would visit but knowing he wouldn't. Eventually, bored out of my mind, I wobbled over to my bookcase and took down *The Hidden Staircase*, an old Nancy Drew mystery I'd loved as a teen. After reading a couple of chapters, I dozed off.

Caro woke me when she opened the door again. "Another visitor," she announced, ushering in Roarke with great ceremony. He bore flowers, too, a professionally-arranged bouquet of color-coordinated chrysanthemums and petunias offset by a sleek calilysis.

"How are you?" He handed the flowers to my mother, who before I could stop her, scurried off to find an appropriate vase.

Not sure how I felt about being left alone with him, I gave him the best smile I could manage. "Fine, except for a headache. And thanks for what you did last night. I owe you one."

"You'd have done the same for me. Frieda would've come along, too, but the poor girl's suffering from morning sickness."

We talked pregnancy and boats until Caro returned, bearing his expensive bouquet in the small Ming vase she'd hidden from the feds during their property-grabbing rampage. "Aren't Roarke's flowers beautiful, Teddy?"

Yes, they were, and too slick for my taste. I preferred Walt's wildflowers. Feeling safer now that she'd returned, I asked Roarke why he'd left the restaurant to usher me home.

"Are you kidding? Those liveaboarders were baying for blood. You didn't show great judgment by leaving right after that drunk fireman."

"The others were as angry as Walt, most of them just as drunk. And they were still there. So why'd you leave Frieda anywhere near them?"

He gave me an accusing look. "Nothing bad could happen to her at Fred's."

"How trusting. By the way, did you happen to catch a glimpse of the man who attacked me? Walt was here earlier and said you reached me first."

He shook his head. "The guy took off as soon as he heard me. Like I told the sheriff, I saw somebody in dark pants and a dark hoodie running toward the parking lot, and Walt staggered after him for a few steps. I don't think either of us could tell you the color of his hair or whether he was tall or short, fat or thin. The fog was too thick."

After Roake left, I lay in my turquoise and lime room staring at the ceiling. It had been two weeks since I discovered Grayson dead in the anteater enclosure, and I was no closer to discovering who killed him than before. All I knew for sure was that it hadn't been Zorah. What if...?

My train of thought was broken when the door opened and my father walked in bearing a big pitcher of orange juice and two glasses. "I wanted to add some champagne to celebrate your great escape, but your mother wouldn't let me. I don't remember her being that bossy."

"Your memory must be failing," I said, as he poured for us.

He laughed briefly, then his face grew grave. "I'm glad you're feeling so perky again, but how many more visitors do you expect? I've been hiding in the attic all morning and I'm wondering if I should go back to Al's for a while. It's been wonderful being with your mother again, but if anyone sees me…"

He didn't have to finish his sentence. With Joe and Chuckles Fitzgerald both on the alert, my father's presence in Gunn Landing was getting more and more problematical.

A hesitant knock at the door sent him scurrying into my closet, where he scrunched himself among plastic and lavender-wrapped prom dresses and riding habits. Putting a finger against his lips, he softly shut the door.

Caro stuck her head into the room, obviously unaware that she'd interrupted my father in the midst of a visit. "Another gentleman caller."

When she opened the door wider, I saw Barry Fields almost hidden behind a huge bouquet of long-stemmed roses. Taken off guard, I pulled up the covers around my neck, which sent Miss Priss flying. DJ Bonz gave the zoo director a brief growl, then went back to sleep.

"My poor Teddy!" Barry rushed toward me, roses flapping. "When I heard what happened…" Considering that he wasn't a professional actor, he gave a pretty decent performance. His voice choked with emotion and he displayed all the appropriate body language, but his eyes were as calculating as an IRS tax auditor's. No doubt he was running an inventory of the expensive goodies he'd seen since entering the house.

I gave him a feeble smile. "I'll be back to work tomorrow."

"No you won't!" Caro rose from the chair. "Not with that disgusting anteater and those vicious bears! You're not going back to that messy boat, either!"

"Yes I am!"

Barry groveled for a few seconds at my bedside, his eyes glued to the Ming. Then, forcing his attentions away from the vase, he took my hand. "Your mother knows what's best for you, dear."

Dear. I almost lost my chorizo omelet. "The dizziness is gone, my vision's cleared, and my memory's back." I snatched my hand away and wiped it surreptitiously on the lime green comforter. "All I need is rest. Thanks for stopping by."

I slid further underneath the covers and closed my eyes. A moment later, I heard the door close.

When it was safe, I peeked out from under the comforter. "Dad, you can come out now!"

He emerged from the closet. "You're drawing too much heat. As soon as that jackass leaves the house, I'm going back to Al's." With that, he left, trailing a scent of lavender.

As soon as the door closed behind him, I crawled out of bed and threw on my clothes. I'd had enough of this.

The *Merilee* might be a mess, but at least she was *my* mess.

The next day I returned to the zoo, my hair combed carefully over the shaved spot. At first it looked like I'd merely exchanged my mother's over-protective behavior for my fellow zookeepers' concerns, but unlike her, they got the message and backed off. All except for Zorah, who insisted on shadowing me during the early part of my rounds.

"I want to make sure you don't keel over," she explained, jumping down from her cart to help me lift feed buckets at the commissary.

"It was just a bump on the head."

"Some bump. Did your mom tell you I stopped by the hospital to see you?"

I vaguely remembered my mother saying something about a big Amazon asking to see me, but I'd been too fuzzy at that point for visits. "Yes, she did, and I appreciate it. But I'm fine now. If I do start feeling sick, you'll be the first person I radio."

"Promise?"

"Scout's honor." I'd never been a Girl Scout.

She inspected my radio to make sure it was functioning. It was.

"Zorah, could I please get on with my work?"

With an unhappy expression, she jumped back into her cart and drove off.

Nothing would ever make me believe that a woman who cared that much for others could murder anyone, no matter the provocation. All right, so she'd once roughed up a man who had attempted to feed a razor blade to one of our animals. But murder? It simply wasn't possible. To think of my friend facing a murder trial...I couldn't bear it.

I would keep searching for the truth, no matter how much danger was involved.

When I arrived at Tropics Trail, Lucy was so busy pacing from one end of her enclosure to the other that she hardly gave me a glance.

Although long fur hid her belly, it seemed to have grown much larger in the two days I'd been gone. Her pacing worried me, too. Now that she was out of the small holding pen she should have settled down, but except for that one brief moment of joy on her first day of freedom, she remained anxious. Perhaps, since her baby was due within the week, she desired a more suitable place to give birth than her old bamboo-covered dog house. With that in mind, I hopped back into my cart and went to pick up more hay. I'd toss a few flakes into her enclosure and let her figure out how to arrange them. Regardless of species, most females preferred to do their own decorating.

Within minutes of my heaving the hay over the back fence, she started fluffing it around, raking it this way and that. When she'd created a large hump a few feet behind her doghouse, she plopped down in the middle and rolled around for a while, manipulating the hay into a giant anteater-sized bed. Once she appeared to get stuck on her back, but finally managed to right herself. With a satisfied grunt, she backed off and began sucking termites from a faux log.

By the time I made it to the wolves' enclosure, I found a crowd gathered near their outer fence. To the noisy delight of several teenagers, Cisco and Godiva were joyously mating as the other wolves watched with varying degrees of interest.

Not everyone was pleased. A harassed-looking mother approached me and begged, "Please do something. I drove the kids all the way up from Carmel to teach them about endangered species, and now…" She pointed to a small group of six intrigued children, whose ages ranged all the way from toddler to middle-schooler.

Our animals' public sexuality was a common cause of complaint. These days, few people are raised on ranches or farms and therefore don't understand that animals had no concept of privacy or shame. I tried explaining the facts of zoo life to the woman, but she didn't get it.

"Put them back in their den until they stop."

"If I tried that, ma'am, I'd get my hand bit off. Cisco doesn't like to be interrupted during his, ah, romantic encounters. But here's a thought. Mexican gray wolves mate for life. It might be a good lesson to teach your children, that lifelong marriage—even among animals—remains a possibility in this promiscuous old world." Although not all that common, I'd begun to believe, remembering promiscuous old Michael.

"So there's nothing you can do?"

"How about…?" I tried to think of an animal guaranteed not to indulge in public mating behavior. Not the monkeys, that was for sure. Or the happy capybaras. But there was one animal whose sexual behavior was as pure as a cloistered nun's. "Our anteater might be a nice animal for your children to visit. She doesn't have a boyfriend, and she's only a few yards away on Tropics Trail. If you want, I'll walk you over there."

A frown. "Are you talking about the animal who killed that poor man? Some life lesson *that* would be!" She gathered her children and pulled them away from the wolf exhibit. With a glare, she headed toward Africa Trail, where I'd seen the giraffes mating a few minutes ago. I was tempted to run after her with a warning, then decided to let the Africa Trail keepers deal with her. One thing was certain. By the end of the day, her children would know they hadn't been delivered via stork.

I was ready to go around to the back of the wolves' enclosure to portion out their meal when I heard an unwelcome voice.

"Ah, spring, with love in the air."

Barry.

He sidled up to me, and slid an arm around my waist. "How's my girl today? Feeling all better? You look like you could use a good steak dinner."

Before I could escape, Jack Spence picked that moment to drive up the pathway in his cart. The last thing I wanted was for the other keepers to get the idea that something was going on between the zoo director and me. I tried to move away, but Barry tightened his grip.

"I have to finish up my chores here, so if you don't mind, I'll get back to work."

Too late. Jack's cart screeched to a stop right in front of us. "Hi, Teddy! How's your head? And, uh, Barry, what are you…?"

Oh, hell. When Jack wasn't telling the spectacled bears about the restoration he was doing on his '76 Chevy Malibu, he gossiped with humans. Soon everyone at the zoo would suspect that my relationship to the zoo director was something other than professional.

I tried to make the situation seem innocent. "Mister Fields stopped by to see how I was feeling. Didn't you, sir?" I punctuated the question with an elbow to his ribs.

Barry either didn't get it or refused to. Hugging me closer, he said, "My girl here sure took a big knock on the head, didn't she?" He then proceeded to make matters worse. "I stopped by to see her yesterday, you know, at her mother's estate in Old Town. Such a beautiful place! I took along a dozen long-stemmed roses. Nothing's too good for my girl."

My girl. His fixation on the phrase did not bode well. All the keepers hated him, and if they thought we'd hooked up, they'd hate me right long with him unless I told the truth. Yet how could I? The real reason behind our dinner "date" would eventually get back to him and he'd take his revenge by penning Lucy up again.

I wrenched out of his clutches and moved closer to the wolves' fence, hoping that his recent encounter with the monkeys would make him nervous about getting too close to animals. It worked. Seeing one of the wolves cast a slant-eyed glance his way, he hopped back into his own cart. Then he drove a final nail into my coffin.

"Now, I don't want my girl to work too hard!"

After Barry blew me a kiss and drove off, Jack Spence gave me a dirty look.

The day grew increasingly difficult. Regardless of my morning's bravado, my endurance began to wane and several times I was forced to sit down and catch my breath. At noon, I braved the stares of the other keepers in the employee lounge as I took an extra-long lunch break. My worst fears about Jack's addiction to gossip were confirmed.

"So you and Barry hooked up, huh?" This from Miranda, the Down Under keeper.

"No, we didn't 'hook up.' I had dinner with him, that's all." I couldn't even look at Zorah, whose frosty expression hurt the most.

Miranda wouldn't let it go. "We thought you had better taste."

I was saved from trying to answer the unanswerable with the arrival of Kim Markowski. The education director announced that she wanted to use us as a test audience for a quick run-through of her revised puppet show, now titled *Little Red Riding Hood and the Giant Anteater.*

Eager to get the spotlight off myself, I volunteered to help set up the small stage. The new puppets weren't finished (the anteater looked like one of the beaky old codgers on *The Muppet Show*), but she explained that she was taking a puppet-making class once a week in San Francisco.

"By the time the show debuts, they'll look more professional," she said. Then, to my surprise, her eyes teared up. "Grayson paid my tuition. Wasn't that a kind thing to do?"

A murmur of assent around the table. Zorah remained silent. She still hadn't forgiven him for not appointing her as zoo director.

Once Kim began the show, I found myself drawn to the tale of an innocent anteater accused of killing and eating Little Red Riding Hood's grandmother. After a brief investigation, Little Red discovered that the anteater was simply hiding Grandma to keep her safe from Mr. Wolf. In a stirring climax, the anteater yanked the sheepskin off a nearby "sheep" to reveal Mr. Wolf himself. Demonstrating a less pacific temperament than the peaceful anteater, Miss Hood whacked him with a shepherd's staff.

Gratified that the idea I'd given Barry had been so successful, I cheered with the rest of the keepers when the wolf ran howling into the forest, chased by the valiant Hood. After Kim took a few bows, the keepers drifted back to work. I stayed behind to help her take the puppets back to the cart. As we worked, I told her what a great job she'd done.

"I can't take all the credit," she replied, her long-lashed eyes bright. "Barry gave me the idea. He said the plot came to him in a dream."

"*Really!*"

"I didn't know he was so creative. Did you?"

"Can't say I did."

As she drove off, I realized that our zoo director's ethics made the Big Bad Wolf look saintly.

By the time the zoo closed for the day and the last visitor straggled out the gate, I was exhausted, but at least the bald spot on my head had stopped throbbing. After the events of the past couple of days, the prospect of a peaceful evening on the *Merilee* couldn't have been more desirable.

At first, the reality lived up to the dream. As I watched Jack Hanna cavort with a wallaby on *Animal Planet,* my pets curled up next to me. The only blot on the evening came when—for the first time ever—I locked the salon hatch. Except for that, the evening passed without incident, although *Animal Planet* grew too fuzzy and I switched over to a rerun of something named *Magnum.* The guy playing the private detective was cute, but the plot didn't seem as realistic as those on *Law & Order.* Or maybe life in Hawaii wasn't as rough as in Manhattan. After the program was over, and the fog had enfolded the harbor in its soft embrace, I sank into bed.

Although exhausted, I couldn't sleep and lay listening to the tide whisper against the *Merilee*'s hull. I tried to empty my mind of its chaos by picturing a soft gray blankness. It didn't work. Since nature abhors a vacuum, more disturbing images crowded in: Grayson's ravaged corpse; Jeanette caressing his old suit; Zorah's face shadowed by iron bars; the lines of pain around Joe's eyes when I told him we needed to put our relationship on hold.

Defying doctor's orders, I went to the galley and poured myself some wine. Once back in bed, I propped myself up on the pillow next to where Priss now lay snoring and tried to organize my thoughts.

With the exception of Zorah and Dr. Kate, most staffers had come in contact with Grayson only on those rare occasions when he attended the zoo's fund-raisers. How could they have a motive to kill him?

Dr. Kate's refusal to discuss the independent vet study worried me. Not only that, but according to zoo gossip, she had once crossed swords with Grayson over the ever-increasing expenses involved in keeping our animals well-fed and healthy. Yet would anyone murder a man over the rising cost of hay?

Moving my focus outside of the zoo, I reviewed a different group of suspects.

Most of the pro-Trust Gunns benefited from Grayson's murder because it effectively ended attempts to break the trust and disperse its funds among the heirs. Now the Gunns would receive their dividend checks in perpetuity. With an increasing sense of discomfort, I remembered Roarke's timely arrival at my side seconds after I'd been mugged. Speaking of the Gunns, what about Henry and Pilar? Something had been nagging me about that conversation, something that didn't make sense.

Nothing came, so I let it go, deciding to revisit the conversation later. One thing was for certain. The Trust was administered by a firm in the City, which probably meant that another drive up there might be wise, even if I had to take a day off work. I groaned aloud at the thought, making Bonz open his eyes and look around. When no action toward his food bowl was forthcoming, he fell back asleep. Priss never stirred from her place on the nearby pillow.

The pillow.

Where only a few nights earlier Joe...

I resumed staring at the *Merilee*'s low ceiling.

Why did life have to be so complicated?

Chapter Seventeen

The next day brought no enlightenment. Hoping to turn my mood in a more positive direction—and to distract myself from my head's throbs—I lingered at the anteater enclosure. With no visitors nearby to make me feel self-conscious, I told her how pretty she was. "Such a fluffy tail! Such marvelous black and white markings! Lucy is the queen of giant anteaters!"

She pointed her long nose at me and grunted in what I imagined was agreement.

"Not only are you more beautiful than any giant anteater alive, but you're a wonderful decorator, too. That nest you made for your baby is exquisite. Would you like to come down to the *Merilee* and decorate for me? I have a sea-animal theme going, but I'm not adverse to incorporating an anteater motif. Do you think I could find the right fabric? Anything's possible." If I had the money. In reality, if I had enough money to redecorate, I'd also have enough to overhaul the motor. Which I didn't. A successful trip to Dolphin Island in order to keep my boat berthed at the harbor remained impossible.

Wrong train of thought. Instead of getting my mind off my problems, I was reminding myself of them. Time to get back to work.

"See you later, Lucy. I'm going to look in on the capybaras. They're —"

An arm snaked around my waist. "How's my girl? Feeling better?"

Barry. As impeccably groomed as ever, the afternoon sun made his perfectly styled hair glow in the morning light. He looked almost handsome, if you were nearsighted.

I stepped out of his grasp. The only thing good about this situation was that Tropics Trail was deserted, and no one would witness his overtures. "Hey, don't…"

He closed the distance between us and drew me back to him. "There's no point in denying the chemistry between us."

In an attempt to set some relationship parameters, however belatedly, I began to peel his hand away one finger at a time. "This is neither the time nor the place."

His smile made him look like a hungry dingo lying in wait for a juicy wallaby. "Anytime's the right time when a man's in love."

"Listen, Barry, you're not in love…"

Before I could finish, he jerked me toward him so hard that I had no chance to pull away before his carnivorous mouth clapped onto mine. Desperate, I freed my hand, grabbed a fistful of hair, and yanked.

To my horror, the top of his head came off.

As I goggled at the hair in my hand, he snatched it back. "Give me that, you…you…"

A chorus of laughter from a zoo cart emerging around the bend snapped me out of my shock. I looked at the zoo director's gleaming bald pate, then at the flap of hair I'd removed, and understood. I hadn't scalped him, merely lifted off his toupee.

Trying my best to dial down his anger, I said, "I didn't mean to do that."

Barry slapped me.

Hard. With the back of his hand.

Without thinking, I hauled off and slugged him in the nose. Blood spattered my uniform.

He drew back his own fist.

While Lucy hissed in alarm, I danced out of Barry's reach. He started after me, but brakes squealed and the cart of zoo workers tumbled out and ran toward us. Even Kim, crutches under her arms, hobbled along as best she could.

"That's enough, you two!" Dr. Kate yelled, waving a clip-board. She looked like she would use it to swat the next person who made a hostile move.

Not being entirely stupid, I raised my hands in the universal signal of surrender. "This isn't what it looks like."

Nearby, the anteater hissed louder. Out of the corner of my eye, I could see her rise to her full height of five feet and extend those long talons, looking every bit the Code Red animal she truly was.

Ignoring her, Barry unclenched his fist, his eyes glittering with hate. "Miss Bentley, you're fired. Your ass better be gone by the end of the day."

He stuck his toupee back on his head and walked away.

I was trying to shake the dizziness away when the others reached me.

"Are you all right?" Zorah put a steadying hand on my arm.

I clenched my eyes shut, then opened them again. Better. "I think so."

"Your concussion. Is it...?"

Yes, my head hurt like blue blazes, but that wasn't what made me feel so miserable. "Did you hear? He fired me!" I wanted to bawl.

"He can't fire you," she snapped. "He grabbed you first, and even if you over-reacted with that toupee-pulling stunt, his response was *way* over the line. If you're sure you're okay I want you to fill out a grievance complaint. Don't worry. You have witnesses."

Jack Spence made it clear where his sympathies lay. "Regardless of the provocation, management can't go around hitting keepers," he said. "Aster Edwina's gonna have a fit if he gets us in trouble with the law or the EEOC."

Aster Edwina. I'd forgotten she remained the final arbiter of all things zoo, so maybe my situation wasn't as bleak as I feared. She'd always preferred animals to people.

"You saw everything?" I threw a glance at the anteater. With the director's departure, she'd returned to all fours and no longer looked dangerous. But the continued hissing wasn't a good sign.

Dr. Kate nodded. "Everything. I saw you resisting what appeared to be unwanted overtures, the toupee removal, the backhand, your attempt at self-defense." She raised her hand to my cheek. "The swelling isn't too bad yet but you might develop a shiner if we don't get some ice on that right away. Come on down to the Animal Care Center and I'll fix you up. And I suggest you see your doctor. That slap can't have been good for your concussion."

As I tottered toward the cart, Zorah added, "Let's call the police, too. We just witnessed an assault."

"No!" I didn't want Joe brought into this. Our relationship was already a mess. "This is all my own fault, anyway." No lie there. With my ill-conceived plot to help the anteater, I'd brought all this on myself.

Zorah snorted. "Every battered woman thinks she asked for it. Tell me what's been going on, Teddy. That was no lover's tiff we just witnessed."

Lover. Since my relationship with the zoo director was now beyond repair there was no point in keeping secrets, so I told them everything. Lucy's distress, the hatching of the plot, the dinner, Barry's behavior in the restaurant's parking lot, the continuous gropings.

Instead of being shocked, Zorah gave me an approving smile. "I suspected something like that. Hell, if it would help our animals, I'd put on fishnet hose and hang out under a street light with a sign saying TWENTY-FIVE BUCKS A THROW hanging from my neck."

Probably envisioning the Amazonian keeper as a particularly ill-dressed hooker, Dr. Kate smiled. "Same here. But there's another way to play this. As you may or may not know, there've been rumors of harassment. Our boy Barry really likes the ladies, whether they like him or not."

Interesting. She'd once asked if I was "having trouble" with him. At the time I'd thought nothing of it but now her question seemed oddly prescient. Notwithstanding the shadows under her eyes, she was still an attractive woman. *Harassable*, in fact.

〈〉〈〉〈〉

The rest of the day passed without further drama. I stopped working only once, to fill out the grievance forms Zorah handed me as I tossed vegetables into the capybaras' enclosure.

While I wrote, she studied my face carefully. "Before you leave tonight, I want to photograph the evidence."

I touched my cheek, which was now as sore as the back of my head. "Do you have to?"

"The more ammunition, the better. And I still think we should call the police."

"I said *no!*" The very idea of Joe finding out what I'd been up to made me ill.

"Okay," she grudged. "But if that creep comes around again, make sure there's another keeper nearby. If there's not, get on the radio and start moving until someone finds you. I don't want you left alone with him for one minute, understand?"

"That means I'm not fired?"

"Of course not. Anyway, I have a plan."

"Care to share?" I handed the signed grievance forms back to her.

"You'll find out soon enough." With a mysterious smile, she walked away.

〈〉〈〉〈〉

Regardless of the vet's ministrations with an ice pack, when I looked at myself at the end of the day in the ladies' room mirror, a ghastly face stared back at me. The area around my eye sported a purple crescent, and my cheek had swollen to twice its normal size. Hardly anyone's idea of a *femme fatale*. As I stood there bemoaning my appearance, the door opened and Zorah walked in carrying a camera. Even with a murder trial hanging over her head, she looked happier than I did.

"Smile for the birdy," she said, following through on her promise to document my injury.

"I don't feel like smiling."

She took one close-up full face, then a profile shot that showcased my inflamed cheek. "Too bad he didn't knock out a tooth."

"Zorah, are you serious?"

"Bigger damage settlement."

As it turned out, she never filed those grievance forms because that night Barry Fields ceased to be a problem.

Chapter Eighteen

Although my swollen face made me look lopsided, I arrived at work on time the next morning, thus ignoring Barry's verbal pink slip. To my relief, the day started as normally as any day at a zoo can, which isn't very. A check of the squirrel monkey's night house revealed we were one female short. She'd picked the lock.

I called a Code Blue on my radio, and soon the grounds around Monkey Mania swarmed with keepers and volunteers looking up into the trees.

"Who escaped?" Zorah asked, as she scanned an overhanging eucalyptus.

"Lana, one of the younger females. She hasn't been herself since Barry slammed into her."

She transferred her attentions from the eucalyptus to me. "You said then that none of the monkeys was hurt." From her tone, I knew she wouldn't have cared if one of the monkeys had bit the zoo director's head off during the attack as long as the animal didn't chip a tooth doing it.

"They were scared, Lana most of all. She's always been shy."

Zorah studied the tree again. "Barry's a menace, all right, but our problems with him may soon be over. I have a nine o'clock appointment with Aster Edwina. She may not like to dirty her hands with the everyday business of running the zoo, but she won't put up with violence against animal or staff."

"She's coming *here*?" It was like Moses descending from Mount Sinai.

"Nah, I have to drive over to the castle." She gave a shudder. "Place gives me the creeps." This from a woman who suffered no qualms working with lions and rhinos.

"Want me to come with you?"

"Not necessary. As Dr. Kate said, you're not the only woman who's been having trouble with our exalted director. All I had to do was talk them into making formal complaints against him. And that was easy."

"Who else, then?"

"You'd be surprised." She refused to say more.

A few minutes later, Lana returned to the night house on her own, apparently deciding freedom wasn't all it was cracked up to be. After inspecting her for injuries and finding none, I fed her a half teaspoon of peanut butter, her favorite treat, and released her to her friends.

We decided to keep the exhibit closed for the day to give the animals a chance to calm down. Before Zorah left for her appointment with Aster Edwina, she promised to order a combination lock, like the one on the gate in the anteater's holding pen. In the meantime, I would triple-lock the night quarters and hope that was enough.

The first indication something was amiss came while I was enjoying a late-morning latte at the Congo Cafe, right inside the zoo's entrance. As I watched the antics of the various visitors—almost as entertaining as watching the animals—I noticed three park rangers running toward the administration building. At first I didn't think too much of the commotion because trouble and zoos aren't strangers. The fact that no radio alert had been issued proved that whatever was going on had nothing to do with an animal's transgression, so I kept sipping my latte and watching the human parade.

I had just directed a bus load of sun-hatted senior citizens to the anteater enclosure when Zorah ran past the cafe, saw me, and yelled, "Be in the auditorium in ten minutes! I'm calling a full-staff assembly."

Judging from her expression as she raced by, the meeting with Aster Edwin must have been uncomfortable in the extreme. "Am I...?" Then I realized where I was, the number of zoo staffers nearby. I shut my mouth before it released the word "*fired.*"

She didn't notice my near-lack of discretion, just continued down the trail toward the administration building.

I gulped down the rest of my latte, and as I tossed the empty container in the trash can, my radio squawked, "Zookeeper One to all zoo personnel. Assemble in the auditorium immediately after following standard safety procedures. Repeat. All zoo personnel, with the exception of concessions staff and volunteers, assemble in the auditorium immediately."

"That's weird," Jack Spence said, making me jump. He'd approached without my noticing him. For such a tall man, he could be surprisingly quiet. "We've got, what, over two hundred people on staff? Granted, not all of them are here today, but still, this must be something really big. I mean, we're using the auditorium, for Pete's sake!"

Energy bills being what they were, the auditorium, which sat behind the administration building, was used only for special events. Firing a wayward keeper such as myself wouldn't rate the room.

"Zorah had a meeting with Aster Edwina this morning," I told him. "Maybe that's what she's going to talk about."

"Let's hope the old bat hasn't decided to dump the zoo."

I stopped. "What made you say that?"

When he kept walking, I ran to catch up. "A hunch," he said. "But I could be wrong."

"The zoo's part of the Gunn Trust. No matter what happens, she can't dump it."

"Like the Trust can't be broken? For all we know, she's had it up to here with the zoo's problems, and now with your and Barry Fields' little brawl, has found a way to cut it loose."

"Are you blaming me for what happened?"

He shook his head. "What else could you do when the creep grabbed you? But it's too bad you couldn't figure out another way to spring the anteater from that holding pen." His big hand slapped my back. "Buck up, kid. For all we know, Zorah's going to announce that China's shipping us a couple of pandas."

But the announcement had nothing to do with pandas.

Once everyone assembled in the auditorium, Zorah, flanked by two park rangers, stepped to the podium. She wasn't used to speaking in public, and sweat trickled from her broad brow. After flicking her index finger at the microphone to make certain it was on, she began.

"Um, this morning I had a meeting about an internal issue with Aster Edwina Gunn. After she heard…after we discussed the issue for a while, she placed a phone call to the zoo director's office."

I tensed. Maybe I *was* the problem.

Her next words eased my concern. "Helen Gifford, Mr. Fields' secretary, informed Ms. Gunn that he hadn't come in to work yet, but once Ms. Gunn told her that…mmm, that the matter was important and he'd better get his ass…uh, that he'd better come up to the castle immediately, Helen jumped in a cart and drove over to his house. So." More perspiration rolled down Zorah's forehead. "Look, I, er, I'm sorry to…" She stopped to wipe the sweat away.

After clearing her throat, she continued. "I'm sorry to inform you that sometime during the night, Mr. Fields, uh…" She raised her eyes and stared at the auditorium's fluorescent lights. One was blinking on and off. She gulped, shut her eyes, and spit out the rest of the sentence.

"Oh, hell, I'm just gonna go ahead and say it. Barry's dead."

Once the cries of shock died down, she continued. "We're all grown-ups here, right? So I'll be straight with you. Helen says it looks like he was mu…uh, she said it looked like, mmm, foul play was involved. The police are on their way here to talk to me and…and…and some other people. If they want to question you, cooperate, okay? And, uh, if any of you have information about what happened to him, please come forward."

She shielded her eyes from the lights with a shaking hand. "That's it for the announcement, but I need to see the following people in my office right away. Dr. Kate Long. Kim Markowski. Jack Spence. Teddy Bentley." With a sigh of relief, she finished, "Everybody else, go back to work. Just do me a favor and don't mention this to the zoo's visitors. What with the media and all, the news will get out fast enough. And let's make sure our animals don't bear the brunt of this, okay? As always, their welfare comes first."

She turned off the mike and left the stage with the two park rangers. They were guarding her, I realized, probably on orders from the sheriff. Did he think she was about to make a run for it?

For a moment the auditorium was strangely silent except for the bear keeper's voice, which climbed so high it could have shattered glass. "Foul play? Did she say foul play? As in *murder*?"

That did it. As the auditorium erupted into chaos, I headed for the exit, Jack hard on my heels.

"Teddy?"

"What?"

"Didn't you hear what I asked?"

"Yeah. She said 'foul play.' And before that, she started to say 'murdered.'"

His craggy face creased with worry. "Are you in trouble?"

I slowed, letting the other keepers stream around us. Of all the people filing past us, not one was crying. The zoo director would not be missed. "Why should I be in trouble?"

He bit his lip so hard I feared it would bleed. "The names she called. You. Me. And everyone else present when Barry, ah, did what he did to you."

And when I'd bloodied his nose. "The police have to start somewhere." Like with people who had motives.

"You're lucky you used to have a thing with the sheriff. This might be time to rekindle the old flame."

I grabbed his arm. "What the hell do you mean by that?"

He jerked his arm away. "You know what I mean."

"You think the sheriff would let a suspect go just because he has a thing for her?"

"It worked with Barry, didn't it?"

I was so furious I stopped talking to him. When we reached the administration building, a small crowd of keepers was milling around Zorah's desk pumping her for more information. While the park rangers hovered in the background, she batted at the keepers as if shooing away gnats. "I don't know, I don't know," she kept repeating. "I promise I'll share whatever news I get, but all I know now is that Helen said there was blood all over the place."

That silenced the swarm for a moment, but they soon started up again.

"Where was the blood? Chest? Stomach? Head?"

"Was the furniture overturned, like there'd been a big fight or a robbery? I saw on a *Law & Order* rerun the other night…"

Zorah caught my eye and stood up, her big bulk towering over the others. "You guys need to leave, because I have to talk to Teddy. Go on now. Get out."

As the keepers filed out grumbling, Dr. Kate battled past them into the office. "Can things possibly get worse around here?"

Zorah nodded. "They're about to." She looked over at me again. "Teddy, I hate to say this, but you know how fast gossip travels around this place. What happened between you and Barry yesterday is already common knowledge. I think that's why the sheriff wants to see you. And the others who witnessed the, uh, argument."

At this, I glared at Jack. The gossip monger had the grace to blush.

Her voice bitter, Zorah said, "I've had some experience with the sheriff lately, and I can tell you that no matter how crazy things sound, you'd better tell him the truth. He's not dumb, and he…"

A deputy picked that moment to enter. "The sheriff wants to see you people up at the zoo director's house."

"Why doesn't he come down here?" Zorah asked. "We can use the director's office now that he's, um, not going to be using it any more."

The deputy frowned. "The sheriff needs to stay on the scene until the crime techs finish up."

After he bundled us into his squad car, no one spoke on the way to Barry's house, located on the zoo's far northeastern boundary. Separated from the public areas by a thick stand of Monterey pine, it was almost invisible from the public area of the zoo. The lush vegetation rendered the house a perfect murder site.

The squad car pulled past a sign declaring ZOO STAFF ONLY, through the sumac-lined lane, and into the gravel parking area. Four other squad cars and a county crime tech van were parked in the yard, along with an ambulance. Deputies and EMTs stood around chatting. No one seemed particularly disturbed except for Helen Gifford, slumped on a chaise lounge. After warning us not to talk to her, the deputy let us out.

The door to the house opened and Joe came out, flanked by three more deputies. He beckoned me over to a picnic table under the shade of an elderly oak. Giving my battered face a careful look, he winced, then recovered himself. Sitting down, he took a small tape recorder out of his shirt pocket and placed it on the redwood table.

"What's that?" I asked, stupidly.

"A tape recorder."

"You're going to record me?"

"You are so astute." When he pressed a button, a tiny red light came on.

I looked over at Zorah and Dr. Kate, who were being interviewed separately, no tape recorders in evidence. "Why are you doing this?"

"Because I hear that you and the zoo director had a lover's quarrel yesterday." His face was devoid of expression.

"That's not tr…"

"We'll follow up with a formal interview at the sheriff's office tomorrow, but for now I want to get everything down while your memory is fresh." He raised his voice and spoke directly into the recorder. "It's twelve forty-five p.m. Friday, May twelve, outside the residence of the deceased, Barry Fields, at the Gunn Zoo. This is the first interview with Theodora Bentley. Ms. Bentley, where were you around two a.m. last night?"

I swallowed. "On the *Merilee*. Asleep."

"Alone?"

My face flamed. "Yes, alone. Joe, what happened to Barry?"

"You don't know?" His eyes looked into mine without the least hint of affection.

"No, I don't. That's why I'm asking."

"Do you own a gun?"

"No!"

"Do you have access to a gun? Through your mother, perhaps?"

"What, you think Caro totes a Magnum to Library Guild luncheons?"

He sat back and crossed his arms across his chest. "Now that's interesting. What made you say 'Magnum'? When I asked if you have access to a gun, I didn't specify manufacturer or caliber."

Oh, God. Was there a Magnum something-or-other lying beside Barry's body? In my panic, the red light on the tape recorder seemed to glow brighter. "Because that's the only kind of gun I know anything about. There was one on that old TV show with what's-his-name, the tall guy with the mustache. I watch the reruns when the reception's too fuzzy for *Animal Planet*."

"Tom Selleck."

"Who's that?"

"The tall guy with the .357 Magnum."

"Joe, was Barry shot?"

"Your words, not mine."

Leaning back, I crossed my arms, too, increasing the distance between us. Forcing myself to ignore the tape recorder, I stared straight at him. "I'm not saying anything else until I call my attorney."

After a silence too lengthy for comfort, Joe spoke again, his voice chillingly formal. "That's certainly your right, Ms. Bentley. Have him or her call me at his or her earliest convenience to set up an interview at the station first thing tomorrow."

He leaned forward and clicked off the recorder.

Chapter Nineteen

As soon as we made it back to the administration building, I ran into a stall in the ladies' room, fished out my cell, and called Tommy Prescott.

"I've been expecting to hear from you," the attorney said.

"You were?" My voice bounced off the bathroom walls, sounding as hollow as I felt.

"Zorah Vega phoned me the minute she found out about the zoo director's death. I hate to tell you this, Teddy, but since I'm already representing her re the other murder, our firm can't represent you. However, Jessica Kimbroe, one of my old law school buddies, is a top criminal law specialist in the City and she's already told me she has room for you on her calendar. She's almost as good as me. Absolutely ruthless."

Funny how we all hate attorneys until we need one. Praying Tommy's assessment of the woman was accurate, I called her immediately. She agreed to contact the sheriff and arrange an interview.

"Don't talk to him until I'm present," Kimbroe warned. She had a young voice, but there was a lot of edge to it. "Without meaning to, clients can blurt out some pretty damaging stuff."

Remembering my injudicious comment about the murder weapon, I swore to keep my mouth shut. We hung up. A few minutes later she called back and said we were scheduled to talk with the sheriff at one p.m. Saturday. I wondered if she charged double time for weekend work. Where was I going to get the money to pay for all this unless I dipped into the pool of my father's ill-gotten gains?

Glum, I went back to the office and found the others grouped in a circle around Barry's secretary. In defiance of sheriff's orders, they were pumping her for information. Helen's middle-aged face, normally not all that creased for a woman in her late fifties, looked ravaged. She acknowledged me with a weak wave, but kept on talking.

"...been banging on the door for a what seemed like a long, long time, I went ahead and turned the knob. It wasn't locked. By then I'd started worrying. Not answering his phone or radio wasn't like Barry, and since both his Beemer and his zoo cart were parked in the drive, I realized he was still inside, maybe sick. You know how he is, *was*. A Type A personality, the type that keels over from a sudden heart attack. So I went in."

She gulped. "At first I didn't see him because he was wedged between the sofa and the wall. It...it looked like he'd been trying to hide."

"Could you tell the manner of death?" This from Dr. Kate.

"Oh, yeah. Since my father was a hunter, I've seen animals sh...uh, I know what gunpowder smells like. Besides, there was blood on the wall near the door, in the entryway, across the carpet —we're going to have to order a new one—all the way to where I actually found him."

If Helen's description was accurate, Barry had been shot as soon as he opened the door. After he didn't go down right away, the killer chased him through the living room to deliver the *coup de grace* as he cowered behind the sofa. I shuddered. Somebody had wanted to make sure he was good and dead.

As Helen wound down, Zorah reached over and tapped me on the shoulder. "I need to talk to you in private."

The others exchanged meaningful looks, but Jack was the first to speak. "On the way back, we compared notes. Most of the questions the deputies asked were about your problems with

Barry, what you did when he hit you, what he said about firing you." He had trouble meeting my eyes.

Dr. Kate seemed uncomfortable, too, but at least she addressed her comments to my face. "The deputy I talked to asked if you had a history of violence. You do have an attorney, don't you?"

I nodded. But something felt odd about this. Since Zorah had already been arrested for Grayson's murder, why were the police focusing on me as the prime suspect? Why not her? Not that I would have it any other way, of course.

While I stood there trying to figure things out, Zorah made a big show of looking at her watch. "You guys better get back to your posts. Helen, there's nothing here for you to do, so go home for the day. And everybody, please be careful what you say. Let's not give the police any more ammunition to use against us."

As soon as the others were gone, I asked her, "Is there something you're not telling me?"

"I have an alibi for this one." She didn't look as happy as she should have.

"I'm glad to hear it." And I was.

"When Barry got shot—the sheriff thinks it was around two a.m.—I was at San Sebastian General Hospital surrounded by a ton of witnesses, some of them even cops. It'll be in tomorrow's paper, so I might as well tell you. My nephew was shot late last night over some kind of drug thing, and I was down there at the emergency ward holding his hand with the rest of the family. There were cops stationed at the door."

When I recovered from my shock, I asked, "Is he all right?"

"The little punk's doing fine but the bullet took off half his earlobe. I just wanted you to know that the sheriff's already checked out my alibi and I'm in the clear on this one. And that he's, uh, he's looking elsewhere now."

Like at me.

"Teddy, think hard. Are you sure there's no one who might have seen you at the *Merilee* last night? Friend? Lover?"

"Just my dog and cat, and they're not talking."

A crafty look flitted across her face. "Come to think of it, I have a cousin who keeps a fishing boat down at the harbor. Maybe he was out walking last night right around the time Barry was killed and saw you fussing around your boat, doing something with a sail. Get what I mean?"

Her clumsy attempt at giving me an alibi made me feel better. "That's very nice of you, Zorah, but I'll be all right. And by the way, the *Merilee* doesn't have sails. She's not that kind of boat."

"Oh."

"I didn't do it, you know. Murder Barry."

She raised her eyebrows. "As if I'd care if you did."

On that friendly note, we returned to our duties.

◇◇◇

Saturday, my attorney made mincemeat out of Joe.

He sat in his office chair, his deeply tanned features arranged in a stern expression. His warm, Irish blue eyes spoiled the effect, though, and Jessica Kimbroe was quick to notice.

The moment he referenced the right cross I'd delivered to Barry's nose, she laughed. "Oh, come on, Sheriff Rejas. So an employee who was the target of a supervisor's unwanted sexual advances defended herself. Big deal. That gives my client no more reason to kill him than all the other employees he harassed." With her long legs, spidery eyelashes, shoulder-length blond hair and enormous breasts, she looked like a Playboy Bunny on steroids, but the overdone look was intentional. Tommy had informed me, in a follow-up telephone conversation that morning, that she was such a killer in court because opposing council kept forgetting there was a brain attached to all that cleavage.

It didn't work with Joe, though.

Ignoring her appearance, he said, "From the new splint the victim was sporting, it looks like she hit him hard enough to break his nose."

"I did?" For some reason, that information loosened the small clog of grief blocking my heart. Poor Barry. Not only had he been murdered, he'd go to his grave wearing a nose splint. "But I didn't mean to! I just..."

My attorney nudged me with her elbow. "Quiet."

Joe's face would have made a poker-player proud. "Is there anything you want to tell me?"

Another nudge. "No, there isn't," Jessica answered.

"But I…"

This time her nudge almost knocked me off my chair. "My client has nothing more to say. Now either arrest her or say goodbye."

"Then goodbye, and make sure your client doesn't leave town."

When we got outside, the attorney smiled. "That went well." She walked so fast on her spike heels that I had to trot to keep up with her.

"You're kidding," I panted, hurrying my steps.

"He's only fishing. I do have one question for you, though."

"Ask away."

We reached the parking lot and found her car, an electric blue Mercedes long enough to haul freight. She opened the door for me and the scent of expensive leather rushed out to mingle with the smell of hot asphalt. As I slid into the passenger's seat, she asked, "Do you and the sheriff have a history?"

"Kind of."

She smiled. "Want some free legal advice? When this is all over, kiss and make up. He's *hot*."

<>◇<>

Knowing that an interview with the sheriff could be rough on the nerves, Zorah had given me Saturday off. Lying on the deck of the *Merilee* with nothing better to do than watch the gulls feast on garbage spilling out of an overloaded Dumpster, I decided that relaxation was overrated. I'd already finished the Jack Hanna book I'd been reading, and the Saturday afternoon TV programming was so bad as to be nonexistent. But as I sat there bored, something my attorney had said popped into my sludgy brain.

That gives Teddy no more reason to kill him than all the other employees he harassed.

Other employees. It was time I found out who else Barry had been bothering.

I grabbed my cell and punched in Jessica's number, but received her answering machine. Then I called Zorah. My attorney's information must have come from Tommy Prescott, and the only place he could have heard it was from Zorah, his own client. Did lawyers exchange information? Or was that against their code of so-called ethics?

When Zorah picked up, I didn't waste time with chit chat. "Who else was Barry harassing?"

A dark chuckle. "I prefer to keep the names of the women involved confidential, but I can tell you this. He was quite the horn dog, a *Hornus canis* of the highest order."

"I need to know their names."

"No you don't."

"Yes I do."

A sigh. "Ask yourself, if you were the kind of guy who saw himself as a stud, who would you set your sights on? Besides you and the Bentley millions, of course." Realizing what she'd just said, she backtracked quickly. "Which is not to say you're not cute enough to attract men on your own."

"Zorah…"

"My mouth is sealed. As much as I owe you, Teddy, I'm not going to betray other women's confidences." With that, she hung up.

More gulls arrived, along with a couple of black-bellied plovers. They haggled over the garbage for a while, but when a charter fishing boat pulled away from the dock, most flew off after it. Watching them disappear over the horizon, I picked up the phone and called Zorah again.

"What now, Teddy?"

"Barry was married and divorced twice."

"Which isn't much, by California standards. What's your point?"

"Give me his ex-wives' names. If you know them."

She thought about that for a moment. "If I do, will you stop bothering me? Erasmus, one of the flamingos, got out again and I need to do something about that stupid enclosure. He's the third runaway flamingo in a month."

I crossed my fingers. "I promise."

"Hang on while I pull his file. I seem to remember…"

She put me on hold and Wayne Newton began singing "Danke Schöen." When he moved onto "Red Roses for a Blue Lady," she came back on the line. "Have a pen?" Without waiting for a reply, she rattled off the names and telephone numbers.

"Those are both San Francisco exchanges."

"Sure. He's from there. Born and raised."

Names and numbers duly written down, I reiterated my other reason for calling. "The other women Barry was harassing. How about Dr. Kate? Kim Markowski? Miranda DiBartolo?"

"Oh, for God's…." She stopped, then started again. "Not Kim. Now I gotta go see a man about a flamingo. Bye." She hung up.

I looked at my watch and discovered it wasn't yet two o'clock, plenty of time to drive up to San Francisco. But first I'd give the ex-wives a call and see if they'd found out what had happened to him.

Sue Fields, wife No. 1, didn't pick up her phone so I left a message, then tried Pamela Curiani, Wife No. 2, a Bay Area yacht broker. Not only was she home, but once I'd explained my involvement with the case and my concern for Zorah, she loosened up. Apparently she felt kinship with any woman who'd been wronged by any man. Especially her ex.

"You're that poor zookeeper's friend, huh? I read about her arrest. Good luck to her, I say, and to you, too. That joker had a talent for spreading misery. He couldn't keep his hands to himself, which is why I'm the *ex*-Mrs. Barry Fields."

Considering the reason for my own divorce, our hearts beat as one on that issue. "How long were you married?"

"Six years, which was way too long. I must have masochistic tendencies I'm unaware of."

"Were there any problems in the marriage? Besides the infidelity, I mean."

A bitter laugh. "All kinds. He liked money, especially mine. He could never get enough."

I sat up straighter. "Was he having financial difficulties?"

"Not really. He was greedy. It came from being raised poor, I think. His mother, who wasn't married to his father, by the way, lived in one of those welfare-subsidy apartments over in Hunter's Point. I'll give the bastard this, though. After he graduated from college—on a full-bore scholarship, I might add—he never looked back. When we first met, I'd recently brokered the sale of almost an entire fleet full of luxury yachts, so I was living the high life. I ran into him at an A-list party where I was trying to sell a few more. He could literally smell money, which I guess is what made him so good at what he did. Right after we married, he insisted we open a joint checking account and to keep the peace I went along. As things turned out, he availed himself of it about ten times more often that I did. And though for a while he earned more than me—the yacht market turned soft for a couple of years—his deposits were always less than mine."

"Was he hiding money?"

"The scum bucket sure was, but my forensic accountant found it. Barry came away with a lot less than he'd counted on, which is why he took that loser job at the zoo."

I winced. Zorah had wanted that "loser job" with all her heart.

"Next time around, I'm getting a pre-nup," she continued, acid in her voice. "If there is a next time."

Before we hung up, she tried to sell me a sixty-five foot Irwin ketch.

I'd gone back to watching the remaining gulls pick through the garbage when my cell rang. Sue Fields, Wife No. 1, returning my call. She, too, already knew about Barry's death, but unlike his other ex, her voice carried sadness. I also noticed she'd kept his last name.

The conversation started off much the same as with Wife No. 2, with me telling her about Zorah being charged with Grayson's murder, and me now under suspicion for Barry's. To my relief, she sounded even more sympathetic than Wife No. 2.

"Barry broke my heart," she said. "Over and over, with each new woman."

"How many, if I may ask?" Although at this point, the question was merely rhetorical.

"Too many to count. Women and money were aphrodisiacs for him. As bad as he was, though, I'd probably still be married to him if it wasn't for the incident with my aunt. Look, I don't feel comfortable talking about this over the phone. That's a San Sebastian County area code you're calling from, isn't it?"

As it turned out, she was talking to me on her cell while driving down the Coast to San Luis Obispo. We made arrangements to meet in an hour at Fred's Fish Market, where she'd planned to stop anyway for boat-fresh salmon. "You can't miss me," she finished up. "I'll be the tall brunette in the pink pants suit. Save an outdoor table in the smoking section."

When she tooled into the restaurant parking lot an hour later driving a ten-year-old Infiniti that needed a paint job, I was sitting at an outside table overlooking the Pacific, batting other people's cigarette smoke away from my face.

She sat down and lit up a Winston. We chatted about women things for a while, then she got down to it. "I'm originally from Lodi, but I'd just started business school at University of San Francisco when I met Barry at a campus kegger. He was about to graduate and had already snagged a job raising money for some charity, and to this country girl, he seemed incredibly sophisticated. I liked the way he talked, the way he looked—this was before he started losing his hair, you understand—and I loved going to social events with him and watching him work the room. He'd get into these deep conversations with people who somehow always turned out to be super important. It was like he had a homing device that let him zoom right in on the real players. Know what I mean?"

I gave her a smile. "He could tell the difference between zircons and diamonds."

Her eyes, rimmed in black eyeliner, moistened. Or maybe it was the cigarette smoke. "That's one way of putting it."

Which begged the question. Nothing about her, from her heavy makeup to her old car, signaled serious money and although she was attractive enough, she was no beauty queen. Given Barry's propensity for "real players," why had he bothered with her?

She noticed my puzzled expression. "My maiden name was Epple."

Ah. Epple Farm Equipment and Supplies, based in Lodi, was the largest farm and ranch supplier in the state, with branches throughout all the inland valleys, including San Sebastian.

"Technically, I inherited everything at seventeen after my parents were killed in a car wreck," she continued. "Four years later, when I met Barry, I was still young and dumb enough to think he loved me for myself. But as you said, he could tell zircons from diamonds." She flexed her fingers, drawing my attention to a ring with a diamond almost the size of her thumbnail. No wedding ring, though. "Anyway, he told me this sad story about being raised by a struggling single mother who lived in government housing, that she'd died while he was in high school, and he'd had to make it on his own. As an orphan myself, it really got to me."

She took another long drag on her cigarette. "Turned out, the whole thing was a crock. His mother was still alive and no longer struggling. She'd married a dentist, but Barry didn't get along with his stepfather so they were estranged. I didn't find out the truth until we were married. Fortunately, my Aunt Evelyn, who raised me after my parents died, was the executor of my parents' estate until I turned twenty-five, and she kept him from getting his hands on most of my money. But that's also what caused the problem that ended my marriage." She stabbed out her half-smoked cigarette.

"On the phone, you said something about an incident with your aunt?"

She shook another cigarette from her pack, muttering, "I need to stop this." She lit her second cigarette in five minutes. "Barry tried to blackmail her."

I sat up straight, though the movement engulfed me in second-hand smoke.

She took two more drags and put out that cigarette, too. When she looked at me again, anger sparked her eyes. "That was his big mistake, because I loved Aunt Evelyn. When I saw what he was trying to do to her…" Another cigarette slid from the pack. This time she didn't light up, just sat there looking at it while seagulls screamed overhead.

"Sue, what did he try to do?"

"I already told you. He tried to blackmail her."

"For…?"

She put the cigarette back into the pack. "I'm trying the Taper Off Smoking Plan. This week I'm limiting myself to five a day. Next week I'll be down to four. But you don't care about my addictions, do you? Okay, here's the deal. When my aunt was a teenager, she got mixed up with a local boy who…let's just say he was a bad influence. Anyway, he held up a gas station, and the attendant got shot. Thank God he didn't die. My aunt was driving the car. She'd been stupid enough to see it as a big adventure, you know, like Bonnie and Clyde, and didn't think beyond that. The shooting brought her to her senses. She broke up with her boyfriend and never told a soul what happened that night until Barry tried to do what he did. But she was willing to go to jail rather than give him access to my inheritance."

For a moment I couldn't speak. Barry had been even worse that I'd thought. Finally, I managed, "How did he find out about the robbery?"

"He had relatives in Lodi and one of them knew the boy involved. You know how small towns are."

I sure did. I tried to picture her aunt as a foolish teenager, then as a sad-but-wiser older woman trying her best to raise another foolish teenager and doing okay until Barry showed up. "When he approached your aunt, what did she do?"

A seagull swooped down and tried to steal a French fry from a nearby table. The man sitting there slapped it away in disgust.

Sue smiled. "He read my aunt wrong, really wrong. Instead of knuckling under, she invited both of us over for dinner, and during dessert, laid out the whole story. She finished by telling me what he'd threatened to do if she didn't funnel the lion's share of my inheritance his way."

"You believed that Barry tried to blackmail her."

"I was young and in love and believed in my husband."

I knew how dumb girls in love could be. "So he denied the whole thing?"

She gave me the saddest smile I've ever seen. "Wrong. He admitted it. He was very self-righteous about the whole situation and said that as a young married couple, we deserved to have my parents' money to 'work with,' as he called it, and not have to wait until I turned twenty-five. As soon as we arrived home, he made me watch as he called the sheriff and turned my aunt in. When I tried to stop him, he hit me hard enough to knock loose a tooth. The next day I filed for divorce."

The seagull came back. This time the man, finished with his meal and enjoying an after-burger smoke, let it have the French fry.

"What happened to your aunt?" I asked.

"She went to the police and confessed. Since the crime was more than thirty years old and the victim had made a full recovery, she wound up serving only a week in jail, plus six months' community service."

"How's she doing now?" Even a week in jail could be hard on a person. Zorah still hadn't fully recovered from her time in the slammer.

The smile brightened. "Oh, she's fine. In fact, her experience with the California corrections system inspired her to start a halfway house for newly-released female inmates with children. It's in San Luis Obispo, which is where I'm headed now. I brought an ice cooler and I'm going to load it up with enough fresh salmon to feed everyone."

I looked back toward her faded Infiniti and was willing to bet that Epple Farm Equipment and Supplies donated a lot more than salmon to the halfway house. Hard times cause some people to turn hard themselves, others to open their hearts.

After we'd said our goodbyes, I returned to the *Merilee* and sat on the deck for a while, wondering if Barry had changed much since his marriage to Sue Epple. That he wasn't above marrying for money, I'd already guessed. That he could be violent toward women came as no shock, either.

But blackmail? That created a whole new motive.

Chapter Twenty

The next day Dad, dressed like a casual yachtsman in chinos and windbreaker, paid a visit to the *Merilee*.

"What, not all bundled up for the cold May wind?" I asked, not halting at my task of swabbing the deck.

"Ha-ha." In the morning sun, his dyed black hair glistened. "What do you have to drink?"

"Just some cheap Riesling. Don't you think ten o'clock a little early to get started?"

"Too early to be drinking sludge, that's for sure." He plopped himself down on a deck chair. DJ Bonz and Miss Priss, who had been sunning themselves on the bow, jumped up to join him so he scrunched over to make room. "Ooo," he ruffled their fur. "Nice doggie, nice kitty! Does ooo remember ooo's Daddy?"

He sounded so much like me that I had to force myself not to smile. "Aren't you going to help me swab?"

"I prefer to watch others work."

"You ought to try it yourself, sometime. Work's good for the digestion."

"There's nothing wrong with my digestion." A pelican trailed by two gulls flew by. He watched them, his head laid back, the picture of contentment. "Anyway, my stomach's not the reason I stopped by. What's this I hear about some of the boats in the harbor losing their berths?"

While I swabbed, I told him about the complaint Maxwell Jarvis had lodged with the harbor master. "And before you bring it up, no, I'm not going to use the money you put in the Caymans account to fix up the *Merilee*."

"You always were a little prig."

"Hey, now! I am not a…" A backfire from the *Texas Hold 'Em*, a Hydra-Sport a few slips over, interrupted my denial. The owner had been tinkering with the engine all morning and it sounded like he was making it worse. When the noise faded, I decided not to bother defending my ethics to my father. It was like speaking Mandarin to a Greek. I changed the subject. "It's not a good idea for you to be sitting out here in the open. What if the sheriff drops by?"

He removed his sunglasses and gave me an unsettling look. "Right now your boyfriend is the least of my worries. I'm here to say goodbye."

"I told you, he's not…" I stopped swabbing. "You're going back to Costa Rica?"

"With Chuckles' goons waiting for me? Hardly. This time I think I'll try Indonesia. I've always liked the cuisine. Or Cameroon. Now *there's* an interesting place."

"Cameroon?!"

"The weather's nice. At times. And they've almost solved that malaria problem. Last night it occurred to me that I could make some serious money there. Did you know they export aluminum? I'm sure they could use some help with that. Best of all, Cameroon don't have much of an extradition agreement with the U.S., so as long as I stay clear of the Bakassi Peninsula—where nobody in his right mind goes these days, anyway—I should be fine. You could come visit. The country's crawling with elephants."

"Dad, I don't…"

Another backfire from the *Texas Hold 'Em*. A splash nearby. Then another. Suddenly I was lying face down on the *Merilee's* deck with my father on top of me. "What are you…?"

"Shut up and stay down! That was no backfire." Before I could say anything else, he'd rolled me into the salon hatch, then tumbled us both down the stairs. Bonz and Priss scrambled after us then headed for the forward cabin, where they buried themselves under cushions.

"How good's the motor?" my father hissed.

"The...the *Merilee's*?" I picked myself up off the floor, but I was so frightened I could hardly speak. "It can barely t-turn over!"

With a curse, he grabbed my cell phone from the galley table and punched in 9-1-1. "Send a patrol car to Gunn Landing Harbor immediately! There's a guy in the parking lot shooting at people. He almost hit someone on the *Merilee* at Slip 34, Teddy Bentley's boat. Hurry!"

"Who shot...?"

He ignored me. "Cops are on their way, but it'll take a while, so you need to hide." With that, he dragged me into the aft cabin.

"There's n-no place to hide in here." My throat was so dry the words hardly made it through.

"That's what you think." I'd never heard his voice so grim.

Before I could protest, he ripped the mattress off the bunk, lifted up the teak platform underneath—which I'd always thought was nailed down—to reveal an empty space large enough for one person. "Get in!"

"But what about —?"

Before I could say "you," he lifted me off my feet and threw me in. He slammed down the teak platform and replaced the mattress and bed coverings, leaving me in the dark. At first I feared I would suffocate, but then I realized there was a breathing hole next to me, probably hidden from the outside.

His voice was muffled but understandable. "Don't make a sound until the cops get here. I'll take care of this."

I heard a familiar snickety-snick. It took me a minute to connect it to some of the cop shows I'd seen on TV, the sound of the slide being pulled back on an automatic handgun. I don't know which shocked me the most: the fact that someone was shooting at us, or that the loving father who'd once read me bedtimes stories had just chambered a round.

"Dad? What's —?"

"Theodora, shut up."

Even I knew better than to argue with a man with a gun, so I shut up.

The hidey-hole was large enough not to be too uncomfortable, but my combination of fear, helplessness and guilt made it a misery. Fear because I didn't want my father hurt, let alone killed. Helplessness because there was nothing I could do for him; I didn't have so much as a hairpin to use for a weapon, only my bare hands. Guilt because I'd been so busy with the zoo, the murder investigation, and my financial problems that I'd forgotten the danger my father was in. If I'd been a better daughter, I would have insisted he stay away from the boat. And Caro's house.

Caro! Was she all right?

I heard a whimper and realized it was me.

I forced myself to remain silent. Whatever was happening to my father, he didn't need the distraction of a weeping woman.

I don't know how long I lay there, trying not to think, breathing stale air, rocking as the incoming tide lapped against the *Merilee*'s hull. I hoped the harbor was so crowded that the hit man wouldn't attempt an outright gun battle. Then again, since he had already taken a couple of pot-shots at my father as he sunned himself on the *Merilee*'s deck, he was probably crazy enough to do anything.

That observation made me so uncomfortable that I stopped thinking.

When what seemed like hours had passed, and I heard footsteps approach the aft cabin, I stopped breathing, too. Whoever it was began to throw aside the bedclothes, the mattress. As the teak platform was yanked away, I tensed, not knowing what to expect. Was I about to die, or be set free?

After the darkness, the light that blazed into my space was dazzling. But not enough so that I couldn't see my father's face.

"Cops are here," he said cheerily, over the sound of nearing sirens. "Now it's my turn!" With that, he hauled me out of the hidey-hole and threw himself into it. "Don't rat me out, Teddy," he said, as I lowered the teak platform.

I made up the bunk as neatly as possible, considering the hurry I was in.

Footsteps on board. The harsh squawk of a police radio.

It sounded like an angel.

The police were milling around the deck when Joe muscled his way onto the *Merilee*, the alpha male snapping at runts. He briefed his men, barked a few more orders, then looked at me with gentled eyes. The anger he'd shown in my hospital room had vanished. "You okay, Teddy?"

"Never been better." I tried a smile, but it wobbled at the corners.

When he put his arms around me, I pressed my head against his chest. "Oh, Joe."

He held me a few moments more, then let me go too soon. "It's too public up here. Let's go below where we can talk in private."

A crowd of liveaboarders, most of them having made their own frantic phone calls to 9-1-1, lined the dock. Snatches of their conversation drifted to me on the soft breeze.

"See, I told you those were gunshots."

"Somebody almost killed her the other night, didn't they?"

"What's this harbor coming to?"

Over my protests, Joe hustled me into the salon and sat me at the galley table. "Who was it?"

I kept my eyes averted from the aft cabin, hoping my father wouldn't sneeze or do anything else to give away his location. "I never saw the…the shooter, but like I told your deputies, it sounded like the shots came from the parking lot. It was probably the same guy who hit me on the head the other night."

"That's not what I meant. Who called 9-1-1 first? The dispatcher said the first call came from your cell phone, but that the caller was a man. I need to talk to him."

When you can't tell the truth, feign ignorance. "Huh?"

I didn't like the look he gave me. "Who was here with you?"

Don't look toward the aft cabin. Don't look toward the aft cabin. "I…I'm feeling faint. Can we go back topside so I can get some fresh air? Please?" Trying my best to act like a swoony Victorian maiden, I clutched at my breast and began to sway.

He didn't buy my act. "Oh, come off it. A woman who jumps into bear pits to save a child doesn't faint. So I'll ask again. We know there was a man with you when the bullets started flying. Who was it?"

Since it hadn't worked, I stopped my clutching and swaying. "Look, there was a guy with a gun out there, shooting. Not once but several times. I was terrified, so when I called 9-1-1 I was probably hoarse." Remembering that the best defense was offense, I added, "What difference does it make what I sounded like, anyway? The important thing is that somebody shot at me. Aren't you going to do anything about that?"

He rose from the table and walked into the forward cabin, where Bonz and Priss were still hiding under the cushions with only their tails protruding. He opened a few cabinets, poked around, and after finding nothing, walked to the aft cabin and repeated the process. Disappointed, he returned to the table. "He must have left."

"Who left?"

"Your father."

At that, I almost did faint. "Who?"

"You must think I'm stupid."

"I don't feel good. Please let me get some fresh air!" This time I wasn't faking.

With a sigh, he led me back outside and over to a deck chair. "Sit down. Take deep breaths." Then he leaned over me, put his lips to my ear, and whispered, "Have Daddy Dearest get the hell out of town, okay? I can't keep pretending not to recognize him."

As soon as the police left, I released my father from the hidey-hole, a dust bunny clinging to his hair. I brushed it away, then remade the bunk. "Sheriff Rejas says you'd better leave town."

"Great minds think alike." Now that it was safe, he sneezed. "By the way, I heard that entire conversation. What I can't figure out is why, with your mother and me as parents, you're such a bad liar."

I let the insult pass. "You have a gun, don't you?" I wondered if it was the same caliber as the one that had killed Barry Fields.

"Certainly I have a gun. I don't exactly fill teeth for a living." He frowned and brushed some dust off his windbreaker. "This'll have to go to the cleaners."

His easy dismissal of the danger we'd been in alarmed me further. "Please don't go back to Caro's. What if…?" Not being able to bear the thought of losing both of them, I couldn't finish the sentence.

Finally acknowledging my distress, he put his arms around me. "I'd never forgive myself if something happened to her. Or you. Apparently my idea that Chuckles wouldn't think to look for me so close to home was wrong. After I leave here I'm going straight to Al's sloop in Santa Cruz and I'll stay there until I can leave the country again. But you know what I was thinking while I was hiding? We're both taking it for granted that the shooter was one of Chuckles' henchmen, but we may be off base there. Those guys are better shots. By the way, have you considered that some of the nonsense you told the sheriff might actually be true, that you were the target and not me?"

I sat down hard on the bunk. He was right. I'd been so concerned about what Chuckles might do to my father that I'd forgotten my own danger. But when I thought more about it, it seemed that both shots had been aimed straight at him. "Dad, sit down. It's time for a serious talk."

"If it's about me, I'm not sure I'm up for anything more serious than a stiff drink." Still, he sat down.

"Have you considered giving yourself up? Now that both the Feds *and* Chuckles Fitzgerald are after you, it might be the smartest thing to do. You could go into the Witness Protection Program."

He shook his head. "I have no information to trade, ergo, no Witness Protection Program. The Feds would just slap me in a federal pen, where Chuckles has many, many friends. Before you could say 'jailhouse rubout,' I'd wind up in the laundry room with a shank in my back. I've got a better idea."

"What's that?"

"It's obvious I'm going to have to blow town in the next couple of days, but you could come with me. That way we'd both be safe and we could have fun!"

I gulped. "Me in Cameroon?"

"The world's a big place. As long as we keep moving, we wouldn't have to stick to non-treaty countries. If Cameroon doesn't turn you on, how about Prague? It's beautiful in the spring."

"Prague." I gulped again.

"Or Iceland, where we could watch the Grimsvotn volcano erupt. If you don't like ice, how about someplace warmer, like Venezuela?" A new energy filled his voice. "You've never been to Caracas, have you? Gorgeous weather year round, only twenty minutes from the beach, great theater and museums. We could ride the cable car up to the top of Mt. Avila and see the…"

"Dad, I'm not going anywhere with you. I'd miss my friends too much."

"Friends like Roarke Gunn? Why, he's a useless, lazy…"

"Lucy. Carlos. Bonz. Priss."

"Oh. Your animals."

"That's right. My animals. I have a wonderful life here and I'm not going to leave it."

"Then promise me one thing, Theodora."

"What?"

"That you'll stop snooping around. It might cut short your wonderful life."

Chapter Twenty-one

As soon as Dad left for Al Mazer's sloop, I called Caro. "Who do you know with a private plane? Someone needs to take a trip." Just in case the Feds were playing loosey-goosey with the wiretap laws again, I didn't name names.

No fool, Caro caught on immediately. "There's Cyril, I guess, but I don't know if our relationship has progressed far enough for me to ask that kind of favor. Why, dear? Is our friend ready to go back home?"

I knew she'd find out soon enough what had happened on the *Merilee.* "Now don't go getting upset or anything because nobody was hurt, but it looks like that funny guy from San Francisco has found him. Our friend was visiting today and, well, some gunfire was involved, but like I said, nobody was hurt."

A strangled noise, then a quick throat-clearing. "I...I understand. A Lear jet, maybe, and a pilot who can keep secrets."

"Yes, that's necessary, too."

"I'll get back to you." She rang off.

I tucked the cell phone into my pocket, and sat there for a moment, thinking about Joe. Why hadn't he told me he already knew about my father being in town and spared me so much misery? The minute I asked myself the question, I knew the answer. He couldn't. If he admitted he knew, he would have to do something about it. By pretending not to recognize my father, he could let him walk around a free man. The heaviness that had weighed down my heart since our hospital face-off went away.

I fished the cell back out of my pocket and began to punch in his number, but before I hit the fourth digit, I clicked off. This wasn't a conversation for a cell phone, either. I'd wait for a while, then drive into San Sebastian and talk to him in person. We could have dinner someplace quiet, then—as we say at the zoo—let nature take its course.

To cool off, I went up on deck just in time to see Roarke and Frieda Gunn approaching the *Merilee*.

"Are you okay?" Roarke called. "We heard there was trouble down here."

"Trouble's over."

After they'd stepped onboard, Frieda enveloped me in a hug, a gesture so unlike her that I was stunned. Had the maternal genes kicked in already? Dark circles shadowed her eyes, and like Roarke's, her hair was mussed. "Teddy, with everything that's happened, you simply can't stay here by yourself. Why don't you pack some clothes and come back with us to the *Tequila Sunrise* until things get sorted out? We have plenty of room."

Moving onto the *Sunrise* might be hopping from the frying pan into the fire, so I thanked them for their concern and politely declined. "But I'm glad you came over, because there was something I wanted to ask you. Everyone's always been curious as to why Grayson gave Barry the zoo director position. Did he ever explain why?"

Roarke snorted. "Grayson never discussed his zoo work with anyone other than Jeanette. Why do you care, anyway?"

"Just wondering."

"Someone banged you over the head, then shot at you, and you're 'just wondering' why Barry Fields got his stupid job?"

I shrugged. "Were Barry and Grayson acquainted before the job interview?"

"How would I know?" he snapped. "Look, I'm getting tired of all your questions. It's time…"

"Roarke, please." Frieda tugged at his sleeve. "She's been through a lot." To me, she said, "No. That was the first time they met. I happen to know because we were at one of Aster Edwina's excruciating Sunday dinners and Grayson—who'd just driven down from the City, where he'd spent a whole week doing interviews—was making fun of some of the applicants and Barry was one of them."

"He actually made *fun* of Barry?"

She grimaced. "He put a napkin on his head and flapped it around like a loose toupee. He even told us he'd decided to promote the head zookeeper to the position, so I was really surprised when only two days later he gave the job to the very guy he'd been making fun of. Especially since he'd already told us the man wasn't qualified for the position and didn't seem to like animals in the first place."

I winced at the thought of the napkin-flapping. So much for Grayson being a nice man. The more I learned about him, the less nice he seemed. But if he'd felt such contempt for Barry, what made him change his mind? I closed my eyes for a brief moment, trying to put things together.

"Teddy? Are you sure you don't want to go back to the *Tequila Sunrise* with us?"

I opened my eyes again. Frieda was so beautiful and now that I knew she was pregnant, the small bump in her stomach was obvious. It's odd how something can be right in front of you and yet you can't see it. "Thanks for the offer, but I'll be fine. One last question. You said that Grayson spent a whole week in San Francisco interviewing applicants. Jeanette was with him, right?"

"Probably. They did go everywhere together."

Roarke cut in. "Not this time. Jeanette told me they both drove up on the weekend but by Monday afternoon, with all the applicants traipsing in and out, she felt a migraine coming on so Grayson hired a limo and sent her home. He interviewed all week, then returned for that miserable Sunday dinner at the castle. I remember because Aster Edwina complained that he hadn't dressed for dinner, just bummed in wearing khakis and a golf shirt. Not that Jeanette cared. She was all over him. You'd think they'd been separated for a year. Between you and me, I don't know how he could stand it, but some men are like that, I guess. Terminally dependent."

So Grayson had spent almost a week by himself in San Francisco. Although this seemed to conflict with something else I'd heard—where?—it clarified other things. But it also raised another question. "Did they have a regular hotel they stayed at? I mean, what with the Trust and all, they had a lot of business in the City, so…"

Frieda raised her eyebrows. "I thought you knew. Aster Edwina keeps a townhouse in Pacific Heights for the convenience of any family members who needed to take regular trips up there. When we're not sailing, Roarke drives up there and meets with his broker every Monday. He spends the night and comes back the next morning. That's where Grayson conducted the zoo director interviews, too, not some anonymous hotel. Roarke and I always stay there when we go to the opera." She paused. "Come to think of it, that week was when we saw *Salome*. You know, the production with the nude scene."

With a wolfish grin, Roarke said, "For once, the soprano didn't look like a truck. Look, does Teddy have to know all this?"

Ignoring him, Frieda continued. "We were going to spend the night at the townhouse, but when we saw they'd already grabbed the master suite, we went over to the Sheraton."

Before they left for lunch, they gave me the townhouse's address, and for the second Sunday in a row, I jumped into my pickup and drove to San Francisco.

The Gunn townhouse, a nondescript, two-story brownstone with a For Sale sign in front, sat on a tree-lined residential street in Pacific Heights not too far from Henry and Pilar's Victorian. Backed up on Lafayette Park, the house felt secluded, at the same time, having good access to the restaurants and shops down the street. After circling the neighborhood several times, I found a parking space only three blocks away. No one answered when I rang the bell, so I walked down the street to Le Bon Appetit, a French bistro I'd passed earlier. While I was too late for lunch— the special was Lobster Newburg, Grayson's favorite, as Jeanette had told me—the waiter did manage to scrounge up a bowl of thick onion soup topped with bread and cheese. He left me alone to enjoy it at an outdoor table.

The weather being balmy, the sidewalk was filled with couples meandering along arm-in-arm, looking as if they were going nowhere in particular. Preteens on skateboards headed for the park at breakneck speed, while a few oldsters clanked along on their walkers, eyeing them with irritation. Michael and I had enjoyed such lazy Sundays, and in my youthful naiveté, I'd thought they would continue forever. How could I have been so blind?

The answer wasn't difficult. The old cliché was true; love *is* as blind as an *Antrozous pallidus*, more commonly known as a bat.

I was staring blankly at the storefronts across the street—a collection of galleries, crafts shops, a puppet theater, and a Starbuck's when two blondes as alike as identical twins exited the coffee shop. Only as they crossed the street and passed in front of me did I realize how different they were: one was a teen, the other at least ten years older. One had blue eyes, the other brown. One was pretty, the other plain.

The waiter, who saw me watching, said, "From a distance, all blondes look alike."

I'd almost made up my mind to return to Gunn Landing when I saw a long limo slide by the restaurant and double-park in front of the townhouse. Ignoring the flurry of honks behind him, a uniformed chauffeur stepped out and opened the passenger door. Aster Edwina swanned out, regal as a queen. The limo departed.

I threw down a ten. After noticing the waiter's offended look, added another five, and ran after her.

"If it isn't little Theodora Bentley," She already had the key to her townhouse in her hand. "What brings you to the Gunn *pied à terre?*"

The question I needed to ask was unforgivably rude, but since she was such a rude woman herself, what did it matter? "Why are you selling your townhouse?"

Her glacial face iced over even further. "Go home, you nosy child." She turned her back on me and unlocked the door. Before I could explain myself, she slipped inside and slammed the door in my face.

But not before I understood that her refusal to answer was an answer in itself. She might be prone to physical violence where grape-stealing kids were concerned, but she never, ever lied.

So I took her advice and went home.

Several people, some yacht club habitués and even a few zoo staffers had gathered for sundown cocktails on the deck of the *Tequila Sunrise*. When I stepped onto the boat, Frieda, surrounded by a group of women admiring her tummy bump, motioned me over. I shook my head, pointing a finger at Roarke, who hunkered alone under the boom. When he saw me approach, he gave an easy smile.

"Gorgeous, humm?" He gestured westward with his wineglass, where the descending sun cut a red and gold swath across the Pacific.

"Can I ask you some more questions?"

His expression hardened. "You're getting tiresome, Teddy. Aster Edwina called and warned that you might drop by. You offended her deeply."

"She's always offended." I lowered my voice further. "You're having an affair, aren't you? Who is she?"

"I don't kiss and tell." He sounded a bit smug. And why not? Men like Roarke felt entitled to the best life has to offer, regardless of how miserable their behavior made their wives.

"That's why Aster Edwina's selling the townhouse, because she's tired of it being used for reasons having nothing to do with business. And your wife knows all about you and your women, doesn't she?" I'd always wondered why such a beautiful woman felt so insecure. Now I knew. Henry Gunn's catty comment about his new wife, Pilar, came back to me, that Pilar had once been after Roarke. To many women, movie star looks connected to piles of money acted as strong aphrodisiacs.

Roarke's smile was mean. "Watch yourself. You can accuse me of anything you want but keep my wife out of it."

I glanced over at Frieda. Other than those dark circles under her eyes, she looked like she'd never had a bad day in her life, but having once been married to a serial cheater myself, I understood her misery.

"Who —?"

He didn't let me finish. Grabbing me by the wrist, he squeezed hard. Too hard for comfort. "For the sake of our lifelong friendship, tomorrow I'll pretend this conversation never happened. But right now, I want you off my boat."

There was no point in arguing, so when he released me I left him to his party. On my way back to the *Merilee*, I went over our conversation again. Who could the woman be? Who was attractive enough, secretive enough? I'd almost made it to my boat slip when the answer popped into my head. Roarke didn't always prefer blondes. When we were teenagers, he'd dated a long series of dark-haired women. And at one of his cocktail parties several weeks earlier, an odd look had passed between him and a brunette I happened to know.

Energized, I headed for the parking lot, climbed into my pickup and drove to the zoo. Bypassing the zookeeper's parking area, I took the back road through the lengthening shadows of eucalyptus trees to Dr. Kate's house. This time I wouldn't let her evasions keep me from the truth.

After my knock, the front door opened, but not by Kate. It was her husband. Although I'd known that Lowell Long had been confined to a wheelchair for the past several months, I was dismayed by his deterioration. The multiple sclerosis that had weakened his muscles had also ravaged his face, and instead of looking like the forty-something Silicon Valley hotshot he'd once been, he now resembled someone's great-grandfather. A pang of guilt hit me so hard that I almost turned around and went home. But remembering that Zorah was still suspected of murdering Grayson, I stood my ground.

"Hi, Lowell. I need to speak to Dr. Kate."

"Inna house. Wanna c...come in?" He slurred like a drunk, but I knew he didn't drink. This was simply more evidence of MS' downward spiral.

Before I could answer, I heard footsteps coming down the hall. Kate, looking harried, shoved a cell phone into her pocket. When she saw me, she frowned.

As he pivoted his wheelchair around, I met her eyes and placed a finger over my lips.

She understood. "Honey, we need to talk about zoo matters. Would you watch the kids? They're in the family room."

"Always g...glad...t...t..." He stopped, simplified his answer. "Yesss."

She bent down and kissed his cheek. "Thank you. I'll be right outside if you need me." She closed the door behind her and followed me to a grouping of lawn chairs set up near a big bougainvillea. Its magenta flowers glowed in the dusk.

Once out of sight of her husband, she dropped her smile and chose the chair across from me, not the one that almost touched mine. "Why so mysterious? I don't like keeping secrets from him."

"If Zorah's freedom weren't at stake, I wouldn't be here. But she's my friend and she's facing a murder charge."

"Then hurry it up."

"Two questions. One, what was in the independent vet study?"

"As I've said before, I can't tell you. It's merely a prelim, and therefore confidential."

"Question two. Where were you when Grayson was murdered?"

Her obvious irritation flared into anger. "In bed with my husband, probably. From what the police said, I'm pretty sure

I'd left the fund-raiser long before Grayson wound up in the anteater enclosure. As if it's any of your business."

"Are you sure you weren't in bed with Roarke Gunn? And wasn't that him on the phone, warning you I was on my way up here?"

To my surprise, she began to laugh, her wild black hair shaking as her shoulders heaved. With an effort, she pulled herself together. Wiping her eyes, she said, "Jesus, Teddy, what have you been smoking and can I have some?"

Startled at her reaction, I tried again. "But I saw the way you looked at him at one of his parties. I know he's having an affair."

The big grin vanished. "Yeah, he is, with some young idiot who thinks he'll leave his wife for her. That'll be the day. Regardless of the bastard's behavior, he loves Frieda. And that 'look' you're talking about? I saw him and his new little hotsy together once, at some out-of-the-way restaurant near Carmel. They were all over each other, so the next time I saw him I told him what I thought of all that screwing around behind his poor wife's back. One more thing. The phone call I was on when you came banging at the door? That was the woman who runs the book club I belong to. She was rescheduling our next meeting because she's having trouble with her recent tummy tuck." She laughed again. "We're reading the new Updike, which as usual, is about adultery. Talk about apropos, huh?"

I felt like a fool and I guess it showed on my face. Before I debased myself further, Kate leaned forward and tapped me on the knee. "Don't take it so hard, Teddy. You're not the only one who thought I was having an affair with Roarke."

An owl hooted from the eucalyptus and I looked around to see that all traces of light had vanished. Something rustled in the bushes behind me, and the owl dove out of the tree. The rustling intensified until a small animal screamed. When the owl flew back into the tree, something wriggled in its talons. Kate ignored it.

The small but vicious wildlife drama finished, I asked the obvious. "Who else thought so?"

"Barry." Her humor disappeared. "Like you, he misread the signs, although he had more to go on. He was having his second job interview with Grayson the same day I happened to be shopping up in San Francisco. I dropped by the Gunn's townhouse to have lunch with Aster Edwina in case she was in, but Roarke answered the door and told me she'd gone home. He invited me in for coffee, and I took him up on it. Now, before you get excited, it was all above board. He never touched me, and I sure as hell never touched him. What I didn't know at the time was that Barry had arrived early for his interview and was killing time by having coffee on the Starbuck's patio down the street. He spotted Roarke walking me out to my car afterwards."

"He recognized you?"

She shook her head. "Not me. Roarke. He'd been to some social function up there that Roarke and Frieda both attended."

"How did you find out he'd seen you two together?"

"One afternoon he cornered me in the Animal Care Center and told me that he wanted to, let's see, how did he so delicately put it? Ah, yes. That he'd seen me with Roarke, and that he 'wanted to sample my considerable charms, too.' If I didn't oblige, he said, he'd tell my husband everything. I told him where he could go."

My mouth dropped. "That's blackmail!"

She gave me a twisted smile. "Sexual harassment, too. Once he pulled that stunt with me, I started watching his behavior with the rest of the zoo's female staff."

"Which is why you were so quick to ask me…"

"If you were having trouble with him. Silly you, for not admitting it. I would have helped."

Adding that remark to my ever-growing list of regrets, I took my leave.

I needed to make one more stop, but since it was on the way back to the *Merilee*, it wouldn't take long.

In the night sky, the castle looked especially forbidding, but I didn't let it bother me. With Aster Edwina ninety miles north in San Francisco, I felt confident I'd get the answer I needed. As it turned out, I was right. In the three weeks since Grayson's murder, Jeanette had calmed down enough so that she didn't sob at the mere mention of her dead husband's name, and she no longer referred to him in the present tense. But his suit still lay on the bed and its condition didn't bode well for her mental health. She looked every bit as ragged as the suit. Her former robust build had shrunken in on itself, her eyes were dull, and her blond hair had lost all its luster. I hoped Aster Edwina would follow through on her plans to take her to a therapist.

Since she refused to move away from Grayson's suit, I sat next to her on the bed. "How are you feeling?"

"I had another migraine this morning, but it's gone now." Her voice was devoid of all affect, and she wouldn't let go of the suit's sleeve, holding it as if Grayson was still inside. The female anglerfish, mourning her vanished mate.

I tried to erase the image from my mind. "Aster Edwina says you'll see a doctor soon, someone who'll help you get..." I'd started to say "get over this," but rephrased it to "...who'll help you feel better."

She gave me a look that bordered on hostility. "I'll never feel better."

Unless she entered therapy, she might be correct. Now I had to make a decision. Comfort her or get what I'd come for. I made the cold-hearted choice but segued into it slowly by spending a few minutes chatting about the zoo and the giraffe's new calf. "It has eyelashes to die for!" Before I could catch myself, I began blabbing about the impending birth of Lucy's baby, that it could happen any day and that the vet had promised to call me the minute the anteater went into labor. Then the picture of what Lucy had done to her husband's body flashed across my mind.

"I'm so sorry! I didn't mean to talk about Lucy!"

Her answer reminded me of her commitment to the zoo and its animals. "I've never blamed the anteater, Teddy. She was only following her instincts. Besides, the medical examiner said Grayson couldn't feel anything by then, that he was already..." A tear leaked out of one red eye. "...gone. You've never really loved a man, have you?"

Her question took my breath away. "How can you say that? I loved Michael!"

Yes, that *was* hostility in her eyes. Remembering her temper from our old Monopoly days, I moved out of slapping range.

"You sure got over him fast enough," she said. "It's only been a year and you're already dating the sheriff."

Sometimes I hate small towns. "I haven't been 'dating' the sheriff. He's an old friend, that's all." I tried to get her back on the subject. "I want you to do something that might help with the mur...with the investigation."

No answer, just another glare.

I kept talking. "The last time I was here, you told me that Grayson was very meticulous about his zoo work, that he made copies of everything."

She began to finger the suit again, and when looked up, her hostility had faded. "You wouldn't believe the amount of files he kept at the zoo. I was always nagging..." Another tear leaked out. "If you're asking me to go over there and poke around, I just can't."

"But he kept an office here at the castle, too, you've said. Maybe he copied the vet report. You know, after that other zoo had its problems..."

"The one where the elephants and red pandas died. Terrible."

"Yes, terrible." Now that I had her attention, I started my explanation again. "Then you'll remember that the National Academy of Sciences sent out a team of vets to zoos all over the coun..."

Her eyes began to drift. "I want to go back to sleep." She lifted the suit sleeve and kissed it.

"But this is important. For Grayson's memory."

Her eyes found mine again. "His memory?"

"Don't you want people to remember him as a man who took his duties seriously?"

She kissed the sleeve again. "Naturally I do. What do you want, then? A copy of that stupid report?"

"If he made one."

The hostility returned. "I *told* you he copied everything. Do you want to see it or not?"

"Yes, I do."

She stood up, albeit wobbly. "Wait here and I'll fetch it from his office across the hall." When she left the room, her face was unutterably sad.

She was gone longer than I'd expected, but upon returning, held a legal-sized file folder in one hand, a sheaf of papers in the other. The papers she gave me were warm. "I copied the report because I'm not letting you take the original away. It's the last thing I have that he worked on."

Worried about her ability to operate a copier in her condition, I asked if I could take a few minutes to compare the copy to the original.

The dullness came back to her voice. "Do what you want." She handed it over.

When I flipped through the two sets, I discovered them to be identical, so I handed the original back.

"Would you mind if I take the copy with me to the *Merilee*? I want to read it more carefully." Either what I was looking for wasn't there, or in my haste, I'd missed it.

She sank back on the bed, wrapping herself in the suit's sleeves; it looked like Grayson's desiccated corpse was hugging her. "I don't care what you do. My husband is gone, and nothing will ever matter to me again."

I left her there and walked down the stairs, expecting the housekeeper or at least one of the maids, to let me out. But the hall was deserted. I guessed since letting me in, the housekeeper had disappeared into her own room to do whatever housekeepers do when their employers aren't watching.

While I'd been inside the castle, the wind had shifted and instead of smelling the Pacific, I smelled the gamy scent of animal. With the zoo now closed for the evening, there were no human sounds on the evening breeze—just a symphony of roars, night bird shrieks, and the trumpeting of elephants. For a while I stood there in the shadows of the castle listening to the music of the zoo, wishing I was there, not here in this dark, isolated place.

Then I climbed back into my truck, turned my headlights on bright, and started the five-mile drive to Gunn Landing. I must have talked to Jeanette longer than I realized, because the winding road was deserted. Even the stream of zookeepers headed back toward San Sebastian and Castroville had dwindled to nothing. I made good time until—with a half mile to go before I reached the main road to the harbor—flashing blue lights loomed in my rear view mirror.

I continued along the narrow road until it widened to accommodate a stand of scrub and live oak, then pulled over. A squad car with SAN SEBASTIAN COUNTY SHERIFF emblazoned along the side drove up and Joe climbed out. He cut his lights and approached my driver's side window.

His stern voice didn't match his grin. "Turn off your headlights and get out of the truck, ma'am."

When I cut the lights, blue flashes from the squad car lent the live oaks an eerie glow. Some other time it might have been frightening, but now it seemed downright erotic. I lowered my voice and tried my best to sound sexy. "Surely I wasn't speeding, Sheriff."

A muffled laugh. "No, Teddy, you've always driven like a little old lady because you're afraid you might hit some jaywalking chipmunk."

"Guilty as charged, Officer. May I ask the reason for this rather ridiculous traffic stop?"

He waggled a finger. "Never sass a police officer or you'll wind up in handcuffs."

A thrilling thought. "And then what?"

"Get out of the truck, Ma'am."

I exited the truck so fast I almost fell flat on my face. Handcuffs!

"That's better, ma'am. Now step toward the police officer."

I stepped toward the officer and felt arms slip around me, soft lips press against mine.

"Oh, Officer, what a big gun you have!"

The officer pulled me tighter.

When we came up for air, he asked, "Why haven't you returned my calls?" Before I could answer, he kissed me again. Then he proceeded to thoroughly search me.

A few minutes later, when we'd both caught our breath, he asked again why I hadn't returned his calls.

"I've been busy. And upset."

"You think *you* were upset." As night birds called around us, he searched me again.

I searched back.

Eventually, he said, "What else could I do but pretend ignorance? Your father didn't exactly parade up and down the street, but one time I saw him buying spices at a bodega over in Castroville. And you know how much he looks like you, even with that cheap dye job. I didn't want to arrest him, but at the same time, I could hardly…"

I put my hand across his mouth. "Do you have to talk so much? Now, about those handcuffs, Officer…"

After leaning into the squad car and cutting the lights, he pulled me into the bushes.

◇◇◇

An hour later, our clothes unbuttoned and unzipped but still more or less on in case his squad car squawked out an emergency, we lay looking up at the stars.

"It's been too long," he said.

"Only about a week."

A chuckle. "I meant since we've really been together. As a couple. Life is just so damn complicated."

"I've been thinking the same thing myself. Let me tell you again how much I love…"

His next words stopped me. "I talked to your mother today."

"You did *what?*" Talk about your cold shower.

"We agreed to bury the hatchet because we're both worried about you. She says you're back on the *Merilee*. She begged me to track you down and make you listen to reason. Ergo, the traffic stop. Which so quickly got out of hand, you criminal, you."

Joe and Caro. Conversing. That those two old enemies were temporarily working together on the same project—controlling me—didn't matter. The important thing was that the two most important people in my life had declared a truce.

As I was still trying to find the proper words to express my combination of delight and disgust, he continued, "Honey, it's not safe for you on that boat, not until whoever's after you has been arrested. Move home. Stop nosing around."

"But home *is* the *Merilee*."

"If you won't do it for yourself, do it for me."

After thinking about that for a second, I said, "All right."

I could read the independent vet report just as easily at my mother's as on the *Merilee*.

Caro, elegant in azure silk, appeared overjoyed to see me even though I carried Miss Priss in my arms and DJ Bonz slobbered at my heels.

"I see the Rejas boy found you," she said, satisfaction in her voice.

"Yep. Rounded me up like a cattle rustler on a busy day. I must say, this is a new direction for you, actually treating him like a human being."

She ignored the dig. "Since he's talked you into abandoning that old boat, I can hardly care what his grandfather did for a living. By the way, I drove over to the harbor earlier but you weren't anywhere around. You saw my note, didn't you?"

"Who could miss it?" Hand-printed on her own embossed stationery, the note had been taped to the *Merilee*'s locked salon door. COME HOME BEFORE YOU GET KILLED. Caro had never been subtle.

I set Priss down on the tiled entryway. She sneezed, shook loose a few hairs, then shot up the stairs to my room. Bonz remained at my feet, but he looked longingly toward the den.

"Is Dad here?"

She shook her head. "He's at Al's. He said he might stop in tonight."

He'd made no firm plans then, which meant that she hadn't yet found a private jet or a pilot who wasn't fussy about flight plans. "I brought several days' change of clothes, too."

She treated me to a pageant-winning smile. "Wonderful. Put them in your room, then come down for dinner. I'll fix you a burger. Unless you want some strawberries and carrots."

"New maid still 'resting'?"

The smile died. "You know perfectly well that I can't bring her back until we get your father out of the country. Until then, I'm doing the best I can, but with eighteen rooms…" She made a helpless gesture. While her own appearance was flawless, the house was a mess. In the three weeks since my father had been back in town, the tiled entryway hadn't been polished, a buildup of dirt grayed the corners of the drawing room, and a hutch of dust bunnies had taken up residence under a Regency satinwood window seat. Animal life had moved in, too. A spider, probably *Achaearanea tepidariorum,* declared his presence by stringing a web from a tall torchiere all the way up to the chandelier. If the maid didn't return soon, Caro would be buried under a mountain of crud.

After eating a burned burger served on a stale white-bread roll, I helped with the dishes, swabbed a few floors, vanquished the dust bunnies and spider webs, and turned the spider loose in the back yard. Feeling like an overworked maid myself, I retired to my room for a more careful read of the independent vet study.

I finished around midnight. While some of the technical terminology escaped me, the report was overwhelmingly positive.

With an exception.

One infraction was found in the zoo's care of its animals, and that was when a keeper neglected to properly close an enclosure gate, which allowed a kit fox to escape. Fortunately, the animal had quickly been captured. The event had happened more than a year ago, before I started working at the zoo, which is why I hadn't known about it.

The negligent keeper's name was Jack Spence.

So *that* was why Dr. Kate refused to talk to me about the report. She'd been covering for him!

From what I'd seen, he'd had learned to be more careful, because he'd been promoted to the spectacled bears.

Other than the kit fox incident, the report was problem-free. It stated that animals' nutritional and exercise needs were more than being met, and the medical care they received far exceeded the usual veterinary standards. The few animal deaths they investigated had occurred because of advanced age or disease, like our cheetah's inoperable brain tumor; or from unpreventable accidents, such as the time an elderly chimp misjudged his leap from the bar on his jungle gym and fell, breaking his leg. Minor cuts, bites, scratches and scrapes didn't count. That sort of thing was daily fodder at a zoo, and the vets had duly noted that our animals seemed less prone to getting in fights than at most zoos.

In fact, the vets had been so impressed that they had even taken the trouble to point out the care with which the groundskeepers groomed each animal's enclosure. On the last page, they gave their summation, signed by all six veterinarians: "With its large natural enclosures, dedicated staff, and state-of-the-art medical facilities, the Gunn Zoo serves as a model for a caring, contemporary animal facility."

I read that sentence again. Unless I was missing something, the positive tone of the report meant that the independent vet study had nothing to do with Grayson's death. If that was true, he and Barry had died for another reason entirely.

Chapter Twenty-two

I skipped my usual Monday morning walk through California Habitat and went straight to the administration building. I didn't know exactly what I was looking for, but I was certain I'd recognize it when I found it. Unfortunately, Zorah was already there, riffling through a stack of papers on Barry's desk.

She looked up with a guilty expression. "What are you doing here?"

"Maybe the same thing you're doing. You don't work Mondays."

Placing her hand on the top page of the pile, she spread her fingers as if to hide what was underneath. "I just came in for a few minutes to finish up some paperwork. And you?"

Zorah wasn't the paperwork type, but I let it go. "I left something in here the other day when I stopped in to see Barry about Lucy. That was before…" *Before someone murdered him.* "How's your nephew?"

"Alejandro? I visited him again last night. Maybe getting shot will make him rethink the thrills of gangsta life." She straightened, but her hand remained on the stack's top page. Not enough, though, that I couldn't read part of it. I was about to say something, when she added, "Not to change the subject or anything, but you have close ties to the Gunns, so I was wondering if you've heard what they plan to do about Barry's job. He didn't do much around here except model designer sports jackets and raise money, but at least he kept up with the paperwork."

I pointed. "Is that an insurance claim under your hand?" The applicant's name was Kim Markowski.

"You're not supposed to be looking at this."

"Neither are you. Insurance claims are confidential."

"Somebody has to get the damned thing off this desk and back into the system! Kim told me...Oh, hell, I never could keep a secret. Apparently Kim's ankle isn't healing right and she needs a second operation, but so far, our insurance carrier has refused to cover it. They claim the only reason that fall in Carmel broke her ankle is because she has a pre-existing condition. The pigs." She fumed to a stop, then resumed. "I take that back. Pigs are very nice animals."

Here was yet another reason everyone at the zoo had wanted Zorah to be appointed director; no matter what the situation, she always sided with staff. "I didn't know she had health problems."

Lowering her voice, she said, "Brittle bone syndrome. She's suffered from it since childhood. Don't tell anyone, okay? I need to find her claim and stick it under the right nose. It's outrageous that the insurance thugs have pulled this."

"Kim really did break her ankle?"

"You thought she was *faking?*"

"She's always smiling, isn't she? When I broke my ankle, I cried for weeks." A slight exaggeration there, since I'd sniffled only once in the emergency room.

"Wimp." But Zorah smiled. "I'll say this for her. That girl's got grit. Surprising, isn't it?"

Yes, it was. In more ways than one.

◇◇◇

While attending to the day's duties, I contrasted this new information against Kim's standard chipper mood. When I tried to reconcile this with my suspicions it didn't compute, which made me even more suspicious. Fortunately, I received a chance to talk to her during lunch break, when I was splitting an anchovy pizza with Zorah, who still wasn't taking advantage of her day off, and hadn't gone home. I'd once visited her tiny apartment, and understood.

We were gobbling down the last of the pizza when Kim crutched into the crowded employees' lounge with a more-polished version of the anteater puppet. Apparently the puppet-making class she was taking in San Francisco had already paid off. Zookeepers are suckers for stuffed animals, so everyone surrounded it with a chorus of *oohs* and *aahs*.

She blushed prettily, and for a moment her pink face reminded me of Jeanette's; their features were not unalike. "I'm glad you all like it," she said. "I've been working really, really hard."

My cue. "How often do you go up to San Francisco for your class?" What I actually wanted to ask her was how often she got together with Roarke Gunn, but with the other keepers present, the question would have been rude.

Unmindful of my suspicions, she chirped, "Every Tuesday afternoon. I've never missed." Her bright face dulled for a moment. "Except for the class right after I broke my ankle."

"The day I found Grayson's body, right?"

The other keepers looked at me.

Ignoring them, I said, "I just asked because you weren't at the fund-raiser."

Kim's lower lip began to tremble. "No, I…I…The car hit…"

When Zorah slipped a steadying arm around her, I noticed they were almost the same height. Strange how a pretty face and bright blond hair could disguise an Amazonian build.

Displeasure colored Zorah's voice. "The car hit Kim on Sunday, the day before the fund-raiser. She was in a lot of pain the next day, which is why she missed both the funder *and* her puppet-making class. Now give it a rest, okay?"

Time to change tactics. "Should she be roaming around the zoo so much? It's been, what, only three weeks since her accident, and what with…" Oops. I almost said, 'that brittle bone condition of hers,' but stopped myself in time.

Zorah noticed. "It's nice you're so concerned about her, but she's getting along fine. Aren't you, Kim?"

Lower lip still trembling, Kim nodded. "Oh, yes. I'm doing fine!" With an obvious effort, she controlled the lip action and summoned up a blinding smile. "Thank you for being so concerned about me."

I felt like a heel.

After that, the day went from bad to much, much worse.

Zorah finally went home—I saw her headed out the employees' exit an hour after lunch—and I was about to lift the latch on the Mexican gray wolves' enclosure when I heard a familiar voice.

"Hold up there, Teddy!" Frieda Gunn, dressed in a drapey gauze blouse and pair of loose-fitting jeans that barely disguised her tummy bump, didn't sound happy.

I relocked the gate, checked it twice, then stuffed the keys into my pocket. Where wolves are concerned, you can't be too careful. "Is there a problem?"

Veins stood out on her slender neck and her fists were clenched. When she answered, a few zoo visitors glanced our way. "There sure the hell is! Stay away from my husband."

My mouth dropped open. "Roarke?"

"Don't act coy with me. I've been through this before!" Sensing that she had an audience, she turned and faced the visitors. "Oh, go gape at an aardvark or something!"

Not wanting to miss this free show, they stayed.

Appalled, I moved away from the gate toward an isolated area near the keepers' trail. As soon as we'd left our gawkers behind, I said, "What's the matter with you? I'm not having an affair with Roarke."

"You think I'm not wise to those so-called business meetings of his up in San Francisco? How could you do this to me, after what you've been through yourself? You know how much I love him!"

I could hardly tell her that the other woman in her husband's life was probably Kim, so I said the only thing possible in the circumstances. "You love your husband as much as I love Joe."

The reference to Joe got through to her. "Then why go after...?"

"I didn't, Frieda. What made you suspect *me*? My god, Roarke and I have known each other since we were kids. It would almost be incest!"

She pulled out a note from her jeans pocket. "You came by the *Tequila Sunrise* yesterday and said something to him I didn't hear, and when you left, he acted really weird. And guess what? Today's the first Monday in ages he hasn't driven off to see his so-called 'broker.' There's more. When I was sorting the laundry this morning, I found this in one of his shirts. I figured you passed it to him when you were on the boat." She handed the note to me.

In a flowery, backward-leaning script no one would mistake for a man's, it said, "Something's come up and I can't make it Monday night. Meet me at our usual place after the zoo closes. We need to talk."

The handwriting wasn't Kim's. It was Miranda DiBartolo's, the dark-haired Down Under keeper.

Instead of arguing further, I walked over to my zoo cart and picked up the clipboard where I kept my keeper's log. "This is my handwriting."

When Frieda studied the nasty scrawl that passed for penmanship, the anger left her face. "If you're not the woman, who is? The note talks about the zoo and their 'usual place' so it has to be someone here. God, I wish I'd attended more zoo functions. The only likely candidates I remember meeting are that big blond education director, she's pretty, and the cute little keeper who takes care of the wallabies. Oh, and the vet. She's good-looking enough to attract Roarke." Her eyes beseeched mine. "Is it one of them?"

Identifying the culprit wouldn't help, so I said, "Talk with Roarke and see if you can work this thing through." Hopefully, he loved her enough to repair their marriage now that a baby was on the way.

"You *do* know who it is, don't you?"

All I could do was repeat my advice. "Talk to Roarke."

Frieda glared at me for a moment, started to say something else, but stopped. Then, shoulders drooping, she turned on her heel and hurried back down the trail.

Heavy-hearted, I went back to the wolves' enclosure and let myself into the keepers' shed in preparation for separating Hazel, one of the less dominant females, from the pack so I could spike her afternoon treat of ground beef heart with an antibiotic. Several days earlier, in what appeared to be an unprovoked attack, Godiva had bitten the smaller female so badly she'd required several stitches. Things seemed to have settled down between the two, so we'd returned Hazel to the pack, watching the reintroduction carefully. All had gone fairly peacefully, the alpha female contenting herself to a pedestrian nip on Hazel's rump.

Relieved by the distraction working with animals provided, I put Frieda's unhappiness out of my mind. After inserting the medication into the beef heart, I looked through the shed's small window and scanned the enclosure for Hazel. At first I didn't see her, only Godiva dozing with her pups in the sunlight. Several wolves were hunkered down in the shade of a cottonwood not too far from the holding pen, but Hazel wasn't among them, so I called her by name. That had always been enough to make her scurry over to the holding pen and snap up her doctored treat before the others caught on, but this time it didn't happen.

At the sound of my voice, Godiva woke up. Instead of showing curiosity about my presence, she lifted her nose and scented the wind. Suddenly she flattened her ears and charged diagonally across the compound. Startled, I looked in the direction she was running and saw her mate Cisco, busily copulating with Hazel, half hidden by a stand of Great Basin sagebrush. Knowing what was about to happen, I ripped the radio off my belt and called for backup. No way would I enter that enclosure alone.

Godiva reached Hazel within seconds. At first, she seemed content to slash at her flank, driving the smaller wolf away from her busted "life-long" mate. But when Hazel made the mistake of defending herself, the alpha female deepened her attack.

All I could do was stand there, flapping a burlap feed sack, trying to distract her, screaming, *"No, Godiva! No!"*

Jack Spence responded first to my radio call, followed by Miranda DiBartolo and three park rangers bearing a collection of safety boards, nets, fire extinguishers and Hot Shots—the electric prods used only in emergencies. More keepers and rangers soon arrived and began directing zoo visitors away from the enclosure. Cisco, the unfaithful male whose wandering eye had started the brawl, slunk back to his confused pups, leaving the two females to fight it out. The more timid members of the pack cowered behind a stand of boulders, howling out their terror.

Now that backup had arrived, I grabbed my safety board and catch pole—a long pole with a loop of rope at the end—and entered the enclosure with the rangers. Rank smells of urine and fear enveloped us as we approached the viciously fighting females. Godiva's snarls were terrible as she ground her teeth into Hazel's neck, but more horrible still were the smaller wolf's screams, which sounded heartbreakingly human.

Netting Godiva and hauling her out of the enclosure was the preferred solution. But if we screwed up and netted the fighting animals together we could make the situation even worse, so our first priority was to separate them. Using the catch poles right now was problematical, too. Godiva had dug into Hazel's neck so firmly that none of us could slip the noose around her head without snaring the smaller wolf at the same time.

The rangers readied their Hot Shots. They didn't want to shock her, because no one can predict the end result of an electric charge. Still, they had to do something.

Distraction was sometimes enough to end an attack, so I stepped forward. *"Let go, Godiva, let go!"*

To my side, one of the rangers blasted an air horn at the fighting animals, while another waved a jacket around his head, screaming, *"No! No!"*

No reaction. Just a continuation of that horrible chewing.

Protected by my safety board, I edged in front of the encircling rangers. Sweat ran into my mouth, the tang of salt blending with the bitterness of my own fear. "*No, Godiva!*" Close enough now, I prodded her sharply in the flank with the non-noose end of the catch pole, but she ignored it and kept chewing away at her rival's throat.

Another movement out of the corner of my eye caught my attention. A nearby ranger pointed his fire extinguisher nozzle at the wolves.

"Now! Use it now!" I called.

He sprayed. With a loud *whoosh*, thick goops of foam immediately covered both wolves. Confused, Godiva released her hold on Hazel. The smaller wolf slumped to the ground, her neck a chewed mess.

With the worst of the noise abated, I heard Zorah on her radio. "Keeper One to Vet One. Attack in gray wolf enclosure, Godiva on Hazel. Possible damage to carotid artery. Rangers and keepers present but medical assistance for wolves needed stat!"

Dr. Kate squawked back that she was on her way.

I couldn't worry about Hazel's condition yet, not with Godiva still in a killing mood. Although she'd dropped the smaller wolf, she was close enough to attack again. With my safety board held in a position to protect my torso, I positioned myself between her and her victim, hoping to hold her off until a ranger with a net reached us. With my free hand, I raised the catch pole and prodded her sharply.

"*Godiva! Down!*"

However habituated to humans they may be, wolves aren't dogs, and she didn't lie down. She whirled around to throw me a hungry look that brought back centuries of Big Bad Wolf lore and raised my own hackles. This was the dangerous part, when a keeper—after distracting an animal from its prey—sometimes finds herself the next target. Still, no decent animal worker gives in to fear.

"*Back!*" I kept my eyes on hers, displaying dominance.

A low growl. She cocked that big, shaggy head at me and looked at my neck.

Oh Grandma, what big teeth you have. I shifted my safety board higher.

"Back!" Stepping forward, I prodded her with the catch pole again, lowering the timbre of my voice to an animal-like growl. "Don't mess with me, Godiva. Back!"

For a few seconds there was a stare-off. I didn't flinch. She did.

Outwolved, she ducked her head in submission and whirled away.

Trailed by Jack and two rangers, I went after her, yelling for all I was worth. "*Back! Back!*"

At one point, she threw me a ferocious look. When I met her glare-for-glare, she ducked her head again.

I should have paid more attention to the direction she was traveling in. Before I knew it, she'd reached Cisco, and to my horror, went for her mate with bloodied fangs flashing.

As she tore into him, their pups scattered, yelping in fright. But Cisco was no Hazel. Before his mate could do him serious damage, he leaped into the air and landed with his neck positioned away from her deadly fangs. At first it seemed that he would merely continue his evasion tactics, but after she slashed at his rump and opened a wound at least four inches long, he whirled around and bared his own fangs.

Cisco was not the pack's alpha male for nothing.

Before I could shout a warning, he lunged for her. His superior weight, added to the lightning thrust of his attack, knocked her onto her side. Ears back, he straddled her prone body with his fangs at her throat.

He was going to kill her.

Godiva, her rage transformed by fear, let out a whine that segued into a high wail.

"*Cisco! No!*" I tried to position the noose end of the catch pole around his neck. He shook it off.

"Say when." I glanced around and found a ranger at my side, Hot Shot in one hand, a net in the other.

As it turned out, the Hot Shot wasn't necessary.

Cisco, having proven his dominance, backed away from his mate. After one final growl, he trotted over to his pups.

I slipped the noose around Godiva's neck and pinned her to the ground. The ranger threw his net.

And just like that, it was over.

Chapter Twenty-three

While Hazel was undergoing surgery and her attacker sulked in quarantine, I went to the administration building and wrote my report. It was a lengthy process requiring not only an account of every animal's reaction, but also that of each human—much of which had taken place outside my sight line. At least I had company. Other keepers and rangers involved in the incident drifted in and began filling out their own reports. Two hours later, I finished. After making several copies and putting them in the appropriate mail slots, I left the others to their red-tape misery and walked shakily to the employees' lounge.

For once, it was deserted. I poured myself a cup of decaf—I didn't need more adrenaline coursing through my body—and collapsed into a chair. I tried not to think about the wolves, but images of the fight kept crowding into my head. The zoo might need to separate Godiva and Cisco permanently, which would be unfortunate because they made a good breeding pair.

Whatever we decided, she'd be fine and would eventually find a new mate. Most people believed Mexican gray wolves mated for life because that's what the popular magazines told them. Wolves can't read. Although they were usually faithful, they strayed whenever they could get away with it.

Kind of like humans, I guessed.

Like Roarke. Like Michael.

But never like Joe.

Remembering his loyal heart, I smiled for the first time in hours. I closed my eyes and let the images come. His mouth. His hands.

Why had I ever feared his love?

Calmer now—and certainly warm enough, with my fantasies—I tossed the remainder of the decaf in the sink and headed toward the capybaras.

Gladys and Myrtle had resolved their jealousies over Gus' attentions, and lay snuggled next to him with the less-aggressive Agnes. They ignored the melon pieces I tossed them and snuggled even closer together. Gus nibbled Myrtle's ear. She, in turn, nibbled Agnes'. Gladys sighed in contentment.

My wonderful, ugly capybaras. Making up, kissing up. Not at all like people, who harbored their grudges forever.

I stiffened.

Not like people?

I looked at the capybara snuggle-group again. If they weren't like people, then why…?

Carefully, I reexamined the events of the past three weeks, the behavior of the capybaras, the anteater, and especially that of the wolves. Hazel. Godiva. Cisco. What they had gone through and would continue to go through.

Then I thought about what a particular human had said and not said, had done and not done.

After I'd filtered out all the lies and the evasions, the only thing left was the truth.

Now I knew what I had to do.

Call Joe.

Dismissing the happy capybaras, I grabbed my cell phone, but my hands shook so badly I dropped it twice and mispunched the number several times. When I connected to the sheriff's office, Deputy Emilio Guiterrez told me Joe wasn't in. After a heavy weekend of car wrecks and convenience store robberies, he'd taken the day off. He was on a boat with his children somewhere west of Dolphin Island, fishing for albacore.

"I'm not supposed to message him unless it's an emergency, Teddy. Is it?"

"No, but if he checks in with you, tell him to call me."

"Will do. Hey, you sound stressed. You sure I shouldn't radio him?"

Spoil one of Joe's few days off with his children? Telling Emilio not to bother, I rang off. To cover all my bases, I then called Joe's house, where his mother, Colleen, answered. This necessitated more casual conversation—we'd always been friendly—but I eventually got around to the reason for my call.

"If he stops by on the way home, have him phone me, okay? Even if it's late. I tend to stay up."

"Surely, Teddy." Almost forty years out of Dublin and she still spoke with an Irish accent. A woman totally without pretense.

Speaking to Joe's mother reminded me of my own, so as soon as I rang off, I called Caro and gave her a sanitized version of the wolf attack before she could hear it from anyone else. I let her vent for a while, then derailed her by saying, "I'm coming back to Old Town tonight. There's too much work left on the house, especially the bathrooms."

There was no way I would return alone to the *Merilee*. Not until I reached Joe and told him what he needed to know.

"Bathrooms?" Caro shrilled. "What do I care about bathrooms? Teddy, I want to talk to you about those wolves!"

Time to distract her again. "Those bathrooms are looking rough, don't you think? After all, it's been a couple of weeks since the maid's been over, and boy, does it look it. The hall bath downstairs, for instance, there's green…" Hearing a gagging sound at the other end of the line, I found something else to distract her with. "Find any transportation for our friend yet?"

Caro was no more interested in talking about Dad than she was in talking about moldy bathrooms. "First it's bears, and now wolves. If you don't quit that job, I'll write you out of my will!" She was nothing if not focused.

After all the danger I'd faced in the past weeks, and perhaps still faced, her threat made me laugh out loud. She didn't like that.

"Teddy, you could have been killed!"

"A tornado could have carried me off to Oz, too, but it didn't. See you tonight." I hung up before she started in again.

One last detail to clear up.

And a warning to give.

I found Kim in the auditorium putting the finishing touches on a brightly colored puppet stage, her crutches propped against the wall. In all the excitement, I'd forgotten that *Little Red Riding Hood and the Giant Anteater* would debut tomorrow to a group of school children bussed in from San Sebastian.

"How's it going?" I asked.

Regardless of her big smile, she didn't meet my eyes and appeared to be trying to keep the puppet stage between us. "Oh, great! Just great!" The strained look on her face had grown worse. No surprise there. Forcing yourself to act cheerful when you had so much on your mind had to be exhausting.

"Let's talk about your accident." I watched her reaction carefully.

"I slipped, that's all."

"What were you doing when you slipped?"

She ducked behind the small stage so I couldn't see her. "Shopping and stuff."

"That's not what I meant. Were you getting ready to cross the street?"

"I don't remember."

"Are you certain of that, Kim? Or do you remember everything and feel too guilty to admit it?"

From behind the stage I heard scrambling sounds, then a loud thud. I peeked around to find that she had fallen over, bringing her crutches down with her.

"Now look what you made me do, Teddy!"

She sprawled on the floor, crying hard. Mascara ran down her pretty cheeks and her lipstick appeared to be bleeding off her mouth. I tried to help her up but she batted away my hands.

"Tell me what happened, Kim. Everything."

She struck at me with her crutch. "Get away! What's wrong with you, bothering me like this? Can't you see I'm in pain."

Yes, I could see that, but someone else was in pain, too. "Let's see if I have this right. You were on the curb, ready to cross the street. The light was red and a big SUV was approaching, speeding up to get across the intersection before the light changed. Then someone came up behind you and..."

"Shut up! Just shut up!" She aimed the crutch at me again. I sprang out of the way. Her reflexes weren't nearly as good as a zookeeper's, perhaps because puppets so seldom tried to tear out your throat.

"You didn't slip, did you? You were pushed off that curb, weren't you?"

Hate blazed from her eyes. "Nosy bitch!"

Sticks and stones. "Stay home tonight, Kim. Whatever happens, don't go wandering around. Especially not in Carmel. I'm afraid—"

A noise from behind interrupted me. Zorah, probably summoned back to the zoo by Dr. Kate so that she could debrief those involved in the wolf incident, opened the door to the auditorium and peered in.

She spotted Kim scrabbling around on the floor, her face muddy with dust and tears. "Hey, you two. What's going on?"

A sniffle. "I tripped. Teddy was about to help me up."

Zorah rushed forward and lifted Kim to her feet. "Oh, you poor thing," she crooned, as if to an injured squirrel monkey. "The day's almost over, so why don't you go home?"

"Good idea," I agreed, with relief. "And Kim, remember what I told you. Watch TV. Play Scrabble. Don't go out."

Giving me an accusatory look, Kim hobbled out of the auditorium.

Oblivious as to what had just transpired, Zorah turned to me and said, "I've been looking everywhere for you. Now, about that wolf incident..."

My anxiety faded while we talked wolves. Zorah insisted on going over to the Animal Care Center to see how Hazel was doing, but the animal wasn't out of surgery yet. From there, we went to the wolf enclosure, which had been closed to the public and would remain so for several days. Cisco was standing under the cottonwood tree with his pups, looking bereft. With the heat of battle already a fading memory, he missed his mate.

"Think we can salvage their relationship?" Zorah asked, studying him.

"You're the wolf expert, not me. I'm just helping out until their regular keeper gets back from vacation, remember?"

"But you're the one who watched the dynamics play out."

She was testing me, attempting to find out how good my judgment was. Not taking my eyes off Cisco, I ventured an educated guess. "We'll need to relocate Hazel. The Phoenix Zoo's been desperate for another breeding-age female, and their Mexican Gray Wolf Conservation Program is as good as our own. As for Godiva, we can't bring her back like nothing ever happened. Too dangerous. If we want to salvage this thing, we'll have to reintroduce her to the pack slowly, like we would any new animal. You know, put her in a cage and move it in a few feet further every day, let everyone sniff around, see how Cisco responds. It's my guess he'll welcome her with open arms, er, paws."

She gave me an approving look and slapped me on the back so strongly I almost fell over. "That's the way to do it! One other thing. From what I hear about your actions during the attack, you were textbook. I couldn't have done better myself. The zoo's lucky to have you."

I flushed with pride. When it came to handling animal emergencies, nobody could match Zorah.

Zorah, who had never murdered anyone.

As the afternoon passed, I tried Joe's office and home several times but answering machines and deputies were the order of the day. With nothing more to do, I decided to visit Lucy. Talking to her always made me feel better.

When I arrived at her enclosure, I found Dr. Kate studying the anteater across the fence with anxious eyes. One look inside and I could see why. Lucy had intensified the previous day's behavior. Without once stopping to suck up the termites I'd hidden earlier, she paced from one end of the enclosure to the other. When she caught sight of me I thought her tense expression softened.

For her part, Dr. Kate appeared even more exhausted than usual.

"You okay?" I asked.

"I'm doing better than Hazel. It took eighty-six stitches to close her wounds, but you saved her life."

Poor Hazel, just looking for a little love like the rest of us. "And Godiva?" For all the ferocity she'd shown me, I didn't hold it against her. When it comes to animals, zookeepers are a forgiving lot.

"Cisco didn't hurt her, but as to bringing her back to the habitat now, we'll have to wait and see. Not to change the subject or anything, I think we should move Lucy into her holding pen."

I didn't like the sound of that. "That's risky."

"We might get a baby tonight. There's no discharge yet, but better to be safe than sorry. I prefer a more controlled environment, especially with a threatened species."

Under normal conditions Lucy would have already been confined to her holding pen for the birth, but ever since Barry had exiled her there, she hated the pen's close confines. Locking her up for a few minutes in order to clean her enclosure was one thing, keeping her there for days something else entirely. But the vet was boss.

I unhooked the radio from my belt. "If you want to move her now, let me call Zorah for some help. She might still be on the premises." And might defend my point of view.

The head keeper arrived a couple of minutes later. "I'm with Teddy on this," she told the vet, after hearing me out. "Attempting to move the anteater will make her more stressed than she already is, but if you insist, I'm willing to try."

There was another reason confining Lucy to the holding pen might not work. Giant anteaters preferred to give birth standing up on their two hind legs, propped by their massive tails. Five feet tall when erect, her nose would almost scrape the pen's wire mesh ceiling.

My prediction about the difficulty of the move proved accurate. Since Lucy was more familiar with me, I was given the honors, for all the good it did. Zorah opened the gate while I, with my catch pole in one hand and my safety board in the other, attempted to maneuver the recalcitrant animal into the pen. She fought me all the way, rearing up and striking out with those deadly, four-inch claws. At one point, she gave my safety board such a blow that she cracked it. Heavily pregnant or not, she could still move faster than we could.

In the end, Zorah and I retreated to the safety of the holding pen while Lucy glared at us, hissing and grumbling, flashing those long talons, threatening to eviscerate us both.

I shouted across the enclosure to the vet. "If we keep this up, she'll probably go straight into labor, and as upset as we've made her, she might even kill the baby." Infanticide wasn't rare in the wild, especially with inexperienced mothers. In zoos, it could occur if the mother was unduly stressed—which Lucy had quickly become.

Dr. Kate studied Lucy, her talons, her long blue tongue that flickered in and out. "Point taken!" she called over the fence. "I'll have the rangers re-rig the camera to focus on her new nest. Teddy, you're sure you want me to call you when she goes into labor, no matter the time?"

After receiving a strong affirmative, she gave us a wave, hopped into her cart and drove away.

Now that the excitement was over, I realized my hands were stinging from the blow Lucy had given my safety board. "I need a new board," I told Zorah as we left the holding pen through its back gate. "One more hit and this thing's gone, me with it."

"There's a spare near the Bengal's night house. Use it until Carpentry makes you another." Then she gave me a wicked grin. "Ever thought about transferring to the lemurs?"

◇◇◇

As soon as six o'clock arrived and the last of my charges were fed and watered, I tried Joe again. No luck. I left for Caro's.

She was ending a phone call as I walked in. At her feet, DJ Bonz gazed at her with adoration. Priss coughed up a hairball in the corner. She paid them no attention.

"You look like hell, Teddy."

"Rough day at the office. Say, that wasn't Joe, was it?"

She smoothed her hair, although every strand of it was already in place. Her eyes shifty, she said, "One of *my* friends."

Which probably meant a male. With money.

I bounded up the stairs to one of the only two clean bathrooms in the house. When I'd showered away what must have been a pound of zoo dirt, I wrapped myself in a towel, padded into my room, and changed into an old pair of jeans and a tee shirt. Casual, yes, but there'd be no parties tonight.

I called Joe's office only to learn he still wasn't back, but this time—the fifteenth call, I guess—Deputy Guiterrez sounded testy. "As I've told you, Teddy, I don't know how many times before, I can contact him on the boat if you really think it's necessary."

"No, no," I muttered, hanging up.

Hearing a growl, I looked around. No Bonz. He was probably still downstairs with Caro. It was my stomach, messaging me that it was time for dinner.

When I returned to the kitchen, Caro was standing in front of the refrigerator, holding an indistinguishable package that looked years old. "How about some Chicken Kiev? I found one of those frozen thingys in the freezer. I'll boil a potato, too. Can you do that with their jackets on?"

Picturing a big baking Idaho served half-raw, half-soggy, I shook my head. "I'll make us a salad instead. Vinegar and oil or Green Goddess?"

"Carrot juice for me. I'm back on the Strawberry/Carrot Diet."

"You're a size three!"

"Size two, after three weeks on the diet. I'm trying for size one, which was my size when I was crowned Miss San Sebastian County. That's when I met your father, remember. He loved my tiny waist. Speaking of, he's leaving day after tomorrow."

I put down the radish I'd been slicing. "Don't tell me you found a plane!"

She nodded. "He's flying out of San Jose International Airport. I hope you'll come say good-bye to us."

"*Us?*"

"I'm going along for the laughs. I'll be back in a month. In the meantime, you keep an eye on the house."

"Mother, you can't be serious!"

She gave me an injured look. "I'm due for a vacation. And quit calling me 'Mother.' "

Vacation? During my last conversation with my father, he'd attempted to lure me with sparkling visions of Cameroon and Iceland. I wondered what delights he had offered her. "You packing mukluks or bikinis?"

She treated me to a mysterious smile. "He told me not to tell you, that the less you knew, the better off you'd be. And him."

That was probably true, but why did he have to involve Caro in his schemes? If he'd been here, I would have given him a piece of my mind. "What about your boyfriend? After all the work you've put in, are you going to dump him?" For months Caro had been trying hard to snag billionaire Cyril Keslar, of the Montecito Keslars, and before Dad had emerged from exile, she'd appeared on the verge of success.

Her expression turned prim. "I asked Cyril to loan me his Lear and he turned me down. He even had the nerve to say it sounded like I was up to something dishonest."

I laughed. "Well, you are."

She pointed a perfectly manicured finger at the cutting board. "Either eat that radish or throw it in the trash. Better yet, have a strawberry."

After dinner, I helped Caro clean—or rather, *I* cleaned while she supervised. When my arms began to ache, I went upstairs to my room. Although it had ten times the space as my aft cabin on the *Merilee*, I felt cramped. Restless and hungering for the scent of the harbor, I sat down on the window seat and opened the window.

It was not yet eight, and the sun's pink glow remained visible on the horizon. I heard the foghorn on Point Gunn, the ringing of a buoy bell. In my mind's eye I could almost see the *Merilee* rocking on the outgoing tide, hear the creaking of the lines tethering her to the dock. Nearby, surfacing otters and sea lions would be blowing water out of their nostrils with a wheezy whoosh; here and there, a careless fish would be leaping out of the water, only to become someone's dinner.

As the evening breeze caressed my face, I breathed in the scents of the home of my heart. Rotting algae. Dead fish. Gull droppings. Over-full dumpsters. Gasoline-slicked water. Why this gamy cornucopia could smell so wonderful was beyond me, but nothing—not even a zoo enclosure—could compare to its perfume. I relaxed for the first time in hours.

What was that old saying, "God's in his heaven and all's right with the world"? Knowing that the *Merilee* rocked on the tide was heaven enough for me. Then I remembered that she was unable to make the trip to Dolphin Island and that my days in paradise were numbered.

But my own troubles paled in light of my father's. At least he would soon fly to safety, still free, still alive.

With darkness descending, Joe would be on his way back from his fishing trip. When he returned my call, I would tell him who had killed Grayson and Barry. The burden of a murder trial would be lifted from Zorah's broad shoulders to descend on someone else's.

My sore heart calmed by the nearby ocean, I drifted off to sleep right there in the window seat.

◇◇◇

The cell phone's chimes woke me.

Glancing at my watch, I saw it was almost eleven. I answered. "Joe? Listen, I need to tell you…"

I received a blast of static, then a garbled word.

"…anteater…"

Not Joe. Dr. Kate.

"…baby…difficulty…needs you…"

The connection was so bad I could hardly make her out.

More static, then a roar that sounded like one of the spectacled bears, who were only a short distance from Lucy's enclosure. The static cleared for a moment and I heard, "…needs to calm down…*hurry!*"

A final burst of static, then silence.

Fortunately, I was already dressed. Stuffing the phone into my jeans pocket, I hurried out of the house, closing the door softly so I wouldn't wake Caro.

Fifteen minutes later I was fumbling with the combination lock at the zookeepers' entrance, the cold metal slippery against my fingers. While I'd expected the lone park ranger working the night shift to let me in, the vet had obviously been too busy to alert him. Not that his absence created a problem. The three-quarter moon was bright enough to illuminate the lock's numbers. After a couple of tries, I managed to open it, let myself inside, and after driving my truck through the gate, locked it securely behind me.

I parked behind the administration building. Pausing for a moment, I wondered if I should get one of the carts from the brightly-lit maintenance yard. But it would take too long to dial my way through another series of combination locks, find the right key for the right cart, start the thing—the carts were frequently stubborn after being left standing for a few hours—then relock all the gates.

So I hoofed it.

A symphony of sounds charged the night. The wind had risen, and palms leaves crackled above. Below, tall grasses brushed against reach other in a velvety whisper. Lions called to those left behind on a faraway veldt, coyotes yipped at the three-quarter moon. Over in California Habitat, Cisco sang of his loneliness for Godiva.

As I ran up Tropics Trail toward the giant anteater enclosure, my own heart ached. After all the misdirection had been cleared away, the solution to the murders had been so obvious, yet so painful. But thinking about the sorrow involved for everyone wouldn't help Lucy now. She needed my focused attention. I forced myself to stop thinking about death and ran, my sneakered feet sending up echoes against the waving eucalyptus trees, causing a flutter of great horned owls.

When I reached Lucy's enclosure I found it dark, with only the faintest glow from the far-off maintenance yard filtering through the trees. I expected to see Dr. Kate's cart parked nearby, loaded with medical supplies, but it was nowhere around.

"Dr. Kate! Where are you?" My voice echoed along the wide trail.

The only answer was a rustle from the enclosure, near the moat.

As if enraged at having her slumber interrupted, Lucy reared up on her hind legs, flashed her talons and rumbled a warning. Her exposed belly revealed she hadn't yet given birth.

"Oh, Lucy, you're all right!"

Another rustle, this time from the lone California buck brush at the side of the trail.

Jeanette Gunn-Harrill stepped out, the pistol in her hand pointed straight at my heart. "You always were ridiculously fond of that anteater, Teddy."

In my concern for Lucy, I had obeyed my emotions instead of my brain, not thinking the phone call through. Common sense should have reminded me that Dr. Kate always messaged me via beeper. As for the "static" on the line, that would have been easy enough to fake. Anyone could hiss.

Somehow I had to talk Jeanette down and stay alive until the solitary park ranger happened by on his nightly rounds. Struggling to stay calm, I said, "Don't do anything you'll be sorry for, Jeanette. Things aren't as bad as they seem." A foolish statement if there ever was one.

The gun didn't waver. "You think I'm stupid? The only man I ever loved is dead and I killed him. That's as bad as it gets. As for Barry…" She waved away the director's memory as if he were an annoying gnat. "Grayson thought I was stupid. Maybe I was for a while, when I loved him, believed in him, allowed him to talk me into pulling out of the Trust. He said it was for the good of our marriage, that we'd buy our own place up in the City where we could concentrate on loving each other without my family making fun of us all the time. But the truth was that he'd grown sick of me and our special relationship. All he wanted was to get his hands on as much money as possible, then leave me for that puppet-waving bimbo."

Kim. The puppet-waving bimbo. I'd noted the resemblance between her and Jeanette, with their tall, sturdy builds and long blond hair. As the waiter in that little San Francisco bistro had said, "From a distance, all blondes look alike." Henry Gunn thought he'd seen Grayson dining there with Jeanette, but he'd really seen Kim.

Poor Grayson. Unlike the free-ranging Roarke, but like so many other faithless men, he preferred one physical type.

A laugh interrupted by a sob. "You want to know something funny, Teddy? I'm the one who suggested she take those stupid puppet-making classes! I mean, did you ever see those raggedy-ass things she made? They were an embarrassment to the zoo, a joke! But in the end, the joke was on me, wasn't it? She and Grayson ran into each other up there. And then they…"

The light from the maintenance yard glimmered on a tear snaking down her cheek. "I wanted to stay in the City with him when he was doing all those interviews, but then I got one of my damned migraines and he sent me home. A couple of days later, when I was feeling better, I borrowed one of the family cars and drove back up to surprise him. That's when…" She choked off, unable to speak.

"That's when you saw them together."

"He betrayed me!" she wailed. "I walked in and there they were, in the bed *we* shared, doing…doing what he was only supposed to do with me!"

Keep talking, Jeanette, keep talking. "Did they see you?"

"They were too busy. That awful townhouse! It's nothing but a brothel."

I was certain Frieda would agree. But that was a different woman, a different broken heart. If I wanted to stay alive, I had to keep this one talking. "Did you confront Grayson about Kim?"

A spiteful smile. "Of course, just before I shot him. He told me that if I loved him, I'd understand, that Kim was his last chance for a normal life!"

The rage in her voice convinced me to change the subject. "How did Barry know…?" How best to say *that you murdered your husband.*

"He saw me slip away from the administration building that night, right after I came back from…from doing what I did. I'd thrown that silly anteater costume on the pile with the others, but he didn't figure out what it meant until the next day, after…" Her eyes welled again.

"He was blackmailing you, wasn't he?"

"The man had no morals. No one's going to miss him. Did you know that only eight people showed up for his funeral?" She laughed through the tears raining down her face. "At least Grayson drew a nice crowd. How many people were there? Fifty? Seventy-five?"

Where was that park ranger?

"I loved him, Teddy. I *loved* him!"

Horribly enough, I believed her. Her grief was real. So real that for too long it had blinded me to the fact that Grayson hadn't been anything like an anglerfish at all, someone so attached to his woman that he'd lost his individuality. He was more like a Mexican gray wolf, faithful *most* of the time, as long as it served his purposes. Godiva's terrible attack, first on Hazel and then on Cisco, had brought that realization home.

"You shoved Kim off that curb in Carmel, didn't you?"

More laughter. "Puppet Girl had it coming. Lucky for her that SUV had good brakes. Otherwise, she'd be road kill."

When Jeanette's attempt at killing her rival failed, she turned on her own mate. Just like Godiva. "How did you know Zorah had a gun in her desk?"

"Just lucky, I guess. I'd already made up my mind to kill him, but I was going to use this one…" I tried not to flinch when she waved it at me. From this angle, the thing looked like a cannon. "It's one of old Edwin's. You've probably seen it hanging in the drawing room a million times. Aster Edwina keeps the collection in perfect working order."

"But you didn't use it. You used Zorah's."

She looked at her great-great grandfather's gun like she'd never seen it before. "Oh. Right. A few days before…before I did it, I was down at the zoo, hoping to catch Kim alone. I had this gun in my handbag, and I was going to…You know what I was going to do. Anyway, I couldn't find her in the auditorium. When I looked for her in the administration building, there was Zorah, acting peculiar about something in her desk. She got a call about some animal and left, so I looked in the drawer and there it was. She all but gave me that gun!"

As distraught over Grayson's unfaithfulness as Jeanette had been, she had recognized the advantage of using a weapon that couldn't be traced to her. I remained confused about one thing, though. "The night of the fund-raiser, you faked your migraine and left, but you returned later. How? No one saw your car."

"That's because I didn't drive. You've been up to the castle often enough to know how isolated it is up there, especially at night. An elephant could stomp around outside and nobody would notice. I slipped out the back, where there's never anyone around after dark, took the short cut through the vineyard, and entered the zoo through the employees' entrance. And before you ask, yes, I know all the lock combinations. You guys should change them more regularly. Otherwise some disgruntled employee could get in and do some damage."

Here she was, about to blow my brains out, but she could still spare a thought for the zoo's welfare. What dedication.

"After getting in, I put on the extra anteater suit I'd ordered—yeah, I was the one who ordered them—and waited in the shadows until Grayson went to the little boy's room. When he came out, I lifted up the mask and told him I had something to show him over by the anteater's enclosure. The lions were roaring that night, making so much noise that I knew no one would hear… Grayson…He…" She gulped. "He never suspected a thing."

Like everyone else, he had mistaken her passivity for stupidity.

"I didn't know…I didn't know shooting him would hurt so much!"

Hurt *who* so much? Her? Or Grayson?

"Oh, Teddy, he made the most horrible noise! And he didn't die right away. He…He tried to run away, but I got in front of him and was going to shoot him again, to put him out of his misery like you do a badly injured animal, but he climbed over the enclosure fence. I guess he thought he'd be safer with Lucy than with me. Or maybe he thought he could hide down there. When he hit the moat he went under the water for a minute, and I thought he was finally dead, but then he crawled out and…" Her sobs were horrible to hear.

Something occurred to me. Here I was, hoping to stall Jeanette until the night park ranger came by to rescue me. But under ordinary conditions, the rangers weren't armed, and Jeanette might shoot him, too. If I wanted to stay alive without getting someone else killed in the process, I'd have to help myself.

But how? Running and hiding was out of the question, because other than the brushy area directly behind her, Tropics Trail stretched straight and broad for approximately twenty yards in both directions. The Trail might be lined with palms, but until it hooked around to the west for the spectacled bear exhibit, it contained no ground foliage dense enough to hide in. As for rushing Jeanette, she stood a good ten feet away from me. I'd be dead before covering half that distance.

Her next words convinced me I had little time left. "Too bad you had to be so nosy, Teddy. And so stubborn. I hoped that after I hit you over the head that night down by the harbor you might back off, but you didn't. Now I have to do what I need to do." Her voice, once jittery with adrenaline, flattened to a dull resolve. Animals displayed this behavior just before they attacked.

I tried one last appeal. "You don't have to kill me, not really. What Grayson did, cheating on you when you loved him so much, a jury will consider that a crime of passion." *But not Barry's murder, they won't.*

She looked at me with distain. "You always did underestimate me, even in Monopoly. I am so tired of people—especially *you*—thinking I'm stupid." She leveled the pistol and squinted one eye.

I raised my hands and tried to act panicked—not difficult, given the circumstances. "Oh, God, Jeanette! Please don't shoot me! I swear I won't tell anyone!"

Then, hoping that for at least a second she'd pay more attention to my words than my actions, I spun on my heel and—practice making perfect—vaulted cleanly over the fence into the anteater's moat.

As I splashed down, I heard a gunshot and the bee-whine of a bullet flying past. Knowing there was nothing else I could do, I dove again beneath the water's surface and stroked hard for the other side. This moat wasn't as deep and nowhere near as wide as the bears', but by the time I reached the bank, two bullets had penetrated the water, missing me by scant inches. My plan was to head for the thicket by the banana tree, and after that— if Lucy let me—use the broad-leafed cover to hide in while I crept toward the holding pen, through it, and out the pen's rear gate. Once I reached the narrow trail used by the keepers, heavy brush would cover me all the way to the administration building, where I would barricade myself in the windowless employees' lounge and phone for help.

But as I sloshed ashore on the other side of the moat, Lucy rushed to meet me, and the growl that issued from her throat wasn't friendly. Enraged at this intrusion, she reared to her full height, long talons flashing. Would she do to me what she had done to Grayson's body? With despair I realized I might not survive long enough to put the rest of my plan into action.

To gain time, I said in the cooing tone I normally used with her, "Does my Lucy want a *banana*?"

The growl faded into a querulous rumble. The red glow of anger in her eyes softened.

"*Banana*, Lucy! *Banana!*"

After taking a half-hearted swipe at me, she dropped to all fours. When I repeated the magic word, she ducked her head and flicked out her blue tongue.

"*Snort?*"

Grateful tears cleared the moat water out of my eyes. "Yes, Lucy *loooves* banana!" One baby step at a time, keeping my eyes on those horrible talons, I backed us both into the shadowy protection of the banana tree thicket where bullets couldn't find either of us. She followed closely, rumbling her greed.

Although it seemed like an eternity, only seconds had passed since I'd jumped into the moat. Jeanette, apparently recovered from her shock that I would dive into what looked like certain death, snapped off a couple more rounds. When they missed, she howled in fury. No stranger to the zoo, she knew that if I reached the back trail, her chances of catching me in its deep undergrowth weren't good.

So she did exactly what I'd done. Emboldened by my safe passage across the anteater's enclosure, she vaulted over the fence.

When she splashed down in the moat, Lucy swung her head around.

I reached the holding pen. Put my hand on the gate. Started working the combination lock. Saw the fire extinguisher in the corner. The shovel. The rake.

I was no longer weaponless.

Behind me, the anteater made threatening noises. I wasn't safe yet, so I kept talking, kept maneuvering the lock. "*Banana* for Lucy. Soft, mushy *banana*."

The last tumbler fell into place. The lock opened.

Jeanette screamed.

Lucy stretched to full height again, talons slashing. This time, Jeanette was the object of her ire. Lucy slashed at her hand, knocking the gun into the foliage.

"Run back to the moat!" I screamed. "She hates water!" Too late. Talons sliced through the air again. Connected.

With little more than a sigh, Jeanette went down.

It could have ended right there. For a moment, a very brief moment, I was tempted to escape through the holding pen, leaving Jeanette to Lucy's mercies. After all, hadn't she killed two people and tried to kill me? Instead, I dashed into the holding pen, grabbed the rake, and without caring for my own safety, rushed to Jeanette's side. When I reached her, I saw blood seeping through her shredded blouse. The anteater towered over her, talons flexing.

I gave Lucy a poke with the rake. "No!"

Those baleful eyes turned toward me again. A hiss.

"I said, '*No!*'"

She looked toward the holding pen, then at me. Her blue tongue flickered.

"*Squeak?*"

Lucy really wanted that banana.

Keeping an eye on the anteater, I grabbed Jeanette by the foot and dragged her into the safety of the pen. As Lucy hissed her frustration, I slammed the gate and screamed for help, hoping the ranger was somewhere nearby.

I heard no answering voice. Just the wind rushing though the trees, an owl's hoot above, an annoyed lion's roar from Africa Trail. The ranger was probably down there, making certain no mischievous teenagers had snuck into the zoo.

Wondering if my cell phone would work after all the abuse it had taken, I fished it out of my pocket. As I started to punch in 9-1-1, it rang.

More out of reflex than anything else, I answered.

Joe's warm voice came over the line. "Hi, there, Teddy. Hope I didn't wake you."

Chapter Twenty-four

Two days later Joe and I stood hand in hand on the tarmac of the San Jose International Airport, watching as a large crate stamped GUNN VINEYARDS: THE BEST OF THE WEST was loaded onto the Gunn family's Lear jet.

"Come kiss us goodbye," my mother said to me, smiling. She was clad in cream-colored linen, her hair freshly tinted. She'd gained back a whole half-pound since my father talked her into quitting the Strawberry/Carrot Diet.

"What, kiss you and Aster Edwina?"

"No, silly." She winked.

"Oh." I snuck a sidelong look at the serene countenance of the Gunn family doyenne, who didn't seem at all disturbed that her grand-niece—who was fine, except for a few scratches on her hand and a superficial shoulder wound—now lay handcuffed to a bed in the San Sebastian County Hospital, facing double homicide charges. But why should Aster Edwina be bothered? The fleet of attorneys she'd hired had all but guaranteed that if convicted, Jeanette would spend her time in a mental hospital, not in prison doing someone else's laundry. After all, Jeanette was a *Gunn*.

"You understand that I can't know anything about this," Joe said, as my mother started for the plane.

I smiled as I leaned closer to him, inhaling his cologne. I would never let anything separate us again.

With my mother's back to us, he snuck me a quick kiss, then whispered, "Hurry up and say goodbye. Just the thought of who's on board makes my handcuffs twitch."

I left him behind on the pavement and followed my mother and her unlikely co-conspirator up the plane's stairs.

While Aster Edwina settled herself in one of the leather club chairs with her well-thumbed copy of Machiavelli's *The Prince* and began to underline various passages, Caro led me toward the seating banquettes in the rear of the plane.

"It's hard to believe she's doing this for you, what with Jeanette under arrest and all," I said. "You two don't even get along."

A dismissive wave. "She said something about us old families having to stick together. Besides, she always had a thing for your father."

Crusty old Aster Edwina and Dad? Well, he always could charm birds out of the trees. Even the harpies.

Lifting the seat cushion off a banquette, Caro said, "Say goodbye to your father."

Dad lay in the storage compartment underneath the banquette, dressed in a golf shirt and broadcloth slacks. Not Iceland, then. From his prone position, he waggled his fingers at me. "Your mother ordered me to order you to quit your job. Oh, and also to break up with that nice boyfriend of yours." Then he smiled his wonderful smile. "I told her you never listen to me."

"You're right." I leaned over and kissed him on the forehead.

"Kiss Al goodbye, too."

I frowned. "Al Mazer? He's going to wherever you're going?"

Dad shrugged, not an easy thing to do when you're lying in the bottom of a hollowed-out banquette. "Since he purposely flubbed that hit on me, he has to get out of town, too."

My mouth flew open. "*Hit*? Do you mean to tell me Al works for *Chuckles*?"

My father had the decency to look abashed. "Not any more. Not after he was assigned to my, um, *case*. Talk about an ethical problem! It's a sad day when duty to your employer dictates you do one thing, but friendship dictates you do another. Al told me

he'd always liked working for Chuckles, who—money launder-
ing and rubouts aside—is an excellent employer. He even gives
freelancers like Al complete insurance coverage, which in this
day and age, counts for something. Now go give Al that kiss."

Caro lifted up the cushion on the facing banquette. Al Mazer
lay beneath.

I didn't kiss him. "You shot at my father, you creep."

He looked contrite. "I made certain I missed. Believe me,
I'm a much better shot than that. Your father was never in any
danger and neither were you. Not from me, anyway."

"You scared me!"

"Sorry about that. I did what I could to make up for it,
though."

It was all I could do not to grab Aster Edwina's copy of *The
Prince* and bash him over the head with it. "Are you *nuts*? How
can you ever make up for shooting at someone?" I could still
remember the whine of those bullets before they splashed into
the water by the *Merilee*, so much like the sound other bullets
had made as they flew by me as I swam for my life in Lucy's
moat. I never wanted to hear anything like that again.

He reached up and grasped my hand before I could snatch
it away. "Remember how worried you've been about the *Merilee*
not being able to make that trip to Dolphin Island?"

"Don't you dare offer me blood money!" I yelled.

From the interior of the other banquette, my father called,
"Pipe down, Teddy. Al understands that you have this silly thing
about ethics." The way he pronounced the word raised my ire
even further.

Al gave me a sheepish grin. "You know Maxwell Jarvis? The
guy who registered the complaint about the liveaboarders?
When you get back to the harbor, you'll find the complaint's
been withdrawn."

"You *threatened* Maxwell?" I didn't have to feign my outrage.
"What, you left a dead horse's head on his pillow?"

"That's unnecessarily harsh." Dad again. "Al merely suggested to Mr. Jarvis, who by the way is deeply invested in some

questionable holdings himself, that he find another harbor for his own yacht since Gunn Landing so offends his sensibilities. He also pointed out that if Mr. Jarvis didn't withdraw his complaint, the Securities and Exchange Commission would soon receive a letter, attached to photocopies and notarized statements."

So the bane of Gunn Landing Harbor was a criminal, too. It made for a certain kind of justice, one crook blackmailing another. At least I didn't have anything to do with the situation. Now the *Merilee* could remain in her slip, along with the *Tea 4 Two*, the *Running Wild*, and all the other floating homes.

"I still think it's shoddy," I grumbled.

A chuckle from my father. "Much of life is, Teddy. We just muddle along the best we can."

He was right. So I gave Al a kiss, after all.

Then I kissed Caro.

As I walked toward the plane's exit and approached Aster Edwina, I was in such a kissing mood that I even thought about bending over and giving her a peck on the cheek, too.

Common sense reasserted itself and I kept moving.

Chapter Twenty-five

The past few nights had been odd, Lucy reflected, as she prowled her enclosure in the early morning sunshine. First, the soft-voiced human thing had attempted to share her enclosure, promising bananas. Lucy had given her welcome, but no bananas had been forthcoming. Then that other human-thing, her voice shrill and squawky, had fallen in.

Maddening!

But this morning…

First came the belly-pain, which was terrible. To ease it, she had reared up on her hind legs and propped herself against her strong tail. The belly-pain didn't go away, just kept up. She grunted and hissed, hoping the soft-voiced human-thing might hear her and bring a banana—that might help the belly-pain—but her friend was nowhere around.

After a forever, something big and wet slid from between her legs. Exhausted, she slumped to all fours and found a wiggling creature snuffling along the ground toward her, its long nose so much like her own.

What's this?

Then she remembered. The soppy-wet thing was a *baby!* Long ago she'd had one of these and oh, how she'd loved it! The baby had suckled at her teats, ridden on her back, played Wrestle with her, sometimes even Chase! When it grew as big as Lucy, it had wandered away, never to return. But sometimes in her dreams, she remembered the feel of its tiny, soft snout.

With a joyous squeak, she trundled over to the baby. Carefully, talons tucked under her leathery pads so not to cause harm, she drew it to the nipple underneath her armpit.

Here, baby, here!

While it suckled, she licked it clean with her long, blue tongue. Soon the baby, its belly full of milk, crawled up on her back, dug in with its tiny talons, and went to sleep.

Proud and happy, her baby safe and warm, Lucy looked down the trail, where she heard the hum of a nearing zoo cart. A screech of brakes, feet running through the brush on the back path, the clank of metal locks being opened, the squeal of gate hinges.

That familiar voice whispering, "Oh, my sweet Lucy!"

Lucy leaned against the holding pen where her friend, the human female with hair the color of flowers, stood laughing and weeping.

Feeling magnanimous in her own joy, Lucy flicked her blue tongue through the metal fence links and kissed her friend's hand.

Wait. Was that...?

Oh, yes, it was.

Banana!

To receive a free catalog of Poisoned Pen Press titles, please contact us in one of the following ways:

Phone: 1-800-421-3976
Facsimile: 1-480-949-1707
Email: info@poisonedpenpress.com
Website: www.poisonedpenpress.com

Poisoned Pen Press
6962 E. First Ave. Ste. 103
Scottsdale, AZ 85251

LaVergne, TN USA
05 August 2010
192236LV00001B/8/P